"Was Stella trying to fix us up?" she asked, feeling incredulous.

Ever since Nick had rescued her on her way into town, she'd been fantasizing about this man, only to find out he was related to her only friend in Mistletoe. Small towns had such an interconnectivity among the residents. She shouldn't be surprised at all.

"Without a doubt," Nick answered, full-on grinning at this point and confirming her hunch.

Harlow covered her face with her hands. "How cringeworthy. My good friend didn't think that I could land a man on my own."

Nick reached out and touched her arm. Her body instantly responded to the contact, and a sigh slipped past her lips. She wondered what it would feel like to be kissed by Nick, to feel his fingers roaming across her skin. It would be heavenly, she imagined...

Falling in *Love* on Sweetwater Lane

BELLE CALHOUNE

FOREVER
New York Boston

Copyright © 2023 by Sandra Calhoune
Cover art and design by Elizabeth Turner Stokes
Cover images © Shutterstock
Cover copyright © 2023 by Hachette Book Group, Inc.

Forever
Hachette Book Group
1290 Avenue of the Americas, New York, NY 10104
read-forever.com
twitter.com/readforeverpub

First Edition: February 2023

Forever is an imprint of Grand Central Publishing. The Forever name and logo are trademarks of Hachette Book Group, Inc.

The publisher is not responsible for websites (or their content) that are not owned by the publisher.

The Hachette Speakers Bureau provides a wide range of authors for speaking events. To find out more, go to www.hachettespeakersbureau.com or email HachetteSpeakers@hbgusa.com.

Forever books may be purchased in bulk for business, educational, or promotional use. For information, please contact your local bookseller or the Hachette Book Group Special Markets Department at special.markets@hbgusa.com.

ISBN: 9781538736050 (mass market), 9781538736043 (ebook)

Printed in the United States of America

OPM

10 9 8 7 6 5 4 3 2 1

For my forever friend, Cheryl Paris Chandler. No matter time nor distance, you'll always be in my heart.

ACKNOWLEDGMENTS

For all the readers who asked for Nick's story. Thanks for the encouragement and love.

With deep gratitude to my agent, Jessica Alvarez, for your wise counsel and listening ear. I appreciate our partnership.

I'm indebted to my editor, Madeleine Colavita, for always being so in tune with the story elements and for asking the hard questions so the finished product can sparkle.

And for my friend Jessica Keller. You are such a wonderful single mother, and like my hero Nick, you work hard to make the world a precious place for your child.

PROLOGUE

Harlow Jones sat in the back seat of her family's station wagon, looking out the window as the two-story colonial house faded into the distance. Hot tears stung her eyes as she whispered words of goodbye to the only home she had ever known. "I'll never forget you."

They had packed up all of their belongings and a bunch of muscled movers had put them in the back of their U-Haul. It didn't seem right that they were leaving an empty house behind.

She would always remember the sleepovers in her petal-pink bedroom, playing double Dutch in the driveway, hide-and-seek with Malcolm, and the great oak in the backyard. She'd fallen out of that huge tree on her sixth birthday. Harlow smiled at the memory of the hot-pink cast on her arm. She had worn it for weeks and been the hit of her first-grade class. Everyone had thought it was so cool. Her entire class had lined up to sign their names on it.

Her brother reached over and squeezed her hand, whispering, "Don't worry, Harlow. We're going to have an even better house in Philly." Harlow looked over at Malcolm. He was smiling at her in a fake way that didn't make it all the way up to his eyes.

She didn't care about a better house. It still wouldn't feel like a home to her. Leaving Chestnut Ridge hurt her heart. Her friends were here. Janie Duckett and Devikah Kumar had been her best friends since nursery school. Best friends didn't grow on trees. She didn't want to even think about going to a new school or making new friends. She'd been the spelling bee champion at Chestnut Ridge Elementary for three years running. Now Billy Dempsey would get the title. She hated him. He was an awful boy who'd said terrible things about her father.

But he hadn't been the only one. That was one of the reasons they were leaving Vermont. Her daddy had been accused of stealing lots of money from his work. And now he was dead. Nothing would ever be the same again. All her mother ever did now was cry and talk about how much she hated Chestnut Ridge. Harlow still loved this town, even though she'd lost her father and now her mother as well. Her mother didn't laugh anymore or make lame knock-knock jokes. And her father was just gone in a car wreck. Harlow hadn't even had a chance to say goodbye to him.

Malcolm kept pestering her to play I Spy to kill time until they reached Pennsylvania. She finally gave in, her mind scrambling to find objects as the vehicle raced down the highway. An American flag. A water tower. A helicopter flying low. A pink house.

"I bet that made you feel better," Malcolm crowed once the game was over.

"I do," she said, lying through her teeth. Stuffing down her feelings was easier than dealing with them. She had learned that lesson on the day of her father's funeral. Her mother had freaked out when she'd burst into tears. So she had stopped crying and held the tears back from falling. *Never let them see you cry.*

It was late that night when they pulled up to their new home in Philly. She took one look at it and knew that Malcolm had been wrong. This oatmeal-colored house wasn't nearly as nice as the one in Chestnut Ridge. It was much smaller, with a tiny yard. Someone had painted the fence an ugly green color. Most important, Daddy wasn't here. And he never would be again.

"We can paint it a nice blue color. The two of you can pick," her mother said once they'd gotten out of the car for a better look at the property. "What do you think?"

"Sounds good to me," Malcolm said, smiling.

"I like this place." They both looked over in her direction, waiting for a response.

"Harlow? Is the house okay?" her mother asked, nervously fiddling with her collar. Harlow would do just about anything to take away the look of worry stamped on her mother's face. She didn't want to be yet another reason her mom cried late at night in her bedroom.

Harlow plastered on the biggest grin she could muster. "I think it's fantastic." She stuck her tongue out at Malcolm. "Dibs on first pick of a bedroom," she called out as she took off running toward the house.

"No fair," Malcolm yelled, racing after her as their mother's laughter filled the air.

Once she was all settled in for the night, Harlow gazed up at the moon from her bedroom window. So far the moon was the only thing that seemed the same. Everything else in her life had shifted.

She had a funny feeling in her stomach that her family would never be as happy as they'd once been in Vermont. All of that had vanished the day they'd driven away from Chestnut Ridge.

CHAPTER ONE

NINETEEN YEARS LATER

One minute Harlow Jones was cruising down the scenic coastal Maine road admiring the gorgeous fall foliage and the next her car was sliding on the wet pavement before slamming through the guardrail. She tried to remember everything she'd ever learned about skidding and how to properly maneuver a vehicle, but it happened too fast for her to react. And now her ten-year-old Saab was dangling between the guardrail and a terrifying drop down below to the frosty Maine waters. Fear gripped her by the throat. How was she going to get herself out of this dangerous predicament?

Don't panic! she warned herself. *Try to breathe.*

People who talked about their lives flashing before their eyes were right. From the instant her tires began to slide, images flashed into Harlow's mind's eye—birthdays, breakups, her family, her dad's accident. Love, loss, heartbreak, Bear. Malcolm. It was all laid out for her like a roadmap of her life. Oh, she'd made so many mistakes along the way, leading up to this gigantic misstep.

This terrifying situation was all her fault. At the very moment she was navigating a sharp curve in the road, a fox had darted in the path of her car. In an effort to avoid the animal, she had swerved to the shoulder and crashed through the barrier. A disastrous decision. It served her right for coming to this hick town called Mistletoe in the first place. She should have just stayed put in Seattle, where things like this never happened to her. The worst thing in Seattle had been a coffee order gone wrong. Wild animals weren't running around the city. She didn't have to worry about veering off the road to save them from becoming roadkill.

But the state of Maine had made her an offer she hadn't been able to refuse. They'd dangled a big old carrot in front of her eyes—spend a year as a veterinarian at a Mistletoe practice in exchange for the erasure of her student loans. For Harlow, the decision had been a no-brainer.

Harlow knew her position at the moment was incredibly precarious. One wrong move and her vehicle could shift, which would cause her to plummet into a watery grave. Could she safely reach for her cell phone to call 911? Fear grabbed her by the throat and wouldn't let go. She didn't want to move a muscle. Surely another driver had seen her lose control of her car and would notify authorities of a crash? Harlow shut her eyes and prayed for someone to rescue her.

"I've called for help. Just stay put," a female voice called out to her.

Stay put? It wasn't as if she had any other options. It was either stay still or plunge to her death. All things considered, she was fine staying put. Honestly, she was too petrified to move a muscle. She didn't dare turn her head to see the woman or even respond. Any movement at this point was risky. She barely wanted to breathe. Minutes passed during which Harlow made countless promises to God, begged, pleaded, cried, and let out a few curse words for emphasis. How on earth had she landed in this predicament?

The fact that her own father had lost his life in a car accident only served to heighten her anxiety. *Please, please, please.* She didn't want to go out like this. She'd barely hit her stride in the world. Beads of sweat pooled on her forehead, and she suddenly wished that she wasn't wearing layers of clothing. The interior of the car felt so hot. She wanted to fan herself, but she didn't dare move in case the car slid. Her seat belt was tight against her chest, making breathing even more difficult. She wasn't sure if it was her imagination, but her breathing sounded labored and choppy.

Time seemed to crawl by as Harlow waited for rescue. After what seemed like an eternity, wailing sirens rang out in the stillness, alerting her to the fact

that help was on the way. Approaching voices announced the arrival of emergency rescue personnel,
and out of the corner of her eye she saw a flash of
movement. Someone was standing right beside the
car. She was too scared to crane her neck to look
over at them.

"Hey there. I'm Nick with the search and rescue
team. We're tying your vehicle to a fire truck to
steady it. You might feel slight movement but just
be aware we're securing you." The low, soothing
voice washed over her, providing her with a much-
needed reality check. She wasn't alone!

"What's your name?" he asked.

"H-Harlow," she said, forcing the word out of
her mouth. She was shaking so badly now she felt
certain her voice must be trembling as well.

"Nice," he said with a nod. "My granddad used to
watch Jean Harlow movies. She was a blond bombshell from back in the days of classic films. Has
anyone told you about her?"

"A few times," she replied. *More like a hundred.*
Basically every time she met someone new over a
certain age they mentioned her namesake.

"Okay, Harlow. Do me a favor. Don't look down.
Just listen to my voice, okay?"

Harlow froze. *Don't look. Don't look.* If he was
telling her not to look, then surely there was a
reason. What would she see if she looked down?
Try as she might, Harlow couldn't resist the urge to
peer down into the abyss.

As soon as she did, Harlow let out a scream worthy of a horror movie. She squeezed her eyes shut as a way of blocking out the terrifying sight of dark water and jagged rocks. She needed to wake up from this nightmare! Her life couldn't end this way. Not when she was on the verge of being debt-free.

"I told you not to look down, Harlow." Nick's voice was as smooth as glass. It felt reassuring. Surely he wouldn't sound like that if he thought she might die.

She let out a moan. "I know you did, but I couldn't stop myself."

"Slowly unbuckle your seat belt, Harlow," Nick instructed. His voice was so close to her now, it felt as if he was talking into her ear. Seconds later his face appeared by her window. Whoa! If this was going to be the last face she ever laid eyes on, she'd hit the jackpot. Leave it to her to appreciate male beauty at a time like this.

Deep-set chocolate eyes framed by jet-black lashes she'd give her right arm for looked at her. Russet-colored skin. A strong jawline and amazing features. He was so close that Harlow could see a small scar resting by his full, nicely shaped lips.

"I know you're scared, but I've got you. I'm going to open the door and get you out. Okay?" he asked in a buttery soft tone. "Make sure you place your arms around my neck. Really tight, all right?"

All she could do was nod. A huge lump was sitting in her throat. It felt impossible to trust this man she'd only just met with her life. But what choice did she have? Before she knew it, Nick had scooped her up in his arms and lifted her from the driver's seat, swinging her back toward solid ground and safety. He gently deposited her on the pavement as a team of EMTs rushed toward her. She was still tightly wrapping her arms around his neck with no desire to let go.

"You're safe now," he said in a low voice as he gently pried her arms away. As soon as he released her, a warming blanket was placed around her shoulders as she was led to the back of an ambulance. After insisting she didn't need treatment, Harlow accepted a bottle of Gatorade and a pack of graham crackers. Once she'd finished them and assured the EMTs that she was fine, Harlow looked around the area to try to spot Nick, but he was nowhere to be found. She really needed to thank him for saving her life. If she didn't do it right now, the opportunity might slip through her fingers.

Harlow walked back toward the group of firefighters, singling out a pretty female with fiery strands of hair peeking out of her helmet. "Have you seen Nick? He's part of the rescue team."

"The tall dude with killer eyes and a rugged build?" the woman asked with a knowing look.

"Sounds about right," Harlow said, noticing the way the pretty firefighter's eyes lit up. It didn't take a genius to figure out she had a thing for Nick. Harlow didn't blame her. He made quite an impression.

"He headed out a while ago," the woman elaborated, grinning hard. "Trust me, I noticed."

"Thanks," Harlow said, swallowing past her disappointment. Not being able to thank Nick didn't sit well with her. It was the least she could do after his heroic actions.

Her life had just been saved by the most swoonworthy man in the entire state of Maine, and she didn't even know his full name. She let out a sigh. Too bad she wasn't looking for even a hint of romance. A man like Nick would check off all the requirements on her list.

Harlow needed to keep her eyes on the prize. She would fulfill the requirements of her agreement to work at Paws and then leave Mistletoe as fast as her legs could carry her.

* * *

Nick Keegan drove along the coastal road toward his hometown of Mistletoe, Maine. A quick glance at the clock on his dashboard confirmed that he would get home just in time to make dinner for his son, Miles, check his homework, then watch one of their favorite television shows together before it was lights-out for both of them.

As a single father of a nine-year-old, Nick always felt as if he were burning the candle at both ends. His career as a search and rescue agent meant grueling hours and emotional assignments. Sometimes he wondered if he was doing a good job raising Miles in the shadow of his wife Kara's tragic death. She had been the magic glue that held their family together. Without her at the center, Nick had struggled for a long time, always feeling as if he was floundering.

The ache of loss was still there, but he was beginning to see the light at the end of the tunnel. He didn't want to be single for the rest of his life, but finding someone he vibed with and who meshed with his life wasn't easy. Sure, he'd put his toe in the dating waters in the past few months, but nothing had come of it. The thought of those awkward dates made him cringe. Nick hadn't felt any true connection or chemistry with any of them.

Had he lost his swagger? Or was he simply rusty at wining and dining a woman? It had been a while, but at least he still looked half decent. Due to his career, he was in great shape. He even had a six-pack. Or at least a four-pack. Not that it did him much good.

Harlow. Seeing such a beautiful woman while on the job was rare. Curly black hair framed a gorgeous face. With her sepia-colored skin, full, rosy lips, and big brown eyes, she was absolutely stunning. And maybe a little bit out of his league, if he was being honest. Nick couldn't help but wonder if she knew how close she'd been to imminent disaster. If the circumstances had been different and he hadn't been on the job, Nick might have flirted with her a little bit instead of keeping his distance. Or maybe he would have invited her out for coffee.

Baby steps, he reminded himself. Getting back in the dating game wasn't easy. But he knew he didn't want to walk alone for the rest of his life. Seeing his younger brother, Luke, and close friend, Dante West, happily settled down made him want a loving partnership for himself. It didn't even have to be a white picket fence and a wedding ceremony. Nick just wanted to be head over heels for someone again and to have those feelings reciprocated.

Nick paused for a moment as he pulled into the driveway of his white colonial-style house with black shutters. It was the quintessential New England family home. Two red Adirondack chairs sat out front, along with half a dozen pumpkins. His mind flashed back to the first time he and Kara laid eyes on this place. His heart had lurched when Kara turned to him and said, "I can see us growing old here." They'd made an offer on the house that very day. And he had planned to live happily ever after with her, until a drunk driver hit Kara's car head-on and snuffed out his wife's life.

Just when he thought that he'd turned a corner, it all came rushing back to him. The shock. The pain. The guilt. A last-minute change in their schedules had forced them to switch up their regular routine, with Kara dropping Miles off at school while he'd been on a rescue. What-ifs and might-have-beens still tugged at him.

"Dad!" As soon as Nick turned the key in his front door, his son came running down the hall toward him. Nick braced himself for impact, then hoisted Miles up into his arms.

"Hey, buddy. What've you been eating? You weigh a ton!" Nick said in an exaggerated manner that caused Miles to grin wildly. He knew it made his son feel like Superman.

"Lots of meatballs and Nana's corn bread," Miles said, laughing.

Nick's mother made incredible corn bread. He and Luke had grown up on it, along with corned beef, collard greens, and banana pudding. To this day, Nick headed over to his parents' house for Sunday dinner whenever he was craving those particular dishes. Thankfully they had an open-door policy.

Miles raised his arm and pulled up his sleeve, showcasing a skinny arm. "Look at my guns," he said, flexing his nonexistent muscle.

"Whoa. Pretty soon you'll be replacing me and Uncle Luke in search and rescue," Nick teased. This banter about Miles being on the search and rescue team was a running joke among the three of them.

Miles's grin threatened to crack his face wide open. "You're pulling my leg," he said with a crooked smile. "That would be so cool though."

Miles had a great relationship with Nick's brother, Luke, who had recently retired from being a Navy SEAL due to an injury he'd sustained while on active duty. Upon returning to Mistletoe, Luke had entered into a faux romance with Miles's teacher, Stella Marshall, in order to get the local match-makers off their backs. They'd ended up falling in love before getting married last year.

"I think he missed you." Van, Miles's sitter, walked down the hall toward them. Tall and sandy haired, Van was a good-looking college student who was paying his own way through school. Watching Miles after dismissal until Nick came home from work was a sweet gig, especially since he and Miles got along like a house on fire. In a pinch, Nick's family always subbed in to watch his son. So far, he was making it work.

"That's only fair, since I always miss him," Nick said, running his palm over his son's close-cropped Afro.

"Hey, don't touch the 'fro, Dad," Miles protested, ducking away from Nick. "I need to keep it tight for picture day tomorrow."

Van made a face at Nick and whispered, "I think he might be crushing on someone in his class. Not sure, but he's been talking a lot about someone named Lily."

Noooooo! Nick wanted to say. His son was far too young for crushes. Time was flying by way too fast for his liking. Nick just wanted things to slow down so he could savor the moments. Pretty soon he'd be dealing with a tween who didn't want anything to do with his father.

Sometimes he wished that he and Kara had made

the decision to have another kid. That way Miles would always have someone to walk through life with. A sibling. A best friend. The way Luke had played a huge role in Nick's life. He wouldn't know what to do without his brother. Honestly, Nick didn't even want to consider that possibility. He wasn't sure he could handle losing anyone else. It might just break him once and for all.

CHAPTER TWO

The day after her car accident, Harlow was busy setting up her new digs and reflecting on the last twenty-four hours. Thankfully, she would be getting her car back next week. She'd awoken several times in the course of the night due to nightmares about the crash. She was acutely aware of how lucky she'd been to survive the accident. Chills ran straight through her at the memory of how frightened and vulnerable she'd been while dangling above the water, all the while fearing the worst.

She had to admit that her new lakefront home was full of charm and infinite possibilities. She had spent the morning setting up her bedroom and kitchen with all the items she'd had mailed to her new address. Her rose-colored comforter, a collection of cozy sweaters and boots, framed photographs, paintings, and an assortment of cookware that she hadn't yet

used. And her air fryer. Harlow salivated just thinking about Malcolm making shrimp and grits for her.
Anything else Harlow needed she would pick up in
town at the local shops.

Her brother, Malcolm, would be arriving in a few
days with her Shetland sheepdog, Bear. Malcolm
and Bear had been hanging out together at his summer house in Cape Cod for the last few weeks while
Harlow resolved things in Seattle with her condo
and the veterinary practice where she worked. She'd
missed her dog like nobody's business, as well as
her brother. As a successful artist, Malcolm had a
lot of freedom with his schedule, so watching Bear
for Harlow hadn't been a burden. Harlow suspected
that Malcolm loved Bear almost as much as she did.
She'd adopted Bear from an animal rescue when he
was barely a year old. Every time she thought about
what her sweet dog had been through before they'd
found each other she wanted to weep.

A knock on the front door alerted her to the arrival
of her afternoon tea date. Harlow rushed toward the
door and wrenched it open, letting out a cry as she
laid eyes on her old friend Stella.

Stella Marshall, now Stella Keegan, had been one
of her college buddies. They hadn't seen each other
in a few years, but they had always remained in
close contact. Once she'd accepted the vet position
at Paws in Mistletoe, Harlow had reached out to
tell Stella the news. Over the course of the next
few months, they'd texted, Zoomed, and talked on

the phone, quickly becoming as close as they'd been in school. Stella had even helped her find this rental property, which was out-of-this-world gorgeous. Situated right by Pinecone Lake, the views were stunning. Between the lake and the mountains, standing on her front porch provided such an incredible visual. Seattle had its fair share of amazing vistas, but even Harlow could admit that Mistletoe, Maine, had its own mind-blowing sights. If only that was enough to offset all the drawbacks of living in a small town.

Harlow immediately beckoned Stella inside. "Come on in. Don't stand on ceremony."

Stella stepped inside and enveloped her in a tight hug. "I'm so happy you're here in Mistletoe! I've missed you."

"Me too, Stella! It's great to see you in person after all this time." Her eyes skimmed over her friend. With mocha-colored skin and big brown eyes set in a heart-shaped face, Stella was lovely. Her kindness radiated from within. "You look amazing. Are you sure you just had a baby?"

"I sure did. It took me twenty-four hours of labor to push out all eight pounds of her," she said with a laugh. "You look wonderful, Harlow. You haven't aged a bit since college."

"You always were too kind," Harlow said with a chuckle. Stella's warm personality had drawn Harlow in from the first time they'd met on the quad one warm September afternoon. They had maintained their friendship postgraduation, even though they'd been living on opposite coasts.

"I mean it. You look great," Stella said with a warm smile. "We're in dire need of more veterinary services. This town is lucky to have you here pitching in."

"Let's go into the kitchen and I'll make us some tea. Then you can tell me all about your yummy husband." The little Harlow knew about Luke was intriguing. He was a former Navy SEAL who'd been awarded the Medal of Honor for valor.

Stella looped her arm through Harlow's and they headed down the hall to the bright, sun-filled room. After boiling the water Stella began to set up the mugs, sweeteners, and creamer. As they sat down, Harlow said, "I'm so sorry that I don't have any muffins or finger sandwiches. I didn't get in until late last night, so I haven't been to the market. Everything I have here was shipped."

"No worries. Oh, that reminds me," Stella said, taking a small box out of her oversized purse. "A few scones and mini muffins from a local bakery you've got to try. It's called Wicked Eats."

"Wow. This is amazing," Harlow said as she began placing the baked goods on a plate. "You saved the day. What's a tea party without a few indulgences?"

As they sat across from each other drinking their Earl Grey tea and devouring the treats, Harlow grilled her friend about meeting her husband. Although

Harlow knew some of the details, she wanted to know more about their romance.

"So, was it love at first sight when you met Luke?" she asked. It was nice to live vicariously through Stella. Her last boyfriend, Neil, had turned out to be of the cheating variety, and it had made Harlow shy away from committed relationships. She was fine being single; this way her heart would remain in one piece. If she was being honest with herself, she hadn't been in love with Neil or any other man. She'd never allowed herself to fall.

"Not exactly love at first sight," Stella admitted. "Although he did cut a mean figure in his Navy SEAL gear. He came to my school to surprise one of my students at our end-of-the-year assembly. His nephew, Miles. When he walked onstage my heart was pounding in my chest."

"So from the sounds of it, he made a great first impression."

Stella nodded. "He sure did. Not just on me, but on most of the ladies in Mistletoe. They all wanted to date him. His younger brother was being hounded around the clock by females in town wanting to get set up with Luke."

Harlow laughed out loud. "Wow. That type of pandemonium says a lot about Luke's appeal."

Stella took out her phone and showed Harlow her screensaver, which was a picture of her and Luke on their wedding day. "Not bad, if I do say so myself," she quipped.

Harlow let out a low whistle. "Oh my goodness. I knew he was totally scrumptious but that photo says it all. And the two of you look like you stepped out of a fairy tale." Not that Harlow believed in fairy tales, but Stella and Luke were a divine couple. "I'm so happy for you. And now that Jade's arrived, you really do have it all."

Stella chuckled. "A lot of sleep-deprivation going on in my house, but it's worth it. My sister and Dante just found out that they're expecting their first child." Stella was grinning so hard, Harlow thought her face might crack. Her joy for the couple was effusive. "Ever since we were little, Lucy and I have talked about our kids growing up together without a huge age gap. That's always been the plan."

"That's great news for Lucy and Dante. Now you and Luke can have a friend for Jade." It was nice seeing good things happen to wonderful people. Harlow wasn't a big believer in white picket fences or vows of forever—her mother had raised her not to believe in romance or wishing on stars or the kindness of strangers—but she didn't mind rooting for other people to achieve their dreams. She was the first person to cheer others on, even though she didn't dream of happily ever after for herself.

It's a surefire way to get your heart broken. Deidre Jones had known what she was talking about. After Harlow's father's death, every ounce of sentimentality had been stripped from her mother's spirit. Harlow had seen the pain and heartache unfold up close and personal. And she'd sworn never to allow her heart to rule her head.

"So, tell me more about your assignment here in town. I know you weren't exactly thrilled about coming to Maine," Stella said, pausing to sip her tea.

Harlow wrinkled her nose. "Don't take it personally. I'm just not big on small towns. I grew up in one, so I'm biased. Seattle suits me. I like big buildings and being so close to other cities, not to mention having the best coffee at my disposal. Not to ding Mistletoe, but it's not a place I would have chosen on my own." She took a bite of a blueberry scone. "So, as you know, I was drowning in student loan debt from undergrad veterinary school. Something truly had to give. I was working nonstop and not even making a dent in it."

Stella made a sympathetic sound.

"So, I entered a program where I was matched up with a town in dire need of veterinary services," Harlow explained. "In exchange, the state of Maine will erase my student loan debts in addition to paying me a salary for my vet work that's competitive to what I've been earning in Seattle."

"Wow," Stella exclaimed. "That's amazing. I knew it had to be something extraordinary to get you to relocate to Mistletoe."

"For a period of one year," Harlow said, making a face. "After that I'm heading back home to the West Coast."

"Who knows?" Stella asked with a shrug. "Maybe

you'll fall in love with Mistletoe and decide to stay put. Stranger things have happened," she said in a teasing tone.

Harlow let out an indelicate snort. "That is highly unlikely. I prefer a city vibe to small towns, although I could get used to this amazing house. The view is spectacular. Thanks for giving me the hookup."

"That's why I love my hometown so much. It was so easy to ask a Realtor friend to work on finding you something to make your own...at least for the year."

One year of working at Paws Veterinary Clinic. One year of being stuck in Hicksville, Maine. She could do it. A lot was riding on her fulfilling her end of the bargain. Financial freedom would be life altering. Harlow could buy a place of her own and help her mother out with her medical bills. She wouldn't be so cash-strapped all the time. Maybe she could even take the vacation to Antigua she'd always dreamed about or buy a new car. Yes! Being in Mistletoe was a means to an end. She wasn't about to do a single thing to screw this situation up.

* * *

Nick counted to ten in his head, all the while taking calming breaths and reminding himself that his brother was, and would always be, his best friend. *Be Zen*, he told himself. Try to remember that your brother is a war hero and a truly good person.

"You can't just bring a dog here, Luke, and try to convince me to adopt him." Nick let out a frustrated sigh as he gazed at the goofy-looking German shepherd sitting next to his brother.

Luke grinned at him. "Why not? You guys need a dog and Zeus is perfect. He didn't quite work out on the search and rescue team, so he needs a new home. The poor guy was booted out of training." Luke made a pouting motion with his lips. "Please, Nick. Take me in," Luke said in a low, growly voice. "I'll be a good boy."

Nick frowned. "Who names a dog Zeus anyway? I always imagined giving a dog a warm and fuzzy name like Barney."

Luke let out a hoot of laughter. "Barney? Sounds like an old man's name."

Nick scowled at his brother. "It's distinguished. Zeus sounds like the name of a WWE wrestler."

Luke laughed, showcasing his perfect pearly white teeth. "I bet Miles would love him."

Luke wasn't lying. Miles was dog crazy these days. He'd been pestering Nick about bringing a dog into their household. With Nick's long days working in search and rescue, he wasn't sure he could pull it off. Dogs needed constant care and attention. He couldn't expect a nine-year-old to be the main caretaker.

"Well, thankfully Miles isn't home yet from his friend's birthday party, so we're not going to find out. If he sees Zeus, he'll want to adopt him."

"So what's the problem?" Luke asked with a frown. "Dogs are great companions, not just for kids but for the whole family."

Maybe that was the real problem. Kara had always longed for a dog, a Labradoodle. Nick's plan had been to buy her one for her birthday. He'd had it all planned out. Only that day had never come. She'd passed away exactly one month before the big day. And he'd never had the heart to bring the dog home.

"So why don't you adopt him?" Nick asked. "Problem solved."

Luke made a face. "We have our hands full with Coco Chanel. She's harder to handle than Jade. I pity the dog who has to share a home with her. It definitely wouldn't be pretty." Coco Chanel was his wife Stella's high-maintenance poodle. So far Coco Chanel seemed to adore his brother and the baby, but she wasn't used to sharing Stella with another canine. Some instinct told Nick that Luke was right. Coco Chanel radiated a vibe that screamed "I don't play well with others."

"How about Dante and Lucy? Or Troy and Noelle?" he asked, throwing out any names he could think of to divert attention away from himself. Troy West was Dante's brother, who'd recently gotten married to Noelle, a single mother. The sound of a door slamming and loud footsteps caused him to freeze. "What was that?" he asked Luke, his gaze swinging toward the hall. Within seconds, Miles appeared in the doorway, his eyes widening as soon as he spotted Zeus.

Miles practically slid across the hardwood floors to get to the dog, ending up on his knees in front of the pup, lavishing him with attention. "Is this your dog, Uncle Luke? Oh man, he's perfect. I wish we could get a dog." He swung his head around to face Nick. "Can we get one, Dad? Please."

"Slow down, son," Nick said with an uneasy laugh. "You're talking a mile a minute. What are you doing home so early?" Nick asked, glancing at his watch. "I thought the birthday party wouldn't be over for another hour at least."

"The birthday girl got sick and hurled all over the place. Projectile vomiting," Miles said, raising his fist in the air. "It was so cool."

Nick thought he might get sick just hearing about it. "Poor Zadia. There must be a bug going around." He made a mental note to check in with her parents later on. Jim and Priya Henderson had always been supportive of their family and he would never forget the many kindnesses they had offered over the years.

"What's his name?" Miles asked as he vigorously patted the dog.

"This is Zeus," Luke said. "Zeus, this is my nephew, Miles. Zeus was supposed to be a search and rescue canine but he wasn't really suited to work with my team." Luke made a slashing motion by his neck. "Unfortunately, he got the axe."

Miles frowned. "So where will he go?" he asked. "Who does he live with?"

Luke darted a glance at Nick. His eyes were pleading with him. Nick had seen this particular look on countless occasions throughout their lives. Luke was looking for a Hail Mary pass from him, one he wasn't getting. "Well…umm," Luke said, drawing out his words. "At the moment he doesn't really have a home."

Why? Nick wanted to scream. Why did you have to give him a sob story? Nick shut his eyes and began the countdown. Ten. Nine. Eight. Seven. Six.

His son let out a wail. "That's so sad. We have to do something to help. Isn't that right, Dad?"

"Sure," Nick said after a brief pause. He knew exactly where Miles was going and his mind was working overtime trying to fend him off. "I'm happy to make a donation on his behalf. Let me get my checkbook." He quickly moved toward his desk, avoiding eye contact with Miles. Nick didn't need to be guilted into adding a four-legged hellhound to their family.

"We need to give him a home, not just throw money at the situation." Miles's voice was solemn and heartfelt. The sound of it made Nick stop in his tracks. All of a sudden his nine-year-old sounded full of wisdom and much older than his years. And of course it was popping up now, rather than when he needed to tidy his room or finish his homework.

"You always tell me not to be a bystander in my

life. This is me trying to help and make a difference. We have to do our part to help dogs like Zeus," Miles continued. "Come on, Dad. You know how much I've been wanting a dog of my own."

Nick let out a groan. His son was using his very own words against him. He was raising Miles to be a good citizen and to care about everyone and everything in his orbit. Now it was coming back to bite him. All thanks to Luke, who seriously deserved bad karma to head his way.

"He's a great dog," Luke chimed in. "A protector. He'll always have your back."

Nick scowled at him. Why had he even let Luke inside? He should have double bolted the door.

That was it! He was going to kill his brother. Slowly. Methodically. Painstakingly.

"Okay, I'll think about it. That's the best I can do," Nick said, knowing he was about to fold like an accordion. Miles flew to his side and launched himself at his chest. Getting hugs from Miles was one of the best feelings he'd ever known. It was almost worth adopting a dog he'd never intended to take in.

"So, should I go get the bag of dog food, his bed, and his bowls from my truck?" Luke asked with a smirk.

"Yes!" Miles shouted, jumping up and down with excitement. "I can help," he said, tugging on his uncle's hand. As Luke walked past Nick toward the front door with Miles by his side, Nick leaned in and said in a low voice, "Payback is coming when you least expect it."

Luke let out a deep-throated chuckle. "What are you, five?" Luke scoffed, shaking his head as if he were the injured party.

Nick made a face at Luke's retreating figure. He headed toward the front door so he could watch the duo as they headed with Zeus to Luke's vehicle. His heart twisted as he noticed his son skipping down the stone path rather than walking. Seeing him so ecstatic about Zeus took some of the sting out of this unexpected turn of events. Adopting a dog hadn't been on his to-do list today, but at least it had given Miles unimaginable joy. And for that, he was grateful.

CHAPTER THREE

Harlow cruised down Main Street during her lunch hour, perusing the quaint shops and eateries in the downtown area. She was still using a rental until her Saab was repaired from the accident. There was something eye catching in every direction she looked.

She had to hand it to Mistletoe. There were loads of restaurants, coffeehouses, clothing stores, and novelty shops. If she had more time, she would sit down at the Lobster Shack and order a nice seafood lunch. Since time was short until her next appointment, Harlow ran into the Coffee Bean and grabbed a bagel with cream cheese along with a hot vanilla chai.

In typical small-town fashion, she received numerous glances in her direction. Some folks openly gawked at her. Harlow might as well wear a sign on her forehead that said in bold ink OUT-OF-TOWNER. Being stared at was the most uncomfortable feeling in the world for Harlow. Even though she knew the townsfolk were merely curious about her, Harlow couldn't separate the stares from her childhood experiences in Chestnut Ridge. *Shake it off*, she told herself. *Don't go down that road. Not now!*

Today was about fresh starts and making the best of life when it handed you lemons. Mistletoe was one big lemon she planned to squeeze dry over the next year. At the end of her stay, Harlow would have made the sweetest lemonade of all time. Tim Gunn's voice buzzed in her ear, urging her to *Make it work!*

At least this little town was visually appealing, with an abundance of New England charm. Maybe she should buy a postcard and send it off to her mother. *Or not!* Deidre Jones would no doubt lecture her about small towns and the terrible things that could happen there. Although she had told her mother about moving to Mistletoe for a year, Dee probably didn't remember. Sadly, she currently resided in a nursing home on Cape Cod due to the progression of her dementia.

Harlow and Malcolm had been raised on that negative mantra about small towns, never being allowed to forget their painful past or the grudge their mother carried against the people of Chestnut Ridge. It was understandable, considering the fact that her upstanding father had been accused of embezzlement and branded as a criminal. For that reason, a mistrust of small towns was imprinted on Harlow's soul like a permanent tattoo. Sometimes small towns made her feel claustrophobic, as if air was being sucked from her lungs.

Stay positive. Being in Maine was far from ideal, but at least she would be able to do what she loved. Being a veterinarian had taken years of hard work and discipline, but putting in all the hours was now paying off. She loved working at Paws.

Paws, her new place of employment, was located a few blocks away from the main drag on a cute tree-lined street. Although it was within walking distance of downtown, she'd felt too lazy to walk. Plus, driving around gave her an opportunity to see all the sights.

The Free Library of Mistletoe rose up to greet her as she drove past, a stately and majestic building. If she wasn't mistaken, that was where Stella's sister Lucy worked as head librarian. Lucy's husband, Dante West, a famous Hollywood actor, had recently filmed scenes from one of his movies there. That was probably as exciting as Mistletoe got. An actual A-list celebrity came back to his hometown for Christmas, fell in love with his high school sweetheart and then married her. If that wasn't a Hallmark movie, she didn't know what was.

Fall had graced Mistletoe with gorgeous foliage on the town green. Bursts of orange, crimson, and gold caught her eye. A quick glance at her watch confirmed she had another twenty minutes to kill before heading back to the clinic. *Why not take advantage of the glorious autumn weather?* She pulled into a parking spot by the town green and headed toward a nearby bench. She sat down and proceeded to eat her bagel while taking in the beautiful landscape stretched out before her.

Her eyes focused on a boy and the adult with him—maybe his father—playing fetch with a large dog. From this distance it looked like a German shepherd, but she couldn't be certain. Harlow loved all animals, but dogs held a special place in her heart. She'd grown up with a rottweiler named Rambo, who'd instilled in her a lifelong love of dogs, as well as inspiring her career as a veterinarian. She couldn't wait to be reunited with Bear later on this afternoon. Things just weren't the same without him. Or Malcolm. Ever since they were kids he'd been her best friend and rock.

The little boy laughed raucously and hurled the ball in her direction. Harlow watched as the ball landed a few steps away from her. For a little kid, he had quite the throwing arm. She stood to retrieve the toy and hurl it back in the dog's direction. When she looked back up, the German shepherd was barreling toward her with abandon. She raised her arm to throw it at him just as he attempted to grab it from her hand.

Ooof! Next thing she knew, Harlow was lying on her back on the grass with one hundred pounds of dog sitting squarely on her chest. He began licking her face and lavishing her with attention. She tried her best to push him off, but he wouldn't budge. What were they feeding this dog? Was this yet another small town annoyance?

"Zeus! No. Off," a little voice commanded. The dog immediately got off her and sat down next to the boy, who was shaking his finger at him. "Bad dog. You need to listen. Now you're really in for it. Here comes Dad."

Harlow sat still for a moment, trying to catch her breath. *Dang!* Was this dog some type of Cujo? A hound from hell? As a veterinarian she'd come across a few over the years. Actually he looked kind of cute, but he weighed a ton. Harlow knew she should really stand up, but she still felt a bit winded.

Someone else joined them, and she registered a low adult male voice reprimanding Zeus. Harlow had a feeling she must look fairly ridiculous lying flat on her back among the leaves.

"Harlow!" For a moment confusion swirled around her. Nobody in town knew her yet, so how was her name being uttered in this deep, sexy voice? Glancing up, her eyes landed on a familiar and un-forgettable face. With the sun glinting in her eyes, Harlow could have sworn there was a golden halo around his head.

"Nick!" His name flew from her lips as soon as she recognized the man who'd rescued her the other day. Was it really him? *Of course it was.* How many

men who looked like this were walking around
Mistletoe? He gave new meaning to the words *tall,
dark, and handsome.* In his gray pullover and dark
jeans, he looked casual and sporty. And 100 percent fine.

He offered her a hand and pulled her to her
feet. "Are you okay?" he asked, peering closely at
her face.

She brushed dirt and leaves off her coat while
trying to appear unfazed. "I-I'm fine. Just a little
startled."

Harlow felt almost as shocked to see him as the
first time they'd crossed paths. If it was humanly
possible, he looked even better than she remembered. *Mistletoe's finest!* He had to be at least six
foot two—maybe even taller—with a rugged frame
that spoke of his job duties...rescuing damsels in
distress from near disaster. His beautiful brown skin
was flawless. Who knew the state of Maine had
been hiding such a fine specimen? She could get
used to this!

"We've really got to stop meeting like this,"
Nick said, his beautiful mouth turning upward into
a magnificent smile. Have mercy! His grin went
straight to her gut, where butterflies began to wildly
flutter around. This man was pure Kryptonite.

"Well, at least this time I'm not dangling over
a cliff."

"It's time we met for real." He held out his hand.
"Nick Keegan. And this is my son, Miles."

She reached out to shake his hand. Her palm tingled with awareness. "Harlow Jones." *Keegan.* Why did that name sound so familiar? It was nagging at her, but she couldn't figure it out. Being in Nick's orbit made thinking straight a difficult task.

He placed a hand on his chest. Nick quirked his mouth. "I can't apologize enough for Zeus's behavior. He just joined our family, so we're still sorting out some issues."

"If it's any comfort, he was definitely going after the toy. I just happened to be in the line of fire," Harlow answered. She'd been around enough dogs to know aggressive types. This dog wasn't that variety.

"Still," Nick said, sounding annoyed, "he used to work with search and rescue. He knows better. Or at least he should. Perhaps that's why he was cut from the program."

Miles shrugged. "Maybe he thought she needed a rescue," he said lamely.

Nick scowled at his son. "Or maybe he needs more training. A bit of discipline."

It was obvious to Harlow that Miles was sticking up for his dog so he wouldn't get in any trouble. It was sweet and endearing. Miles frowned at her, giving Harlow the impression that he was blaming her for the incident.

"So, what brings you to town? Did you relocate here?" Nick asked, his voice tinged with curiosity. "I don't recall seeing you around Mistletoe."

"The day you saved my bacon I was heading to Mistletoe for the first time. I just started a job at Paws Veterinary Clinic. I'm a veterinarian," she explained. Harlow couldn't help feeling a burst of pride every time she uttered the *v* word. Despite her past, she'd managed to make something of herself. She hadn't given up. She had persevered.

Nick chuckled. The sound of his laughter was nice and light. "Believe it or not, I was just about to make an appointment there for Zeus. We need to get him up to date on his vaccinations. Welcome to Mistletoe, by the way. I hope you'll like it here."

"Thank you," she murmured, feeling all tingly inside. Whatever magic Nick possessed, if he bottled it up and sold it he could make a fortune. Harlow couldn't recall the last time a man had made her weak in the knees.

If Nick Keegan was Mistletoe's welcome wagon, women would flock to this town in droves. Maine eye candy alert!

"I'm going to make an appointment for Zeus," Nick said. "Is it all right if we ask for you?"

She was flattered. It would be nice to build up a client base while she was in Mistletoe. Establishing a solid reputation in her profession was crucial to long-term success. "Sure thing. I'd love to check you out." Harlow sputtered. "I'd love to check him out. Meaning your dog. Not you." She wanted to slap her palm to her forehead. Talk about a slip of the tongue! Duh!

Nick shook his head and let out a throaty laugh. "I knew what you meant."

She was glad at least one of them did. Yep, it was high time she slunk away before she made a total fool of herself. As it was, Nick probably already thought she was flakier than a croissant.

"Okay, I've got to head back to work. It was nice officially meeting you, Nick." She turned toward Miles, who was playing with Zeus. "And you also, Miles. See you soon, Zeus."

Miles lifted his hand to wave at her before turning back to his dog. It didn't take a genius to see that he was over the moon about his new pet. There was nothing sweeter than a child and their dog. When she was Miles's age, Rambo had been everything to her.

As she got behind the wheel and began to make her way back to Paws, her mind took her straight back to Nick. Something about this man tugged at her. She hadn't felt this way in years. Not since he who should not be named under any circumstances. Harlow bit her lip.

Wait. She had totally fangirled over Nick Keegan without pausing to check his ring finger. Was tall, dark, and chocolate already spoken for? Hmm. The clues were all there. He had a son. He was scrumptious. Super charming. But she'd detected a slight flirtatiousness in his manner toward her. Or had she imagined it? Perhaps it had simply been part of his welcome-to-Mistletoe shtick. She was far from an

expert on men. What Harlow knew about relationships wouldn't even fill up a postage stamp.

Maybe it was time to get back in the game. Being
single was getting old. A man like Nick Keegan
might be fun to go out with—if he wasn't already
taken. If he was, Harlow would just drool from afar.
The last thing she wanted to do was catch feelings
for a man who already had a woman.

* * *

By the time dinner rolled around, Miles had fed
Zeus, taken him on his nightly walk, and played
with him in their fenced-in backyard. Even though
he'd grudgingly made Zeus a part of their family,
Nick had to admit that his son was doing an amazing
job taking care of his new pet. Nick didn't think
he, at nine years old, would have had the discipline.
But it was clear that Miles adored Zeus. He'd even
allowed the dog to sleep at the foot of his bed. Nick
must be getting soft, because he didn't have the
heart to banish Zeus to the playroom.

"Are you still mad at Zeus?" Miles looked over
at Nick with a crestfallen expression etched on his
face. Since the day he was born, Nick hadn't been
able to resist his son's soft brown eyes. His son
really knew how to work all of his assets.

"I wouldn't say mad exactly," Nick hedged. He
had been treading lightly on the subject of Zeus,
unwilling to let his son see how annoyed he was

at their new family member for tackling Harlow at the park. Getting acclimated to the boisterous pup wasn't easy.

"Pissed off?" Miles asked with a smirk.

"Miles," Nick said in a warning tone. "We talked about not saying the *p* word."

"Sorry. It slipped out." Miles put a forkful of mac 'n' cheese in his mouth and closed his eyes. He let out a sound of satisfaction. "Dad, I gotta hand it to you. This mac 'n' cheese is slammin'." He gave Nick a thumbs-up. "I'll definitely be having seconds."

"Well, thanks. High praise indeed coming from a mac 'n' cheese connoisseur like yourself," Nick said as he dug into his own meal. Yum. It was pretty tasty, he decided. It had taken him a long time to get the mac 'n' cheese right. Miles had gotten so used to Kara's recipe that nothing Nick ever whipped up could compare. Finally, after many months of trial and error, he'd come up with a winning recipe that Miles devoured. If he was being honest with himself, Miles's reaction made him feel like a rock star, which wasn't always the case these days. Miles was at that age when he was beginning to question his dad's cool quotient. Knowing he had scored a home run with dinner was gratifying.

After doling out seconds of mac 'n' cheese for Miles, Nick began collecting the dirty plates and placing them in the dishwasher.

"I have to head out soon to work, which means Aunt Stella is coming over to stay with you."

Miles loved hanging out with Aunt Stella, who had been his second-grade teacher a year ago. Long before she'd married Luke, Stella had held a special place in Miles's heart. Even though he adored Stella, Nick knew from past experiences that Miles hated when he had to be away from him overnight.

"I wish you could tuck me in," Miles said, sounding wistful. "Will you be here when I wake up in the morning?"

At moments like this, Nick felt completely torn. He needed to work so he could keep a roof over their heads and food on the table, but he hated being away from his son, especially overnight. Nick wanted to be there if the nightmares came back, the ones that had tortured Miles in the weeks and months after Kara's death. "Bud, I'd love nothing more than to stick close to you twenty-four/seven, but I've got to put my cape on and protect the people in Metropolis from danger."

Miles began to giggle. "Dad, you're not Superman."

Nick widened his eyes. "I'm not?" He pulled open his shirt in an exaggerated fashion, pretending to look for his uniform. "I don't know what happened to my uniform. Maybe it's in the wash."

Miles threw back his head in laughter. "You are so lame, Dad. But in the best way ever."

That's all Nick needed to hear. Maybe one day in the future, when Miles was an adult, he would look back on this moment and laugh. So many of Miles's young memories were tied up in profound loss. Nick considered it his job to add lightness and laughter to his son's world. For the moment, he'd accomplished his mission.

The sound of the front door opening and closing, followed by heels clicking on his hardwood floors, announced Stella's arrival. Within seconds she appeared in the kitchen doorway with a huge smile stretching across her pretty face. Sometimes it still felt jarring to Nick that his childhood friend had married Luke.

Miles jumped up from his seat and catapulted himself against his aunt's chest. Nick's heart squeezed as he watched. Stella placed her arms around Miles and pressed a kiss on his head. Although Nick knew it wasn't the same as a mother's love, Stella sure did a great job at mothering his son.

"Hey there, Zeus," Stella said as the German shepherd raced to her side with his tail wagging fast and furiously. "You're such a good boy. You need to have a play date with Coco Chanel soon."

Nick let out a snort. He'd love to see that meeting of the canine minds. Stella would have a heart attack if Zeus got overly playful with her precious poodle. "Let's not go there just yet. Zeus needs some home training first. He just knocked down some poor woman in the park who was simply minding her own business." Just thinking about Harlow lying on the ground covered in leaves and ninety pounds of dog made him feel sheepish. She'd been so calm and understanding, which told him a lot about the woman. He made a mental note to make that vet appointment. Nick was very curious about Harlow Jones. She'd piqued his interest from the first time he'd seen her car dangling over a cliff, and now he had the perfect opportunity to get to know her better.

"I'm going to get my new Lego set, Auntie Stella. We can play with them in the TV room," Miles said before running out of the kitchen.

Before Stella could even respond, Miles had vanished. Nick and Stella laughed in unison at his speedy disappearance.

"He's fast on his feet when he wants something," Stella noted.

"You should see him when he's trying to escape chores," Nick said.

"Hey, Nick," she said, walking toward him and placing a kiss on his cheek. "How's it going? You look great," she said, giving him a once-over.

"Thanks for coming over, especially since it takes you away from the cutest baby in Maine." His niece had been blessed with two very good-looking parents.

"Oh, it'll be good for Luke to have some bonding time with Jade. Your brother has mastered the fine art of dodging dirty diapers. Since I'm staying overnight, it's going to be impossible to ignore any diaper explosions." She let out a throaty chuckle. "I can't wait to hear the stories. It's amazing how a funky diaper can take a retired Navy SEAL down."

A mental image of Luke battling baby spit up, poopy diapers, and crying meltdowns made him grin. Luke deserved a little agony after unloading Zeus on him.

"I keep meaning to tell you that I have someone I'd like you to meet," Stella said in an excited tone. "She's an old friend of mine from college."

Nick let out a groan. He hated fix-ups. Not that he'd ventured too deeply into the dating pool, but it seemed that every single person in Mistletoe wanted to set him up with someone. For a long time, he'd resisted because he'd still been grieving Kara. As time went on, Nick had warmed up to the idea of dating, but so far, he hadn't felt a single spark.

Nothing remotely like what he'd felt for Harlow! He couldn't seem to stop thinking about the woman. Learning she was Mistletoe's newest veterinarian only served to pique his interest. Nick appreciated a woman who made a difference in her community.

He'd wanted to ask her out at the park, but doing so with Miles standing a few feet away would have felt uncomfortable. He had no idea how Miles felt about the possibility of him dating, even though he was a pretty chill kid. Nick hadn't tested the dating waters enough to know how Miles would respond.

"I appreciate you thinking of me, but—" he began.

"But it's time you got out there," Stella said, cutting him off.

"I'm out there. I've been on a few dates," he

protested. They'd all been pretty lame, but at least he had ventured into the dating pond. He'd tried his best.

"All of those went nowhere. Did you ever go on any second dates?" Stella asked with her hands firmly placed on her hips.

"Not exactly," Nick admitted. *What was the point of going out on a second date when he'd barely survived the first one?*

"Just trust me on this. I promise that you won't regret it." She was gazing at him with puppy-dog eyes, and he saw so much hope in their depths.

Nick didn't want to hurt his sister-in-law's feelings or crush her dreams of playing matchmaker, but he didn't think he would enjoy another fix-up. It just wasn't his style. He needed to see someone across a crowded room and feel sparks. Or look into a woman's deep-set brown eyes as he was saving her from near death. In his entire life Nick had felt sparks with only a few women. Harlow had been the most recent.

"I did meet someone I'm interested in," he admitted. Nick knew it was wrong of him to dangle it out there, especially since he hadn't even asked Harlow out or gotten her number, but he also knew that this would make Stella back off.

Right on cue, Stella let out a high-pitched squeal. Bingo. She'd reacted just as Nick imagined she might. Pure excitement, bordering on hysteria.

"What's her name? Have you taken her out yet?

Can we meet her?" Stella hurled out question after question at the speed of a pro baseball pitcher.

He held up his hands. "I don't want to jinx anything by talking about it, but you'll be the first to know if anything happens," Nick promised. "Now I really have to head out." He leaned in for a hug. "Have fun with Miles."

Just then Miles ran back into the room holding up a box of Legos. "I'm back with reinforcements," he shouted. "You're in for a fun night, Auntie Stella."

"On that note I'm out," Nick said, choking back laughter. After grabbing a duffel bag and his keys, Nick headed toward the front door, turning around to catch one last glimpse of his son. With his cinnamon-colored skin and big brown eyes, he was resembling his mother more and more every day. Noticing the resemblance didn't hurt as it once did. It simply made him happy that he'd loved and been loved by Miles's mother.

CHAPTER FOUR

A breeze swept over Harlow and she closed her eyes to let the October sun warm her up. Maine weather didn't seem to want to make up its mind. The temperature vacillated between chilly and balmy. Today was a sweatshirt day with no jacket required.

"I don't think you realize how much I've missed you," Harlow said to her twin brother as they sat outside on the patio of the Coffee Bean. Bear sat at her feet, just chilling out and watching the world go by. Being reunited with Malcolm and Bear had been just what she needed to rev up her spirits. Moving to a brand-new town after being so settled in Seattle was disconcerting.

"I missed you more," Malcolm said before taking a lengthy sip of his espresso.

"Not possible," she said, repeating their child-hood exchange.

"So far Mistletoe seems pretty nice," Malcolm said as he sat back in his chair and surveyed the downtown area. "You can definitely indulge in some retail therapy here. Although maybe I shouldn't tempt you, since your goal is to be debt-free."

"I look forward to shopping till I drop with Stella. She's been such a big help to me. Without her I wouldn't be living in a house on the lake." Although Harlow still wasn't sold on Mistletoe, or any other small town for that matter, Stella had given her the hookup with a fantastic rental.

"I can't believe she's married," Malcolm said with a frown. "To a Navy SEAL, no less," he muttered.

"And she's also a new mother," Harlow added, smirking. For some reason, Malcolm was experiencing major regret about not romantically pursuing Stella. As much as she loved Malcolm, she'd never been able to imagine the two of them as a couple. Since Malcolm had attended SCAD (Savannah College of Art and Design), he had been only a four-hour drive from their Spelman College campus. He and his college buddies had frequently done road trips to Atlanta, where they'd hung out with Harlow and the Spelman girls. He'd been smitten by Stella at first sight.

Malcolm scowled. "Don't rub it in. I'm still kicking myself that I didn't shoot my shot with her."

Harlow snorted. Her brother was a serious player, going from one woman to the next. "You're being ridiculous. How many women have you dated since Stella and I were at Spelman? You haven't exactly been pining away for her."

Malcolm shook his head at her. He placed his hand over his heart. "You're enjoying my pain, aren't you?" he asked.

"Always," Harlow said, leaning over and tweaking her brother's cheek. When she swung her gaze up, Nick was walking out of the coffee shop with a tray of drinks in his hand. Their eyes met and a smile began to spread across Nick's handsome face. Harlow sucked in a deep breath. Every time she laid eyes on this man her pulse began to race and her thoughts ran wild.

He stopped when he reached their table. "Hey, Harlow. It's good to see you."

"Hi, Nick. Fancy meeting you here," Harlow said, inexplicably feeling tongue-tied. What was going on with her? She was never at a loss for words.

Nick's gaze slid to Malcolm, who nodded in Nick's direction. "Hi, I'm Malcolm. Harlow's twin brother."

Maybe it was wishful thinking, but Nick seemed relieved to find out that Malcolm was her brother and not a date. She might be imagining it, but suddenly Nick seemed a lot more relaxed. His shoulders were hanging lower now and his eyes twinkled.

"Hey, Malcolm. Nice to meet you," Nick said with a friendly smile.

"Malcolm, Nick is the person I was telling you

about. The one who rescued me after my car slid off the road," Harlow explained. She'd told Malcolm all about her brush with death and Nick's heroic actions. He'd been very impressed and grateful. Harlow had also been on the receiving end of a lecture about dangerous driving practices. For once, Harlow had listened without a word of protest. She was simply grateful her life had been spared. She'd tried to put the incident at the back of her mind, but it had been terrifying.

"Hey, man. I can't thank you enough for everything you did for Harlow." Malcolm let out a low whistle. "That was some superhero stuff from what Harlow told me. Good looking out."

"I was just happy to help before things took a turn for the worse," Nick said. "I've seen a lot of fatal accidents." Nick winced, as if remembering the tragic scenes he'd witnessed. He looked down at Bear. "And who is this big boy?"

Harlow reached down and patted the top of Bear's head. "This is Bear. Malcolm's been watching him for the past few weeks, but now he's here to stay."

"Bear, not me," Malcolm said with a grin. "I'm only here for a few more days."

"Do you live nearby?" Nick asked Malcolm.

"I'm living in Boston, which is a lot closer to Mistletoe than Seattle," Malcolm answered.

"You got that right!" Harlow said, relishing the fact that her twin would be no more than a three-hour drive away. Being on the same coast as Malcolm was comforting. He was her version of a human security blanket. Things were always better when he was around.

"Well, you've discovered the best coffee place in town, so it seems like you're getting the lay of the land." He held up his coffee tray. "I better finish my coffee run. It was nice to see you, Harlow." He nodded at Malcolm. "Nice to meet you. I hope you enjoy your time in Mistletoe."

"See you around," Harlow said. "Don't forget to bring Zeus in."

"Will do," Nick said, flashing a smile. "I haven't forgotten."

Harlow's gaze trailed after him as he placed his tray on the top of his black SUV before opening the car door, reaching up for the tray, then sliding into the car. Within seconds he'd zoomed away, causing longing to sweep over her. Harlow didn't know what to make of her feelings. She barely knew Nick Keegan.

"Take a picture. It'll last longer," Malcolm said, reverting to his ten-year-old self.

"You're so funny I forgot to laugh," Harlow said.

Malcolm wiggled his eyebrows. "You like him, don't you? I can tell."

"He's nice," Harlow said, trying not to smile too much. Malcolm was like a shark who could smell blood in the water. "Not to mention he saved my life. That's pretty badass, right?"

"I like him too, Harlow. He seems like a cool guy. Personable. Laid back. Humble." Malcolm gave her a thumbs-up. "I'd love to see you with a guy like Nick."

"He has a son. And I'm not one hundred percent sure he's not married," she sheepishly admitted.

Malcolm let out a groan. "That man was not giving out married vibes. He's into you, sis. And he wasn't wearing a wedding band." Malcolm winked at her. "I checked. Can't have you out here slipping."

She let out a little shriek and threw herself against Malcolm. "You're the best. Have I ever told you that?"

"A few times here and there," he said, wrinkling his nose. "You know I'll always have your back. You're my little sister."

"By five minutes," she said, rolling her eyes. "But I do appreciate you looking out for me."

"That's never going to change," Malcolm said. "Now don't be shy. Go after what you want. Life is too short to sit on the sidelines."

Go after what you want. It had been their father's mantra. Harlow tried to ignore the painful twisting sensation in her gut. She had been thinking of Jack Jones a lot lately, not only missing her father, but feeling cheated out of so many years with him. Sometimes when she least expected it, grief grabbed her by the throat and wouldn't let go. Sometimes when she saw a father and daughter duo a fiery rage came over her. *It wasn't fair! She and Malcolm had been robbed of a childhood and their precious father!*

"I still miss him too." Malcolm's voice interrupted

her thoughts, bringing her back to the here and now. "That feeling of loss won't ever go away, Harlow. But it doesn't mean we can't be happy. It doesn't mean we don't deserve to find love."

"You're right," Harlow said, reaching out to tightly hold Malcolm's hand. "I hope we both find our true north."

Maybe, just maybe, if she said it enough times to herself in the mirror she would finally start to believe it.

* * *

For the entire ride over to Miles's soccer game, Nick found himself wishing he'd bitten the bullet and asked Harlow out when he'd seen her earlier. He tried to tell himself it would have been awkward with her brother sitting there. When had he become such a chicken? Maybe somewhere around the time he'd been forced to bury his wife. Being with Kara had always been effortless. They hadn't been perfect, not by a long shot. They had bickered and nagged at each other like most couples. But not a day had gone by during which they hadn't been a couple. Nick missed the simple things, like having someone warming up a plate of food for him after a long shift. Receiving a text for absolutely no reason at all. Having his and her sides of the bed. Being so in tune with another person that you finished each other's sentences.

Nick wanted to experience all those things again. He wanted to be in love. He yearned to hold some-one's hand and ask them how their day had gone. Nick had no idea what might happen with him and Harlow. It might never get off the ground. She might laugh in his face when he asked her out, but he was going to try.

He'd been relieved to discover that Malcolm was Harlow's brother. When Nick had first spotted Harlow sitting on the patio with a handsome guy who looked like a male model, his stomach had plummeted. She'd looked so happy and comfort-able chatting with her companion that he'd almost walked off in the opposite direction. But he was glad he hadn't.

By the time Nick returned to the field, half-time was over. He quickly made his way over to Luke and their parents, as well as Stella, who'd just arrived with baby Jade. Nick handed out the coffees and peered down at his little niece in her baby carriage.

"How's the little princess doing today?" Nick asked, breathing in the scent of baby powder and sweetness.

"My granddaughter is amazing," his mother said, reaching down and picking Jade up and cuddling her. Betty cooed at her grandchild, who gazed up at her with sparkling brown eyes flecked with caramel.

"We need more grandkids. You two need to get

cracking," Willie said, sending a pointed look at both of his sons.

"Hint taken," Luke said, locking eyes with Stella.

"Don't look at me," Stella said, twisting her mouth. "I'm not even thinking about bringing another life into the world anytime soon. I'm still breastfeeding!"

Nick shook his head. "Don't even start with me. I'm as single as a dollar bill."

"Kara is a hard act to follow," his mother said, "but you'll find someone, Nick." She reached up and tweaked his chin. "You're the handsomest bachelor in Maine. Any woman would be lucky to have a man like you."

"Aww, Mom. You're so sweet," Nick said, pulling her in for a hug. She had always been one of his biggest supporters, and she continued to rally for him and Miles. Having that type of support had been crucial in the weeks and months after Kara's death. As a single dad, Nick always tended to doubt himself. Was he doing enough for Miles? Was he making sure he kept Kara's memory alive for his son? In the absence of another parent in the house, was Nick enough?

His mother blinked back tears. "I speak nothing but the truth."

"Aww, Betty. You're an old softie," his father said as he placed his arm around her shoulder and pulled her close.

"Who you calling old?" she asked with a frown.

"I'm two years younger than you. Be careful you don't squish the baby."

"I'm not going to smush my grandbaby," Willie said in a raised voice.

Nick and Luke exchanged a glance as their parents began to fuss at each other. They loved each other like nobody's business, but their marriage wasn't perfect. There had been bumps and hiccups along the way, but they were still together, fighting the good fight. His parents had once told him and Luke that they wanted no less for the two of them.

He'd had it once before. Did lightning strike twice in a lifetime?

"Just a reminder that we're having a small do at the house Saturday after the baptism," Stella said. "Nice and intimate."

"We can't wait to celebrate Jade," his father said.

Nick appreciated the reminder. Luke and Stella had asked him to be Jade's godfather, which was an incredible honor. Stella's sister Lucy was godmother, so he'd half expected them to ask her husband, Dante, to serve as godfather.

"Dad!" Miles waved to him from the field, jumping up and down to get his attention. In his black-and-orange uniform, black cleats, and knee guards, he looked like the quintessential soccer player. His son hadn't always been super athletic, but he'd made great strides since last year. Extra practice time and participating in a few leagues had helped him immensely. Nick knew it was Miles's most ardent wish to make a goal today. Nick remembered all too well the feelings of wanting to be successful on the field. As he'd suited up for football games, Nick had prayed to make touchdowns and lead his team to glory.

"Hey, Miles. Get it. Chase that ball down!" Nick yelled as his family cheered on Miles. As the game kicked into high gear, Nick kept his eyes glued to number 10. With his lanky frame and long legs, Miles was fast on his feet but a tad hesitant. The action ensued with possession of the ball going back and forth between the teams as the score tightened. Nick winced when an opponent knocked Miles to the ground.

"He's all right," Luke said, clapping Nick on the back. "I think he was just winded."

Nick relaxed as Miles stood up and demonstrated that he was fine. Seconds ticked by, with the opposing team making a shot that tied up the game. Nick and Luke let out groans as they watched the clock tick away precious seconds. Suddenly, Miles had the ball and he was making his way down the field, where he passed it to another teammate.

"Way to go, Miles. Teamwork," Nick shouted. "C'mon, Hawks."

Luke grabbed his arm as Miles once again had the ball. Nick watched as his son positioned himself in front of the goal and lifted his leg up to take a shot. Time seemed to stand still as the ball flew into the air and landed in the netting.

Pandemonium ensued as Miles was swept up by his teammates in a swarm of celebration as the crowd cheered. Luke and Nick began to scream their lungs out as Stella covered the baby's ears. Miles's grandparents were jumping up and down and high-fiving each other.

Nick waited on the sidelines, watching Miles experience one of the major highlights of his young life. His son deserved this golden moment of victory. Life was too short not to cherish the good times. If it were up to him, Miles would have hundreds of moments like this his whole life long.

* * *

Harlow stood in front of the full-length mirror and studied herself from all angles. She hadn't been to many christening parties, but she was excited about going to a social event in Mistletoe. Malcolm had just gone back to Boston yesterday, and she was already experiencing withdrawal. Having her brother in town had been wonderful. Nobody got her the way Malcolm did. Although she wasn't a big fan of marriage, Harlow had always told herself that if she could find a man who deeply understood her, she might just have found a life partner.

Since she was stuck in Mistletoe for one solid year, Harlow needed to socialize and develop a net-work of folks here in town. Harlow couldn't expect

Stella to be her constant sidekick, because she had a
newborn to take care of.

"I think this works," Harlow said out loud as she
admired the bright red dress against her dark brown
skin. A pair of tan low-heeled pumps would round
out her attire. Her curls were a little bit out of
control today, but she poured some product into her
palms, then ran her hands through her hair. A light
application of foundation, along with red lipstick
and eyeliner, completed her look.

Harlow left her lakeside home and followed her
GPS directions to a gorgeous coastal road that over-
looked the waters of Blackberry Beach. A beautiful
gold-and-azure sign highlighted the beach area,
which was visually stunning. All Harlow could see
for miles was a large expanse of ocean and sand.
The beach was devoid of people, most likely due to
the chilly temp of the ocean in fall. It was easy to
imagine swimming here in the summertime. It was
definitely something for Harlow to look forward to
in the coming months.

As her vehicle wound around twisty roads, she
let out a gasp as she reached a portion of road where
she could look down and survey all of Blackberry
Beach. A few minutes later her GPS alerted her that
she was approaching her destination. After parking
her car, Harlow stepped out of the vehicle and
soaked in her surroundings. She walked over toward
the edge of the property so she could get a glimpse
of the ocean.

Stella and Luke's seaside home sat right next to the beach. The house itself was a charming cottage that seemed to have come straight from a fairy tale. Beautiful flowers in brightly colored pots sat on the front porch. Marigolds and sunflowers, and Harlow spotted what looked like mums. Everything she knew about flowers had come from her mother, who'd nurtured a garden when she and Malcolm were small. That had all changed when they'd left Chestnut Ridge in disgrace.

The sound of a car's tires crunching over the pebbles in the driveway garnered her attention. A man stepped out of the car and began walking toward the house.

No, it wasn't. Seriously? Surely there couldn't be more than one man in town who was as gorgeous as Nick Keegan. Dressed in a navy-blue suit and a crisp white shirt, he looked impossibly handsome and debonair.

This was wild! She'd been thinking about Nick so hard lately that she'd conjured him out of thin air. She was gazing at him so intensely that she noticed the very moment Nick spotted her. He stopped on the path and simply stared at her as if he couldn't believe his eyes.

His entire face lit up, and he quickly made his way to where she stood on the porch steps.

Nick let out a low whistle. "You look incredible, Harlow."

The compliment went straight to her head, making

her feel practically giddy. "You clean up very nicely yourself, Mr. Keegan."

"Thanks. It's been a hot minute since I've put a suit on," Nick said, smoothing down his tie.

Harlow hoped she wasn't drooling, but Nick was wearing the blue suit like a boss. She liked his casual attire as well, but seeing him like this brought to mind a Black James Bond or a *GQ* model. Either way, he was fine with a capital *F*.

The door swung open and Stella stood there, greeting them with a wide smile.

"Harlow. Thanks for coming." She swung her gaze to Nick. "Nick! Where have you been? We thought you were following behind us after we all left the church."

"I forgot Jade's present at the house, so I sent Miles ahead with my parents," Nick explained. He reached into his suit jacket pocket and pulled out an envelope and a small, gaily wrapped present. He handed it over to Stella.

"Well, don't stand on ceremony," Stella said, waving them inside. "It's a lot warmer inside. Come on in."

Stella and Nick seemed pretty close, Harlow thought. Almost like family. Harlow racked her brain trying to remember if Stella had a cousin or a close friend named Nick. She was drawing a blank. Nick made a motion for her to enter the house in front of him, then followed closely behind her.

The home exuded a warm and cozy vibe. Delicious

aromas wafted in the air. A picture of Stella and Luke on their wedding day sat on the entry hall table along with a photo of their sweet-faced baby girl. Harlow looked around her. The hues dominating the decor were eggshell, robin's-egg blue, and taupe. Her first impression was that love lived here. It hummed and pulsed all around her.

"Let me introduce you two," Stella said, with a twinkle sparkling in her eye. "Nick, this is my college friend Harlow Jones. Harlow, this is my brother-in-law, Nick Keegan. Harlow is new to town and she's a veterinarian working at Paws. Like myself, Nick grew up in Mistletoe, so he knows it like the back of his hand."

Keegan! Ugh! She'd known that his last name had sounded familiar, but she hadn't made the connection. Nick was Luke's brother. Two achingly handsome men in one family really defied the odds. Normally when there was one incredibly handsome brother, the other one had gotten shortchanged in the looks department. *Not this time!*

"So this is your friend you wanted me to meet?" Nick asked Stella.

"Yes," Stella said. "And now you have, which makes me very happy. Why don't the two of you get something to eat? I'm going to put Jade down soon, since she's getting a little fussy." She turned to Harlow. "I'd love for you to meet my little angel when she wakes up. And Luke as well."

With a smile, Stella turned on her heels and

walked toward the room where Harlow could see guests were gathering. Harlow looked over at Nick, who couldn't seem to contain his gigantic smirk.

"Was Stella trying to fix us up?" she asked, feeling incredulous. Ever since Nick had rescued her on her way into town, she'd been fantasizing about this man, only to find out he was related to her only friend in Mistletoe. Small towns had such an interconnectivity among the residents. She shouldn't be surprised at all by the link Stella and Nick shared. After all, Mistletoe was the quintessential small town. Harlow was on the fence about this aspect of living here. She was a fairly private person who didn't like the idea of so many overlapping connections. It was easy to see how gossip might thrive in a community like this one.

"Without a doubt," Nick answered, full-on grinning at this point and confirming her hunch about Stella's playing matchmaker.

Harlow covered her face with her hands. "How cringeworthy. My good friend didn't think that I could land a man on my own."

Nick reached out and touched her arm. Her body instantly responded to the contact, and a sigh slipped past her lips. She wondered what it would feel like to be kissed by Nick, to feel his fingers roaming across her skin. It would be heavenly, she imagined.

"Trust me, it's more about me than you," Nick continued. "I've been out of the dating game for years. My whole family is trying to hook me up with someone."

Had she heard him right? Years? For a man who looked like Nick it seemed near impossible. What was wrong with the ladies in Mistletoe?

Maybe Nick was pulling her leg. Unless, of course, he had a creepy reputation or he'd been involved in something sordid. Wild scenarios ran through her head at the speed of light. Was he an ex-con, one of those smooth-talking men who swindled women online? Maybe he was divorced and his ex-wife had blackballed him all over town.

Finally, Harlow decided he'd been teasing her. He didn't look like a serial killer, although these days, who really knew.

She cocked her head in order to study him. "Years? Come on. I don't believe it."

"Is this the face of a liar?" Nick pointed his finger at his face and gave her his most winning smile. "Have you ever seen *Sleepless in Seattle*?"

Had she? Harlow had gone through a serious rom-com phase where she had binge-watched the most notable films in this genre. *Sleepless in Seattle* was hands down the best.

"Of course I have," she said, sounding a bit incredulous. "Who hasn't? It's the quintessential rom-com. Single widower dad. Adorable son who goes on the radio to find his dad a romantic partner. Meg Ryan at her perkiest. It's a classic."

"I'm the Tom Hanks character. My wife passed

away." Nick threw out the information like a little stick of dynamite. Harlow felt all the air rush from her lungs. Nick was a widower! Why hadn't she even considered that possibility? At one point, she'd wondered if he was married or divorced, but widowed hadn't even crossed her mind. It was too sad. Nick was way too young to be the main character in such a tragic storyline. And sweet Miles had lost his mother at such a young age. Harlow didn't consider herself to be a sentimental person, but hearing Nick refer to himself as a widower tugged at her heartstrings.

Words failed her. For someone who was never short on something to say, Harlow couldn't muster up a single syllable. All of a sudden, she was reminded of growing up without a father and all of her mother's struggles as a widow raising two kids. Her family had been gutted by her father's tragic death. Their lives had been turned upside down, and they'd fumbled around in the dark for years.

"Sorry, I didn't mean to be a buzzkill. Did I make you uncomfortable?" Nick asked, locking eyes with her as he spoke. "If so, I'm sorry about that. I still haven't figured out how to slide that information into a conversation."

Harlow bit her lip. "Nick, please stop apologizing for something devastating that happened to you... and Miles. I'm just surprised, and honestly I froze because I didn't know what to say. That's on me. I'm not usually so tongue-tied. Or awkward."

Nick let out a laugh. "I'm used to feeling that way. Miles calls me lame at least once a week."

"Ouch!" Harlow said, wincing. Kids were rough. "That kind of talk must keep you humble," she said with a chuckle. Nick had such an easy manner. He was comfortable in his own skin and didn't mind laughing at himself. Even when bringing up the delicate topic of being widowed, he'd tried to put her at ease. This man was growing on her by the second.

Harlow wasn't interested in a serious relationship or anything that might tie her to Mistletoe, but she was attracted to Nick. What would be the harm in getting to know him better?

CHAPTER FIVE

Life was full of serendipitous moments. If Nick had learned anything at all in his life, it was the importance of chance and fate. Harlow Jones kept popping up in his orbit. Granted, Mistletoe was a small town, but crossing paths with her at his brother's house made Nick feel as if the universe was trying to tell him something. He couldn't think of the last time he'd had such a whimsical feeling about a person. On a normal day, Nick didn't sit around thinking about such things as destiny, but today was different. He was different.

Everyone in Mistletoe knew that Nick was a widower as well as the tragic details of Kara's death. After dropping off Miles at preschool one morning, the car she'd been driving had been hit head-on by a drunk driver running a red light. He wasn't used to telling people about being widowed. It was common knowledge in his hometown. Sharing that information with Harlow made him feel as if he'd taken a few steps forward.

Much to Nick's surprise, Miles had turned on the charm and greeted Harlow like an old friend the moment he spotted her.

"I remember you from the park. Zeus acted naughty and jumped on you," Miles said, shaking his head at the memory. "I didn't say it that day, but I'm sorry he acted up."

"It's okay. Zeus seems like a sweetheart. I work with dogs on a regular basis, so I know they can be a bit unpredictable," Harlow said with a smile. "One time I had a dog come in covered with porcupine quills."

Miles shuddered. "Ouch. That sounds painful."

"For real," Harlow said with a nod. "I took out every quill one by one, making sure not to hurt him." Harlow's features were animated as she spoke. "Right after I took out the last one, he bit me." For dramatic effect, Harlow widened her eyes.

"Noooooo," Miles said in a disbelieving tone. "That makes Zeus look like an angel. Did it hurt?"

Harlow shook her head. Her dark curly hair bounced around her shoulders. "Not really. He barely broke the skin. He was scared and that was his way of letting me know. It taught me to always expect the unexpected with animals. So all things considered, Zeus isn't a bad dog. He just needs a little training."

Miles looked up at him. "Did you hear that, Dad? Zeus is a good dog."

Nick frowned. His son was twisting Harlow's words a bit. It remained to be seen if Zeus was going to walk the straight and narrow in the Keegan household. This morning Nick had found his leather slippers chewed up and destroyed. It had taken all of his restraint not to yell at the dog. "That's not exactly what Harlow said, Miles, but I see where you're going with this." Miles was afraid that Nick was going to send Zeus back, so he felt the need to constantly hype the dog up.

"He's my best friend. I've got to have his back," Miles said, looking over at Harlow for approval. She smiled down at him and said, "That's great."

Nick tamped down a burst of jealousy. Once upon a time, he'd been his son's best friend and Miles hadn't hesitated to tell anyone who would listen that he was the best dad in the world. He knew that Miles was growing up and that it was normal for his son to branch out and shift allegiances, but for Nick, it was a little bit of a heartbreak. He'd gotten used to it being him and Miles against the world.

A few minutes later, Luke walked over to Nick and pulled him into the kitchen. Once they were alone, Luke didn't waste any time getting down to business.

"Hey. Stella wants me to ask you what you think of her friend. I get the feeling she's playing match-maker," Luke sheepishly explained.

"Harlow," Nick murmured. "Her name is Harlow."

Luke raised a beer to his lips and took a long sip of the amber-colored ale. "Right. Harlow. So, what do you think?" Luke was no doubt waiting to report back to his wife, who might potentially tell Harlow what he'd said.

"I think she's incredible." The words slipped out of his mouth before he could rein them back in.

Luke let out a laugh. "Seriously? She must have made quite an impression. You just met her."

"Not exactly," Nick admitted. He hadn't previously mentioned the daring rescue to Luke or the stunning woman who had been in harm's way. There had been a lot of action with search and rescue in the last few weeks, including ones that had ended up being recoveries, so their focus had been on those events.

"When did you meet her?" Luke asked, his brows knitted together in a frown.

Nick hesitated for a second, then said, "Harlow and I met on a rescue."

Luke's reaction was immediate. His eyes practically bulged out of his head. "Get out of here. You're pulling my leg."

He shook his head. "I'm not. Remember Brandon and Mandy were talking at work about the rescue where a woman had crashed through the guardrail?"

"That was Harlow?" Luke asked in a loud voice.

"Will you stop talking so loud?" Nick asked, feeling annoyed at his brother. "I'm not trying to spread her business all over town. She strikes me as a fairly private person. And it sounds like she didn't mention it to Stella, so clearly it's not something she wants to advertise."

"You're right about that. Stella would have passed it on to me." Luke shook his head. "What a small world. The woman you rescued is Stella's close friend."

Nick reached into the aluminum cooler for a beer. "You don't know the half of it. She's also going to be our vet at Paws. Heads up, since I'm sending you the first bill."

"Okay, I deserve that. Cheers," Luke said, raising his beer bottle and clinking it with Nick's. Luke began to laugh, with Nick joining in along with him. It felt like old times between them when laughter would break out for the silliest of reasons. Little by little, Luke was recovering from PTSD, and with the help of a therapist, Stella, and his family, his older brother had a new lease on life. Being a part of the search and rescue team had given Luke a sense of purpose. Becoming a father had shown him the best parts of himself. His capacity to love had sky-rocketed into orbit the moment baby Jade had been placed in his arms.

Stella popped her head around the corner. "Luke. What are you doing hiding away in the kitchen? You need to be out here mingling. That goes for you too, Nick."

"Sure thing, sweetheart," Luke said, walking

toward his wife and pulling her against him. He leaned down and placed a smoldering kiss on her lips. When Stella came up for air she fanned herself with her hand. "To be continued," she murmured.

"Oh, get a room," Nick said, covering his eyes. He loved Stella and Luke, but he didn't want a front-row seat for their tonsil hockey exhibition. TMI.

"Hater!" Stella said, giving him a pointed look. Her tinkling laughter followed Stella as she departed the kitchen.

"So, you never gave me a straight answer. Are you interested in Harlow?" Luke asked. "Stella's going to grill me later on about it."

A sudden sound in the doorway caused both him and Luke to turn their heads. Harlow was standing on the threshold with an empty serving tray in her hand. "I'm sorry to crash into your conversation. I was trying to be helpful."

One look at her face told Nick that she'd over-heard their conversation. She wasn't quite making eye contact, which didn't seem to be her style. From what he'd seen so far of Harlow, she was a confident and direct woman, qualities Nick admired.

"Let me take that," Nick said, moving to take the tray off her hands.

"I better get back to...mingling," Luke said as he beat a fast path out of the room. So much for Luke's being a big, bad former Navy SEAL.

After placing the tray on the kitchen counter, Nick turned back to Harlow. He wasn't going to ignore the elephant in the room. That would only make things more uncomfortable.

"So, I'm guessing you heard us talking," Nick said, quirking his mouth. This felt like holding one's hand to a hot fire and hoping not to get burned.

"Pretty much," Harlow said, making a face. Uh-oh. She seemed a bit displeased. "I hate being talked about," she admitted. Nick hated the hurt expression etched on her face.

"It wasn't like that. I promise," Nick quickly pointed out. "Let's face facts. Stella is trying to play matchmaker between us."

Harlow let out a groan. "I literally just got to town. And I'm only here for a year, which may be a year too long."

"Whoa," Nick said, holding up his hands. "Do I detect some hostility toward Mistletoe?"

"Oh, it's not just Mistletoe," Harlow explained. "I'm not a big fan of small towns in general."

Nick furrowed his brow. "And yet you decided to live here for a whole year?"

"Yes, but there's a catch. In exchange for working at Paws, all of my student loans will be paid off by the state of Maine. Getting booed up with someone isn't my main objective. I thought I'd made that clear to Stella."

Her tone radiated a saltiness that stung Nick a little bit. Maybe she wasn't interested in him despite the chemistry he'd been feeling between them. Her words made him feel as if he'd just run into a brick wall.

"Trust me, I know what it's like to be in the crosshairs of matchmakers." He emitted a groan of his own. "After a discreet period went by, every matchmaking mama in town tried to set me up with someone."

A small smile played around Harlow's lips. She seemed to be a lot more relaxed. "So how did that work out?"

"Until very recently, I was able to play the widower card. I told them that I wasn't ready to date. Truth is, I wasn't. My heart just wasn't in it." There was no expiration sticker on a broken heart. The very idea of being with someone—going out on a date, holding hands, kissing—had scared the hell out of him. If he was being totally honest with himself, Nick still felt unsure about moving forward in his romantic life.

"And now? Has that changed?"

"Yeah, it has. And if you hadn't interrupted us, you would have heard me saying yes to Luke. I do like you, Harlow." Harlow's beautiful brown eyes widened. Her ruby lips slightly parted. Nick thought he might have heard a sigh slip past them. "And if you're agreeable, I'd love to get to know you better." He held up his hands. "I'm not trying to tie you down or take the focus off your main objective, but there's no saying you can't have fun while you're in Mistletoe."

"True," Harlow said with a nod. "I don't have a single objection to having fun while I'm here."

That was exactly what he'd wanted to hear from Harlow's lips. It would be a shame if she cut herself off from being social because she was here in town on only a limited basis. From the sound of things, he and Harlow were on the same page. Being permanently booed up with someone was not on Nick's agenda, although he was definitely ready to put his big toe in the local dating pond. Harlow intrigued him, and he was excited about spending more one-on-one time with her. Nick had no idea where things would end up between him and Harlow, but he was ready for the journey.

* * *

By the time Harlow got back home from Stella and Luke's house, the sun was beginning to dip below the horizon. Bands of orange and purple colored the sky, reflecting on the lake in shimmering waves. Harlow took a few moments to breathe in the crisp autumn air and behold the beautiful lakeside view. It was sheer perfection. She let out a sigh. In other circumstances, this place could be a home, a dwelling she would proudly call her own. Harlow hadn't lived in an actual house since she was a kid. Her condo in Seattle had been nice, but it hadn't ever felt like a warm, cozy home. Home was Crock-Pot mac 'n' cheese, a fire blazing in the hearth, and the smell of vanilla potpourri infused in the atmosphere.

In some way, Harlow knew she had been searching

for home ever since the age of twelve. Being up-rooted from Chestnut Ridge after her father's death had been akin to having her heart ripped out of her chest. Her family had lost everything. The town—friends and all—had cruelly turned on them. That's when Harlow had given up on white picket fences and happily ever afters. Those dreams had crashed and burned.

Today had taken Harlow by surprise. She'd imag-ined the party might be slightly awkward, since Stella was her only real connection in town. Thank-fully, that hadn't been the case at all. Nick had been as charming as ever, and they had finally exchanged cell phone numbers with the expectation of meeting up for coffee. She'd gotten the chance to talk to Miles about her work at Paws, which seemed to fascinate him. Harlow sensed that he might have a future in veterinary medicine.

Meeting Stella's hot husband and seeing the pair so happy together had been heartwarming. And she'd actually met Dante West! A megastar. He hadn't put on airs or acted like a big-time celebrity, which Harlow found refreshing. Lucy was just as amazing as Stella, with a heart as wide open as an ocean. She had been a bit envious, seeing Stella's parents and her in-laws fawning over baby Jade. It caused a little hitch in her heart just knowing she would never experience a moment this precious with her own parents. Although her mother was still alive, her health was precarious at best. She

and Malcolm had been forced to make some hard
choices regarding her day-to-day care. The simple
truth was that her mother's health had been failing
for a number of years. Dementia had done a number
on her mind.

One year ago, Harlow and Malcolm had placed
her in a nursing home on Cape Cod. Bay Shore was
one of the best facilities in the country, and it was
located not too far from where Deidre had grown up.
Malcolm was only an hour-and-a-half drive away,
while Harlow had flown in from Seattle as often as
she could in order to see her. Being in Mistletoe
would make those visits easier.

Harlow loved taking her mother for walks on the
beach and eating clams at Tugboat's, overlooking
Hyannis Harbor. She loved seeing her mother smile
as she looked out across the ocean and told Harlow
stories about learning to swim at five years old in
Cape Cod water. How Harlow wished things could
be different. Stolen moments were all they had now
as her mother's memories began to fade.

Just as she let herself inside, her cell phone began
to buzz and she looked down at the screen, smiling
as she glimpsed Malcolm's number. She picked up
the phone, eager to hear her brother's voice and see
his face.

"Hey there, good looking. What's up?" Harlow
asked as her brother's irresistible face popped up on
the screen. His mahogany skin and strong features
were as familiar to Harlow as observing her own

face in the mirror. Seeing him served as an instant pick-me-up.

"Just checking on you. How are you making out?" Simply hearing Malcolm's voice and knowing he wasn't on the other side of the country was comforting.

"I'm actually doing pretty well. I went to the celebration for Stella and Luke's baby. Believe it or not, I was very sociable." Harlow was pretty proud of herself. Making new friends in a small-town setting wasn't her thing. Malcolm knew that better than anyone.

"You look pretty," Malcolm said, letting out a low whistle. "I know you mean business when you pull out the red dress."

Her twin knew her so well. Red was her go-to color. Just wearing her favorite hue made Harlow feel empowered. In many ways it was a suit of armor.

"Thanks, bro. Something unexpected happened." Harlow bit her lip.

"Let me guess. You didn't turn into a pumpkin at midnight," Malcolm teased.

"Stop it," she said, laughing at the faces he was making. "Nick was there. And it turns out he's Stella's brother-in-law."

She watched as surprise registered on Malcolm's face. "Get out of here. It doesn't get any more small town than that," he said with a chuckle.

"Ain't that the truth!" Stella said. "Six degrees of Nick Keegan."

She could see that Malcolm was in his art studio, working on his next collection. As always, she was awestruck by his massive talent. Even as a child, he'd exhibited signs of being an artistic genius. Getting noticed in the art world hadn't happened overnight, but thankfully Malcolm was now a rising star. His pieces were in demand all over the world.

"Did you confess to Stella that you have the hots for Nick?" Malcolm asked with a playful grin. She knew Malcolm was poking her to see her reaction. Little did he know she didn't have time for games today.

"No, but I did tell Stella that you have the hots for her. Oh, wait. I think our connection is going out." She began to make crackling noises with her mouth. "I'll talk to you later, Malcolm."

"No. Wait. You didn't really tell Stella that, did you? Don't hang up on me," Malcolm pleaded as she disconnected the call. Harlow burst out laughing at the panicked tone in his voice. Always cool, calm, and collected, Malcolm had sounded rattled. In a little while she would text him to let him know she'd been joking.

Harlow noticed via a notification on her phone that she had a voice mail. Harlow hadn't looked at her cell phone once during the party, so she hadn't seen any missed calls. She tapped her screen and listened to the message, which came from a Cape Cod number.

"Good evening, Miss Jones. This is Aretha

Simmons at the Bay Shore Rehabilitation Center. I'm calling about your mother. I hate to tell you that things aren't getting any better. Matter of fact, they've taken a turn for the worse. If you could please call me at your earliest convenience, we can discuss future steps."

Feeling numb, Harlow called Aretha back and listened to the update. Her mother's care team was recommending a transfer to the unit for patients with severe dementia. Harlow hung up after making plans to head to Cape Cod within the next few days. She didn't have the heart to call Malcolm tonight to break the news to him. He would immediately know what this meant, and it would shatter his heart. Their mother's condition was declining rapidly, and she was considered at a terminal stage.

Pain spread throughout Harlow's body, blinding her to anything else but the need to curl up in a little ball. It wasn't fair. Harlow wanted to rage against the unfairness of it all. Her mother had lost so much, only to be dealt a terrible hand with her dementia diagnosis. All of a sudden, Harlow was catapulted back to the terrifying moments after her father's death, when her family had imploded. She had done her best to stuff down all of these feelings in an attempt to bury the pain. But now, when she hadn't expected it, those emotions had come back with a vengeance, threatening to bury her all over again.

CHAPTER SIX

Nick drove along Main Street and tried his best to immerse himself in the fall decorations gracing all of the store windows. Pumpkins were beginning to pop up everywhere. Halloween outfits were on display at the toy store. A witch's hat and broom were hanging on the door of the novelties shop. Autumn was in full effect. Nick wished he could soak it all in and enjoy his favorite time of year.

He really needed a hot shower and some coffee. Days like this were tough. Every time he went out on a search and rescue mission Nick reminded himself that success wasn't guaranteed. Knowing that fact still didn't prepare him for failure. Nick took it personally that he hadn't been able to rescue a hiker, Larry Zabo, who had gotten lost at Acadia National Park. A fall from a ledge had resulted in catastrophic injuries. Try as he might, Nick couldn't get the image of the hiker's devastated parents out of his mind. Their hearts had been shattered.

All he really wanted to do right now was scoop his own son up in his arms and never let him go. But Miles was at school and that embrace would have to wait till this afternoon. The most difficult part of being a single parent was the fear that something might happen to him, leaving his son an orphan. Many times he had pondered the wisdom of continuing in his profession due to the inherent risks involved in high-stakes rescues. But each and every time, Nick had come to the conclusion that he was serving a higher calling by working in search and rescue. Nick helped people on a daily basis. What could be better than that?

He loved his profession, but on days like this it dredged up agonizing memories of his own loss. Although he knew Kara had died on impact, it still gnawed at him that he'd been working a rescue when she had been killed. How many people had he rescued in his years in search and rescue? More than he could count.

As he drove past the Coffee Bean, Nick made an impulsive decision to pull into a free space out front and head inside for a cup of molten hot java. He was going to need it to stay awake for the next few hours so he could pick up Miles after soccer practice.

As he entered the shop, Nick closed his eyes and breathed in the heavenly aroma of coffee beans and baked goods that assaulted his senses. The smell alone was enough to give him a pick-me-up.

A familiar head of springy black curls drew his attention to a customer standing at the front of the line. Once he heard the honeyed tone of her voice as she ordered an espresso, he knew for certain it was Harlow. A rush of adrenaline pulsed through his veins. His heart began to beat wildly in his chest. He couldn't remember the last time a woman's nearness had caused such a variety of physical reactions.

Although it was nice to see her again, Nick wondered if she would feel the same way about him. All of a sudden, he felt like a teenager.

As she walked by with coffee in hand, Nick reached out and gently tapped her arm. "Hey there. I was beginning to think you'd gone back to Seattle," he teased.

Surprise registered on her face. "Nick! It's good to see you."

Was it? Nick asked himself. He had messaged her a few times over the past few days and she hadn't responded. Maybe she'd taken his number only to be polite. If that was the case, it was better to know now rather than waste either of their time.

"If you have a few minutes, we can sit down and catch up after I order my coffee," he suggested, practically holding his breath while he waited. If she wasn't interested, he would have his answer. Nick wasn't going to make a nuisance of himself pursuing a woman who wasn't interested.

"Sure," she said, a smile turning her lips upward. "I'll just grab a table outside. The weather is way too nice to ignore."

"Sounds good. I'll be right out." Nick breathed a sigh of relief as he ordered his coffee and waited for it at the counter. This felt better than making a slam dunk when he'd played on his college basketball team.

* * *

Harlow picked a table outside that would allow her and Nick to talk while the sun provided some warmth from the autumn chill. She felt a little bit guilty about not reaching out to Nick. He had texted her a few times while she was out of town, but she'd had her hands full with care issues related to her mother. Harlow should have told him she had a family emergency, but she'd simply ignored his messages, telling herself she would contact him once she returned to Mistletoe. But she had been too busy catching up at the clinic, and now he probably thought she'd been avoiding him, which was by no means the case.

Tears pricked her eyes just thinking about her mother's condition. She hadn't recognized Harlow at all. She'd thought Harlow was her sister Jane, who'd passed away many years ago. Harlow hadn't known what to do, so she'd played along and pretended to be Aunt Jane. Anything to make her mother happy. If she could capture the moon from the sky and gift it to her, Harlow would do it. It was crystal clear to her that her mother was fading away from them and it hurt so much.

She wasn't just emotional about her mother. Harlow was exhausted. Making the drive to Cape Cod and back, along with meeting with the care team and her mother, had worn her out both physically and emotionally. Malcolm had reamed her out for not telling him about the crisis until she was already at Bay Shore. Harlow and Malcolm were never on the outs, so it was an unsettling feeling to be on the receiving end of his anger and extreme displeasure.

"I don't need you to protect me, Harlow. I've been dealing with this stuff my whole life," Malcolm had shouted at her.

His words had been explosive. Harlow sniffed back raw emotion. She needed to hold it together so Nick wouldn't see her losing it. Of all the people she hadn't wanted to run into when she was weepy and super emotional! Nick was at the top of the list. She wiped the tears from her face just as Nick appeared at their table.

"I've been dreaming of this salted caramel macchiato all day," Nick said as he sank down into the metal chair across from her before taking a long sip of his drink. He let out a sound of satisfaction. "Great table choice by the way."

"I needed some sunshine today," she said, her thoughts going back to her mother. Even a walk on the dunes with the sun shining down on them hadn't been possible.

"Are you okay?" he asked, peering closely at her face. "No offense, but you don't look all right."

"I'm fine," she said, blinking back tears. "This too shall pass." But would it? Her mother's condition was terminal and there was zero chance of improvement. And now she had to wonder if she'd irreparably damaged her relationship with Malcolm.

Nick placed his drink down and splayed his hands on the table. "Want to tell me about it? I'm a good listener."

"Not really," Harlow admitted. "It's kind of heavy."

"Are you sure? Why don't I tell you something that I'm going through? Maybe that will make you more comfortable."

Harlow shrugged. "Only share if you want to. It's your choice."

He let out a ragged sigh. "I just came off a rescue, only it turned into a recovery."

"Recovery?" Harlow asked. "Does that mean the person didn't make it?"

Nick nodded. "That's the worst part of my job, which I actually really love. I always focus on the rescue, never allowing my mind to go to a negative space. So on the rare occasion that a rescue isn't possible, it's truly devastating. A real gut punch."

"I'm so sorry, Nick," Harlow said in a soft voice. She could hear the pain laced in his voice and see the hurt radiating from his eyes. He was a helper, one who rushed toward danger when others fled. In her eyes, he was a bona fide hero. "I wasn't blowing you off by not responding to your messages," Harlow said. "There was an emergency with my mother. I had to go out of town to deal with it." *Please don't tear up. Please don't tear up.*

"Oh, no. I'm sorry to hear that," he said, reaching out and touching Harlow's hand. "How is she doing?"

"Not well. We lost our dad when we were kids, so she's the only parent Malcolm and I have," Harlow acknowledged. She quickly told him about her mother's medical condition and how she'd kept it from her brother.

"Sounds as if you were trying to protect Malcolm," Nick said, narrowing his gaze as he looked at her.

"Yes," she said with a nod. "He's taken so much of this on the chin in the last few years while I've been living in Seattle. For once, I wanted to carry the weight of it on my shoulders. At least for a little while." Saying it out loud made her realize how wrong she'd been. All Malcolm wanted was for her to openly communicate with him at all times. She should have known better than to try to take matters into her own hands and withhold the truth.

"But he doesn't quite see it that way. Am I right?" Nick asked.

Harlow bowed her head. "He's furious at me."

"I can see his point," Nick drawled.

Harlow raised her head and met Nick's gaze. "Whose side are you on?"

Nick held up his hands. "Yours, of course. Just hear me out. He probably thinks you weren't being straight with him. I'd feel the same way if Luke did that to me. But I'd also get over it pretty quickly. You and Malcolm seem really tight."

Harlow pushed her coffee to the side. It was piping hot and she didn't want to burn her tongue drinking the steaming brew. "We are. He's my best friend," she acknowledged. Through thick and thin. They'd walked through childhood trauma side by side with only each other to confide in. In the quiet hours between darkness and dawn, they'd whispered secrets and hopes and dreams that they could share only with each other.

"You're twins, right? That makes your bond even more special."

"It does," she said, bobbing her head in agreement. "I'm lucky to have him. Don't know what I'd do without him." She didn't even want to think about it. Malcolm was the peanut butter to her jelly. Neither one made sense without the other.

Nick grinned at her. The corners of his eyes crinkled as he smiled. "I'm guessing he says the same about you."

She smiled back at him. Talk about an instant mood lifter! Nick's grin should be bottled and sold. He would make a small fortune if it were. *Good Golly, Miss Molly, this man had charisma for days.*

"Harlow, just talk to Malcolm. It'll all get straightened out. With regards to your mother, the two of you are going to need each other to navigate these waters. Trust me, I know."

Nick's words hinted at his own suffering. Harlow wasn't going to ask about his wife's passing. She hoped at some point he might feel comfortable telling her about it. He was so strong and well adjusted. Nick didn't wear his sorrow on the outside. That's how she had been with her father's death. Sometimes you had to scratch a person's surface to get a peek at their insides. Harlow wasn't sure she wanted Nick to get a look at hers. He might think she was a hot mess.

"Believe it or not, I don't usually share personal stuff with people I don't know that well," Harlow admitted. That was putting it mildly. She never talked about her painful childhood or her mother's dementia. The very idea of doing so always made her anxious. There had been so much judgment directed toward her family in her childhood, which resulted in Harlow being deeply wounded and marginalized. Those early experiences had taught her not to easily trust people, especially small-town folks. Maybe it wasn't a fair assessment, but Harlow always considered them to be narrow-minded.

"Malcolm says I'm guarded," she blurted out. "I like to say I'm private, but that doesn't mean I have to always hold things in. You made it really easy to talk to you, so thanks."

"You're very welcome." He took a lengthy sip of his drink as Harlow looked on. *How could someone look so sexy simply drinking coffee?*

"I know you're going through a lot, but I'd really like to take you out. Maybe show you a little bit of Mistletoe." Nick leaned back in his chair. With his thick navy sweatshirt, dark jeans, and five o'clock shadow, he exuded a rugged air. Despite the slight shadows resting under his eyes, he looked amazing.

"So, I guess this could count as a first date," Harlow teased. She didn't know what superpowers Nick possessed, but being with him—talking things out with him—made her feel better. She was still grieving her mother's diagnosis and apprehensive about future steps, but she no longer felt as if she was spiraling. Nick had grounded her.

He chuckled. "You're not getting off that easy. This is pure coincidence that we ran into each other."

"What do you have against spontaneity?" Harlow found herself laughing at the look on Nick's face.

His eyes flashed with amusement. "Not a single thing, but when we spend time together I want it to be a little more special than grabbing coffee."

The intensity of his gaze slightly unnerved

Harlow. Looking into Nick's eyes gave her the
sensation of swimming into the depths of the ocean.
She was a pretty good swimmer, but water could be
dangerous. Harlow liked Nick, but she didn't need
any complications during her year-long assignment
in Maine. All she wanted was to work at Paws and
have her student loans erased. Being romanced by a
single dad didn't really factor into her plans.

She owed it to Nick to be straight with him. That
way there wouldn't be any misunderstandings.

"Well, I don't mind going out with you, Nick, but
I have to be honest. I'm not looking for anything
serious. I'm not like some of the women here in
Mistletoe who are itching to walk down the aisle. I
signed an agreement to work at Paws for a year, and
then I'm heading back to Seattle."

Nick reached out and patted her hand. "Well,
bless your heart. Now it's my turn to keep things
real between us. I just wanted to hang out with you,
Harlow, not put a ring on your finger." He slowly
got to his feet, taking his coffee cup with him. Nick
quirked his mouth. "To be honest, I'm not feeling
very good about hanging out with someone who
doesn't mind going out with me." He made a face.
"So I'm going to back off. You have my number.
If you ever want to genuinely spend time with me,
give me a call."

Before she could even muster a feeble apology,
Nick had walked away.

Without meaning to, she'd acted like a colossal

jerk and offended her newfound friend in Mistletoe. She couldn't think of the last time she'd felt like such an idiot. Without raising his voice or lashing out at her, Nick had told her off. And he'd done it in a classy way.

What in the world was wrong with her?

CHAPTER SEVEN

Nick walked away from Harlow with disappointment weighing on him. So much for his good vibes about Harlow. The woman was beautiful and intriguing, but she was frustrating as hell. She was a bit all over the place, which should serve as a bright red flag. Had he been giving out vibes that he wanted a serious relationship? Harlow's reaction made him second-guess himself. He'd been out of the dating game for a long time, so maybe he'd messed up in some way.

No! Stop blaming yourself. It wasn't on him if Harlow didn't feel a connection. It was just the way the cookie crumbled. No big deal! What was that saying about other fish in the sea?

His heart went out to her regarding her mother's illness, although he sensed there was a lot more resting under Harlow's surface. What made her tick?

Why was she so unwilling to put herself out there? She piqued his curiosity, and Nick had been looking forward to peeling away her layers, but that seemed unlikely now.

Nick had no intention of seeking her out again. As it was, his ego was slightly crushed. *I don't mind going out with you.* Dang! As if he would be a pity date. He should have told her about all the women in Mistletoe who'd been trying to date him for the last three years. He wasn't some lovelorn loser desperado. Was he open to finding love again? For the first time in three and a half years he could honestly say yes. The fog of deep grief had finally lifted and from what he could see, Miles was well-adjusted and happy.

Nick let himself into his house, slightly startled by how quiet it was when Miles wasn't around. Normally their home was a hotbed of noise and movement. Zeus was at doggy day care until Van picked him up after his class got out. Luke had surprised Nick by arranging for six months of doggy day care—four weekdays for half a day—and paid for it. Something told him Stella might have twisted his arm. Whichever way it had gone down, Nick appreciated it. Having a still environment all to himself for a few hours would allow him to recharge his batteries after a draining day.

After a quick shower and a change of clothes, Nick headed to the den, where he turned on the television and sank down on a comfy oatmeal-colored sofa.

He landed on a ridiculous reality show where one man was accused of fathering four different babies. The show was a train wreck, but oddly enough, watching the unfolding drama made him feel really good about his own life.

"You are not the baby's father," Nick said out loud in unison with the host. Nick laughed so hard he had a stitch in his side. The sound of his doorbell pealing drew his attention away from the screen. Maybe he should just ignore it. With his luck it was a door-to-door salesman selling time-shares. With a groan, Nick reached for the remote to turn the television off before heading to his front door.

Who was ringing his bell in the middle of the day? He was usually at work right about now. Maybe someone had seen his vehicle in the driveway and decided to pay him a visit. If it wasn't someone he knew and liked, Nick would just tell them to kick rocks. This had already been a day from hell.

Nick opened the door, letting out a sound of surprise as he came face-to-face with an old friend. Gary Shirtock was a local prosecutor in their county. Tall and completely bald, Gary reminded Nick of the actor Stanley Tucci. He had put Frank Baker, the individual who'd killed his wife, behind bars. He'd deserved much more time than his ten-year sentence to rot in prison, but Nick was well aware that all too often drunk drivers got a slap on the wrist.

"Hey, Nick. Sorry to come by unannounced, but I took a chance you might be home." Gary had an excellent reputation for prosecuting the bad guys and making sure the community was safe. He was a hero for justice in Nick's eyes.

"Come on in, Gary," Nick said. "It's been a while."

Gary walked inside and turned toward Nick. "I didn't want to tell you this over the phone. I knew that I owed you a face-to-face meeting."

Nick frowned. A very bad feeling swept over him. Gary hadn't come all the way over to his house to shoot the breeze. "What's going on, Gary? You don't look so great."

"I'm so sorry to tell you this, but Baker's been released from prison," Gary said, his features pinched in anger.

A tight feeling spread across Nick's chest. He felt almost light-headed. "That's not possible. He's been locked up for only two years. He was sentenced to ten."

Gary let out a frustrated sound. "The system doesn't always work the way it should. Believe it or not, his sentence was shortened due to overcrowding. He qualified for early release due to so-called good behavior."

Nick felt as if his head might explode. He let out a growl. "Good behavior? This punk killed my wife and robbed my son of a mother. The system is broken at its core to even entertain the notion of letting him out." Bile rose in his throat. *How was*

this actually happening? "I thought that I would
be notified in advance of anything like this taking
place. Was there a parole hearing?"

"Nick, you should have been informed that this
was in the works several months ago. But with all of
the overcrowding issues, this case slipped through
the cracks." He held up his hands. "I know how
you feel—"

"Do you? Really?" Nick asked in an explosive
tone. "Unless your life was ripped apart the way
mine was, you cannot possibly understand how this
feels."

Honestly, his knees felt weak, and for a moment,
he thought they might give out on him. All the air
seemed to have left his lungs. *Am I having a panic
attack?*

Silence hung in the air between them. Nick tried
to take deep calming breaths. Getting upset would
only serve to hurt Miles if he was carrying this type
of anger around.

"Tell me what I can do to help," Gary said.
"You're a friend, Nick. I hate this situation more
than words can express."

"I'm sorry for going off on you," Nick apologized. He began pacing back and forth on the
hardwood floors to expend some of this negative
energy. "More than anyone else, you fought for
Kara to make sure her death wouldn't be in vain. I
know this isn't your fault."

Gary nodded. "I know this is devastating news.

It's beyond unfair, but I'm asking you not to take matters into your own hands."

"What are you talking about? How would I even do that?" Nick asked, feeling confused by Gary's comment.

His friend's mouth hardened. "He's living in the Mistletoe area. It's one of the reasons I came over. I didn't want you to be blindsided if you crossed paths with him."

Disbelief crashed over him. "You've got to be kidding me! Of all the places in Maine he could live, why pick Mistletoe?"

Gary placed a steadying hand on his shoulder. "I know, Nick. Try not to let this bring you down. You've come so far over the last few years. You and Miles both."

After Gary left, Nick focused on centering himself. He wasn't sure what was up with the universe today. The hits kept coming. But Gary was right. Nick had come too far over the past three years to risk backsliding. He was angry about Baker's release, but he couldn't wallow in it or let Miles know that he was torn up about something. Nick refused to have his son's world rocked by this news.

By the time he picked up Miles after soccer practice Nick was in a better frame of mind. When Miles spotted him waiting outside his car and ran toward him at breakneck speed, Nick thought his heart might crack wide open. This was all that truly mattered. If Miles was good, everything would be right in Nick's world.

"How was your day?" Miles asked from the back seat.

"It was great," Nick fibbed. "But the best part was coming back to you."

"I know what you mean, Dad. Sometimes when I'm at school I miss you so much," Miles admitted. "It's like a little ache in my chest."

Just hearing what was resting on his son's heart nearly did him in. Tender moments like this one always seemed to come out of nowhere. Each and every time Miles said something poignant, Nick was blown away. His throat was clogged with emotion. He must be doing something right if he had nurtured such a wonderful soul as Miles.

"Buddy, I was thinking we should do something kind of wacky, just for fun."

"What's that?" Miles asked, leaning forward toward the front seat.

"Ice cream before dinner," Nick said, looking in the rearview mirror so he could see his son's reaction.

Miles let out a deafening scream. "Seriously? For real?"

"For real," Nick said, chuckling at his son's enthusiasm. "YOLO, right?"

"YOLO," Miles yelled. "Best. Surprise. Ever."

A few minutes later they were standing at the counter of Sweet Dreams ordering mint chocolate chip for Nick and cookie dough for Miles on waffle cones. Today had been a beast of a day, so in Nick's mind this was the perfect way to salvage it. Being spontaneous and making his son smile lifted him up to the stratosphere.

As soon as they got home, Nick drew a bath for Miles, then threw some laundry in the washing machine while trying to come up with some ideas for dinner. Just as Miles sat down to do his home-work, footsteps sounded on the floorboards. Luke, Stella, baby Jade, Lucy, and Dante walked into the kitchen.

"Uncle Luke!" Miles called out, jumping up from the kitchen table and wrapping his arms around his waist. "I didn't know you guys were coming over. Are we having a party?" Miles asked, wide-eyed as everyone trooped in, rapidly filling up the space.

"Not a party," Dante said, placing his arm around Miles. "Just family getting together to support one another."

Miles leaned into Dante's chest. "Just like at my soccer games. I love spending time with you guys."

"You still have to do your homework," Nick said, chuckling as Miles let out a groan.

Luke walked over to stand next to Nick. "Gary called me. We decided you needed some Thai food," Luke said, holding up a few brown bags.

"And some TLC," Lucy said, reaching out and hugging him.

Stella put the baby carrier down on the floor and

quickly made her way to Nick's side, pressing a kiss to his cheek. "We're so sorry, Nick," she said in a low whisper. He knew she was making sure Miles didn't sense anything was up. Nick had no idea when or how to even broach the subject with his son. Like most parents, he wanted his child to hold on to his innocence as long as possible.

Being surrounded by his family had turned an unbearable day into one filled with support and love. For so long Nick had stuffed down his anger about Kara's accident, but he couldn't very well continue to do so now that Frank Baker was a free man. The injustice of the situation nagged at him. Thankfully, he was buoyed by the support from his loved ones who wouldn't let him wallow over the situation. He wasn't battling this alone. And that meant the world to him.

* * *

A quick look at today's schedule had shown Harlow that Nick was coming in this morning with Zeus. She still hadn't recovered from their encounter at the Coffee Bean. All she'd wanted to do was set up a boundary so she and Nick were on the same page from the beginning. Instead, she'd inserted her big foot in her mouth and ruined everything in the space of a few seconds.

"Come on, Harlow," Malcolm had said when she told him about it. "You wear this suit of armor in order to protect yourself from getting hurt. It's way more about you than Nick."

A sigh escaped her lips. She folded her arms tightly across her chest and blew out a huff of air. "I didn't say it was Nick's fault. And why are you so sure it's about me? Maybe I was just being clumsy with my words."

"Because it's true. Tell me this. When was the last time you were in love with someone?"

Harlow rolled her eyes. "That's a cheap shot. You know I've never been in love." Every time she said it out loud, Harlow experienced a twisting sensation in her gut. She always flashed back to the pint-sized version of herself—the little girl who'd played dress-up bride and dreamed of a fancy wedding. She'd forced a reluctant Malcolm to play the role of groom by giving him her allowance.

Where had that little girl gone? she wondered.

You know where she went, a little voice buzzed.

"That's my point. You're afraid to fall. You're scared to be vulnerable. You run when things get real."

Harlow let out a hoot of laughter. "Thanks for the analysis, Doctor Jones. What are your hourly rates?"

Malcolm scoffed. "Laugh all you want, but I'm right," Malcolm said. "Isn't it time you faced it?"

Silence sat between them for a few moments. She wasn't wriggling out of this one. Her twin knew her too well.

"So what should I do…about Nick?" Harlow felt awkward asking Malcolm for romantic advice, but she was stuck. She drew the line at asking Stella how to make things right with her brother-in-law. It was a bit humiliating imagining that Nick might have told Stella about their encounter. She didn't want her only friend in Mistletoe to think she was obnoxious.

"The question is…what do you want to do?" Malcolm asked.

The call ended with Harlow mulling over the question with no answer in sight. And now, she was minutes away from coming face-to-face with Nick. Should she act über professional and pretend as if the other day hadn't happened? Quickly apologize and extend an olive branch? Perhaps she would fly by the seat of her pants and live in the moment.

Harlow walked into the exam room with a grin plastered on her face. Nick, with his tall stature and broad shoulders, seemed to dominate the small space. His mini-me, Miles, was at his side. Zeus was pacing around the room, showcasing his pent-up energy.

"Good morning, guys," she said, trying to sound chirpy.

"Morning, Doc Harlow," Miles said, making her feel sluggish in comparison. He was all smiles and full of little-boy energy. His sweatshirt said it all—GOOD VIBES ONLY. Could he be any more adorable?

"Harlow," Nick said with a nod, giving off a slight chill as they locked gazes.

Yikes! He clearly hadn't gotten over her comments. Suddenly, it was colder in the room than Christmas in the North Pole.

She leaned down and patted Zeus on the head. "Hey, Zeus. You're looking good." The German shepherd radiated the same raw enthusiasm she often saw in young dogs. He was panting heavily and eagerly wagging his tail.

"He's got lots of vim and vigor," Harlow said, using one of her grandmother's expressions. She felt ancient using that description, but it was accurate. As far as she was concerned, Zeus was absolutely charming.

"Too much if you ask me," Nick muttered.

"Just enough if you ask me," Miles chimed in. "He's perfect."

Harlow's lips twitched with amusement. Miles really was Zeus's hype man and protector. Nick seemed unimpressed, which made her wonder why he'd gotten a dog in the first place.

"So let me just get his weight and then I'll get him caught up on any shots he might need. If he was in the search and rescue program he may be up to date, but I'll need to check his file. In the meantime, you can tell me if you have any concerns or questions. Is this your first family dog?" Harlow asked.

"Yep," Miles said, smiling. "My uncle Luke got him for us. Zeus was supposed to work in search and rescue like my dad and Uncle Luke, but he got the boot." Miles shrugged. "I guess he had too much personality."

Harlow looked over at Nick, who shrugged. "Luke said he wasn't suited for it." He twisted his mouth. "I'm beginning to wonder if that wasn't code for something." Nick made a face. Harlow was getting the impression that Nick wasn't Zeus's number-one fan.

Harlow busied herself weighing Zeus and beginning the examination. She listened to the pup's lungs and checked his heart, both of which sounded perfect. "You're a healthy boy," Harlow murmured in her most soothing veterinarian's voice. "He has a gorgeous coat. I don't see any hair loss or patches. Do you brush him, Miles?"

"Yes, every day. And I also feed him dinner and take him out to do his business," he said proudly. "Dad helps out and my babysitter, Van, does too."

"You're doing a great job, Miles," Harlow said, wanting to encourage him. As much as he clearly loved Zeus, it was nice to see he was taking responsibility for the pup. "Dogs depend on their human families so much. Water. Food. Walks. Playtime. And more than anything, love."

"He gets plenty of all of those things. And hugs," Miles said, looking up at his dad.

"I think you might have a future veterinarian on your hands," she said to Nick, trying to engage him in conversation.

"I think his current aspirations are veering toward soccer," Nick acknowledged, placing his palm on top of Miles's head.

"Maybe I can be a soccer player who is a vet on the side," Miles suggested. Harlow and Nick both laughed, which eased the tension hanging in the air.

"What are you doing?" Miles asked, coming closer to get a better view of her movements.

"Well, I'm examining his eyes to make sure they're healthy. From what I can see there are no problems. No discharge or redness. They're nice and bright with no cloudiness or tearing. All the better to see you with."

Miles tugged at Nick's sleeve. "Dad, we need to tell her about the lump."

Harlow swung her gaze away from Zeus. "He has a lump?" Miles nodded. "Can you show me?" Miles reached down and pointed to the dog's foot, where Zeus had a medium-sized tumor.

She placed her fingers on Zeus's foot and began to palpate the mass. To the human eye, it appeared angry and red. A definite area of concern.

"If it's okay with you, Nick, I'd like to do a fine needle aspiration so we can find out what's going on with this lump." Harlow didn't want to use the word *tumor* in front of Miles, in case it might scare him.

Nick knitted his brows together. "Of course you can."

"Is he going to be all right?" Miles asked, looking

to his dad for reassurance. Nick didn't answer but
sent Harlow a questioning expression. For the first
time since she'd met him, Nick seemed uncertain.
Harlow knew he wanted to make sure Miles wasn't
going to get his heart shattered if something happened to Zeus. This little boy had already been
through so much.

"We need to make sure it's not anything problem-
atic, but that's standard procedure. This is a great
way to take care of Zeus and make sure he stays
healthy for a very long time. Okay?" she asked,
placing her hand on his shoulder. "I'm really impressed with how you pointed out his lump. It shows
that you're a wonderful owner and friend."

Miles was beaming after hearing her praise. "So
just a few shots and the needle aspiration before you
guys can get out of here. I'm sure you have a list of
exciting things on tap for today."

As Harlow gave Zeus his shots, Miles talked
a mile a minute about everything under the sun—
school, soccer, pizza, and the upcoming fall festival
to be held in Mistletoe.

"Slow down, buddy," Nick said, chuckling. "I
know you're excited about pumpkin fest, but Doc
Harlow is new in town, so she needs to understand
all the nuances."

Miles scrunched up his face. "Nuances. What's
that?"

"The special touches," Nick answered. "What
makes it one of a kind."

"Oh, I get it," the little boy said before continuing to speak. His features and hand gestures were animated as he spoke. "So, it's this amazing event with contests and games and lots of great food, like fried dough and cider doughnuts and lobster bites."

"Lobster bites? Where can I sign up for that?" Harlow asked, eager to sample her very first Maine lobster. Just the thought of devouring lobster dipped in butter made her stomach grumble in appreciation. The delicious crustacean was an item she'd often treated herself to in Seattle.

"And there's a contest for biggest pumpkin and smallest pumpkin," Miles rambled on. "There's also a cutest dog Halloween costume contest that we're entering this year. And we're definitely going to win. Right, Zeus?" A noise came from Zeus that almost sounded as if the dog was responding to Miles. Harlow let out a laugh at the same time as Miles. She wasn't surprised that Miles was wild about his pet. Zeus had an oversized personality that was endearing.

"Zeus is all done and he was a rock star. He didn't even flinch when he got his shots," Harlow said as Nick stepped forward to lift Zeus up off the table before placing him on the floor.

"Didn't I tell you he was the best dog ever?" Miles asked as he got down on the floor and lavished Zeus with affection.

"There're goody bags at the front desk for all of

my patients," Harlow said. "If you ask nicely, Tina might even give you a lollipop for the road." The doggy treat bags had been a big hit at Paws, not only with the dogs but with the owners as well.

"Let's go get one, boy," Miles said, zooming off before Harlow could even say goodbye.

"Well, thanks for everything, Harlow," Nick said, before turning toward the door. She knew that she needed to catch him before he left, to say something before too much time went by. Apologies were meant to be given sooner rather than later.

She cleared her throat. "Nick, can you wait a second?" Harlow asked, reaching for his arm. Holy smokes! This man had muscles for days. His arm was rock solid. Awareness flooded her. There was no way in the world she could ever deny Nick's raw sex appeal. He was in a league of his own.

The look he gave her was skeptical. "Sure. What is it?" He frowned. "Is it something about Zeus that you didn't want to say in front of Miles?"

"No, this is about the other day at the Coffee Bean," Harlow said, shifting from one foot to the other and wringing her hands. Why did this feel like she was facing the guillotine? Maybe it had something to do with the dour expression stamped on Nick's face. He certainly wasn't making it easy for her to eat crow.

She took a deep breath. "I didn't handle things well when we talked the other day. I'm sorry about that."

"Don't worry about it. I've forgotten all about it," Nick said, his expression shuttered.

"Have you? Because I think that I might have hurt your feelings with my clumsy wording. What can I say? I'm not very smooth." She took a deep breath. "The truth is that I do want to go out with you. Very much."

"You do?" Nick asked, his tone showcasing his surprise.

"I've been thinking about it since the moment you rescued me. Confession. I tried to hunt you down that day at the crash site, but you'd already left," Harlow admitted. She was going for broke here, essentially admitting she was crushing on him, despite how uncomfortable it made her feel. But it was too late to turn back now. She had dipped her big toe into chilly Maine waters.

"Really?" Nick asked. "I made that good of an impression, huh?" He was smirking, seemingly very pleased with himself.

"I wanted to thank you for saving me, but I also thought you were pretty cool."

Nick smiled at her, a full-fledged, megawatt smile that let her know she'd smoothed things over between them. "You liked me."

"Okay, don't get a big head about it. You had your Superman cape on that day, for sure. And every time we've run into each other it seems that the universe is trying to tell us something."

"Maybe giving us a little nudge."

A nudge? For Harlow, it sometimes seemed like a huge push into the deep end of the pool. The way he was smiling at her caused butterflies to swirl around in her stomach. He exuded a masculine swagger that made her a little weak in the knees. The fact that Nick was acknowledging their connection emboldened her. At this point she had nothing to lose but a part of her dignity if he turned her down.

"So, why don't you come over for dinner?" Harlow blurted out.

Nick folded his arms across his chest. "So you want to cook your way back into my good graces?"

"Only if it works," Harlow quipped. "Warning. I'm not going to cook a four-course meal or anything over the top."

"It's a date. Whatever you serve will be fine. Tell me what and when."

"How about Thursday?" she suggested. "I'm living at 17 Sweetwater Lane."

"Down by the lake? That's a beautiful area. I had my first summer job there as a lifeguard back in the day."

Nick as a lifeguard must have been quite something. Her teenage self would have loved to be rescued by him. It probably would have been the most exciting summer of her life. Instead, she and Malcolm had been stuck at sleepaway camp in the Berkshires.

Miles popped in the doorway. "Dad. What's taking you so long? Zeus is getting antsy."

"That's my cue to leave before Zeus tears up your waiting room. Talk to you soon," Nick said, shaking his head and quickly exiting the exam room.

A date night with Nick. Harlow was tempted to jump in the air with a fist raised in celebration. She couldn't think of the last time she'd been so stoked about a date. Adrenaline coursed through her at the thought of spending some alone time with the gorgeous single dad.

There was only one problem. Harlow couldn't cook. Not a lick. She had zero abilities in that department. Nick had gotten her so flustered she'd forgotten about her terrible kitchen skills. If she told Malcolm about inviting Nick to dinner, her brother would bust a gut laughing about the situation.

Harlow had no idea how she was going to pull this off, but she had a feeling it might involve a takeout meal disguised as home cooking.

CHAPTER EIGHT

S o you have a date with Harlow tonight," Luke said with an approving nod. "Good move. She sounds really great according to Stella. Plus, she's gorgeous." He handed Nick a hard cider as they settled onto the living room couch to watch the Patriots game.

"She is," Nick said. "Did you know she's a veterinarian? She's working at Paws."

"I think Stella mentioned it the other day. That's quite a winning combination. Looks and smarts." Luke flashed him a thumbs-up sign. "And it's pretty convenient now that you're a dog owner."

Nick frowned at Luke. Was he really going there with the dog thing? He was still trying to wrap his head around having Zeus thrust on him as a permanent member of his household.

"Too soon?" Luke asked, smirking.

"Way too soon," Nick said. As far as he was concerned, it would always be too soon to joke about the way Luke had manipulated him into adopting Zeus.

"So, back to your date," Luke said, swiftly changing the subject.

"I'm looking forward to it," Nick said. He was trying to play it cool and not reveal how excited he was about his date. If he didn't keep his cards close to the vest, Luke would definitely tell Stella, who might pass it on to Harlow.

Luke raised a brow. "But? I hear a but coming."

"She can be a bit guarded," Nick admitted. "I really want to get to know the real Harlow. There's so much resting under the surface." Maybe he was just being impatient. Getting to know someone took time. But being with Harlow made Nick want to breathe in every little facet of her.

"And you don't think you're making any headway?" Luke asked.

"She gives me don't-get-too-close vibes sometimes," he said with a shrug. "But then again, she's the one who asked me out, so that's got to be a good sign."

Luke nodded his head. "That's what I'm talking about," he said, letting out a throaty laugh.

Nick joined in on the laughter. He'd known Luke would approve of Harlow having made the first move.

"Maybe she's had some bad experiences," Luke

responded. "All she needs is a Keegan man to loosen her up a little bit. Charm city, baby."

Nick chuckled. "I'll try my best."

"Ugh. Do you hear yourselves?"

Nick and Luke both whirled their heads around at the sound of a young girl's voice. With her curly head of hair and warm brown skin, Tess Marshall looked a lot like her sisters, Stella and Lucy, and she was a champion at throwing shade.

"Tess," Luke said with a groan. "Didn't anyone tell you it's not nice to eavesdrop?" •

"I wasn't eavesdropping," she said in a huffy tone. "I was heading into the kitchen for a root beer refill when I happened to hear your enlightening conversation."

Luke made a shooing motion with his hands. "Go get your drink and stay out of grown folk's conversations."

Sometimes it boggled Nick's mind to consider that Tess was Luke's sister-in-law!

"You sound like two Neanderthals. Women don't need men to fix them. We are fully capable of managing our own selves, thank you very much," she retorted, hands on hips. There was no question that Tess was the feistiest member of the Marshall family.

"We?" Nick muttered. Tess was twelve going on forty. She happened to be a pal of Miles's. Although there were plenty of gossips in Mistletoe, Tess was one of the worst offenders. She took ear hustling to an entirely different level. Nick knew Luke got annoyed from time to time with her precocious manner. There was an incident when she'd engineered a dognapping of Stella's poodle, Coco Chanel, and made Miles her accomplice by stashing the dog at Nick's house. On the bright side, her heart had been in the right place and she'd hatched the plot to reunite Luke and Stella. That caper was proof of her mastermind abilities.

"If you really want to impress Harlow, you should start with her mind," Tess said. She shook her head and made a tutting sound. "You probably don't know, but the brain is the most erogenous—"

"Tess, don't you dare finish that sentence!" Stella had appeared out of nowhere and was now standing toe to toe with her little sister. Stella looked as if she was moments away from strangling her.

Tess opened her mouth, then closed it. For a few moments, Tess and Stella engaged in a staring contest with neither one budging. Tess broke eye contact first, looking away and letting out a dramatic sigh. "I'm going to get some root beer," Tess said before walking away.

"You better eat your Wheaties," Nick said, looking at Luke. "That type of sassiness might trickle down to Jade." He had to smother a chuckle at the look on his brother's face. Luke seemed scared to death. Big bad Navy SEAL taken down by a little girl.

"Stella assures me that Tess broke the mold in that regard," Luke said. "Right?" Luke looked to his wife, sounding panicky as he awaited an answer.

"Let's just say that if Jade ever starts acting like Tess, she's going to be grounded for life," Stella said.

"That's what I'm talking about," Luke said with a growl, pulling his wife by the waist onto his lap. "I love it when you get tough." He pressed a kiss to her lips.

"So, are you all ready for tonight?" Stella asked Nick.

"Yeah, although it's pretty much me showing up at Harlow's place isn't it? It sounds like a low-key first date."

Stella frowned. "Well, you don't want to be too casual about it. What about bringing her flowers or candy? Maybe you can bring dessert or a nice bottle of wine. Those are thoughtful gestures."

"Stella, don't mother him. He's got this." Luke drew his brows together and turned toward Nick. "You do have this, don't you?"

Nick rolled his eyes. "I thought I did before the two of you began fussing at me."

"Sorry," Luke and Stella said in unison.

"We just care about you, Nick," Stella added, while Luke jokingly made a heart with his hands.

"Should I be freaking out or something? Because I'm not nervous at all. It's just dinner and getting to know each other better." Nick was excited by the idea of exploring all facets of Harlow. He found her to be way more intriguing than most women in Mistletoe. She was witty and stunningly beautiful. She wasn't the type of woman who would just nod her head and go along in order to get along. Harlow had her own opinions and she held fast to them. She didn't sugarcoat her dislike of small towns. Her passion for animals affirmed that being a veterinarian was a calling and not simply a job. Maybe part of it was that Harlow wasn't tied up in his past with Kara. Everything between them would be a blank slate, unlike the women in town he'd been out with. He loved Mistletoe, but everyone in his hometown knew everything—the good, the bad, and the ugly—about one another. Nick wanted to explore a woman and make new discoveries about her each and every day. He wanted to be emotionally and mentally stimulated. According to Harlow, she wasn't sticking around Mistletoe after her year was up. Was there a part of him that was hoping she might change her mind and stay?

"We know it's been a while since you went out with someone," Stella said.

"Not exactly true. I've gone on several dates in the past few months," Nick said, correcting his sister-in-law.

"Not with someone you really like," Luke added. He sent Nick a pointed look. The truth was, more times than not, Nick had gone out on the date without truly feeling a connection. He'd felt the pressure of everyone's expectations for him to get back into the dating world. So he had caved and gone out with women he had zero interest in. In the end, doing so hadn't helped him move forward at all. And he'd disappointed several women who'd deserved better from him.

"Good point," Nick said after a few moments of thinking his brother's comment over. "But here's the thing. Either Harlow and I hit it off or we don't. We either enjoy spending time together or we nix a second date." Nick shrugged. "Considering the things I've been through in the last few years, it doesn't seem like a huge deal."

Nick said his goodbyes and thanked Stella for arranging a sleepover between Miles and Tess. Now that Luke and Stella were married, the two kids considered themselves to be honorary cousins.

Nick went home to change. A quick shower and shave made him feel like a brand-new man. He put on a nice pair of slacks and a dark sweater. "Not bad, Keegan," he said out loud as he checked himself out in the bathroom mirror. "You clean up well."

A quick stop at the florist yielded a stunning autumnal bouquet of roses, sunflowers, poms, and eucalyptus, and then he was heading to Harlow's. Since it was fall, the roads were already shrouded in darkness. He could barely see the lake around him.

When his GPS led him to Harlow's house, Nick parked out front and walked up her front steps. One quick knock later and Harlow was opening up the door and welcoming Nick inside. Bear gave him a once-over with a sniff test. Harlow wore an oatmeal-colored sweater with a pair of slim-fitting jeans. She looked amazing.

Once he stepped inside, Nick held out the flowers and the bottle of wine he'd tucked under his arm. "I couldn't decide on what to bring, so I went with both," he said.

"I won't complain about that," Harlow said, admiring the flowers. "They're gorgeous. And I've never met a wine I didn't like. Let me go chill this and put these flowers in a vase."

"Something smells great," Nick said, inhaling the wonderful aroma as he trailed after her down the hall. Harlow must be a world-class cook. He couldn't identify the spices floating through the air, but he knew it was a blend of several. Saffron. Curry. Chili. Paprika. Nick couldn't wait to find out. His stomach was doing somersaults in anticipation.

The kitchen was nice and airy, with large windows that he imagined let in plenty of sunshine in the daytime. Everything looked nice and tidy, considering Harlow had cooked dinner for them. The color scheme was white and taupe, with gleaming silver-colored appliances.

"Let me show you around," Harlow said, leading him toward the living room.

Nick looked around him at the beautiful decor. The place looked fantastic. "Was this fully furnished when you moved in?"

"Yes, but I added a few touches, such as the love-seat and ottoman, as well as the curtains and most of the paintings on the walls."

"You've really created a nice home away from home for yourself," Nick said approvingly.

"Thank you. Art is such a personal thing, so I packaged up my favorites from home and shipped them here. I didn't want to be apart from them for a solid year."

Nick stopped in front of an oversized painting of a beautiful jungle. The colors jumped out at him—reds, violets, yellows, purples. "This one is incredible."

A radiant grin spread over Harlow's face. "That's Malcolm's work. I have a few more of his upstairs, but this one is my favorite."

Nick let out a low whistle. "He's incredibly talented." Malcolm Jones. He ran a hand over his face. He hadn't even made the connection until right now. "I should have placed the name. We went to his exhibit in Boston a few years ago. I'm kicking myself for not investing in one of his paintings back then."

"He's really been on the rise in the last few years," Harlow said. "His prices have skyrocketed, which is a bummer for those trying to acquire his work, but I'm so happy for him. He's worked so hard to get to where he is." An abundance of pride rang out in Harlow's voice.

Harlow led him upstairs to show him the remainder

of Malcolm's paintings. They were bold and dynamic, each one more stunning than the next.

Nick looked around to see if Harlow had a candle burning. An acrid odor was now swirling around in the air, replacing the heavenly aroma that he'd first smelled. The sound of Bear barking from downstairs echoed throughout the house.

"Bear! What's going on?" Harlow called out.

Nick suspected that Bear might be trying to tell her something.

"Harlow, you might want to check your stove. Something smells like it's burning."

* * *

"Noooooo," Harlow shrieked as she bolted down the stairs, her shoes sliding across the hardwood floors. She had to catch herself so she didn't fall and land on her butt. The minute she rounded the corner and crossed the kitchen threshold she saw smoke filling up the room.

"Good grief," she said as she grabbed oven mitts and opened the stove door. Smoke blasted her in the face and she swatted it away with her hands.

"Do you have a fire extinguisher?" Nick shouted from behind her.

"Under the sink," she said, coughing as the smoke fog enveloped her. Her dish was literally on fire inside the stove.

Just as she moved to pull the tray of seafood

paella out of the oven, Nick sprayed it with the extinguisher. "Don't take it out, Harlow. You're going
to burn yourself. Just shut the door."

Harlow did as Nick instructed, then turned off
the oven.

"Why didn't the smoke detector go off?" she
asked, looking up at the ceiling. Just then it began to
blare like a siren. "Of course," Harlow said. "Now
it wants to warn me."

"I'm going to open the back door and a few
windows," Nick said before disappearing.

Maybe this was karma. She hadn't cooked a
single morsel of the seafood paella. A few hours ago
she had picked it up in town at a fancy-schmancy
restaurant.

"I think it's safe to say that dinner is charbroiled.
What was it anyway?"

"Seafood paella," Harlow said. "Exquisitely
cooked seafood paella." She wasn't responsible for
making the dish, but a gourmet chef at L'etoile
restaurant in town had done the deed. All she'd done
was pick up the order and put it in the oven. She had
no idea what had happened. Not a clue. Now she
would have to call a service person to come by and
check the oven.

"I appreciate the effort," Nick said. "And if it
means anything, it smelled incredible when I walked
in the door."

Guilt clawed at her. She was being ridiculous. A
poser! For someone who always prided herself on

keeping it real, she was acting like a Julia Child imposter.

"There was no effort," she blurted out.

"C'mon, that's not true. Seafood paella is a tough dish to make."

She bit her lip. "I wouldn't know. I can't cook. This came from L'etoile."

Nick's eyes widened. "You're kidding me," he said, a burst of laughter coming from deep inside of him. It was full-throated and seemed to go on and on. "Why did you pretend you'd made it?"

She shifted from one foot to the other. "I offered to make you a home-cooked meal, so I was trying not to backtrack on that promise," she said feebly. "Plus, it's pretty lame that I'm useless in the kitchen. This is so humiliating. The truth is I can't cook, Nick. Like, not at all. I've even had trouble making boiled eggs," she confessed. She threw her hands up in the air.

"I like to eat, Harlow. That doesn't mean it has to be homemade. I can't believe you went to all this trouble," he said.

She leaned back against the counter and folded her arms across her chest. "What can I say? I'm a dork," Harlow said sheepishly. Now that Nick was saying it out loud Harlow was able to see how foolish it all was.

"So why did you ask me to dinner at your place?" He let out a loud laugh. "We could have just eaten at the Lobster Shack. They make great seafood paella."

Nick covered his mouth as his shoulders shook with laughter.

"You're never going to let me live this down are you?" Harlow asked, letting out a groan and covering her face.

She felt Nick's hands on her wrists drawing her hands away from her face.

"Harlow, I'm just teasing. I couldn't care less about home-cooked or takeout. But we do have a problem." He let go of her hands and rubbed his stomach. "I'm pretty hungry. What do you have in your fridge?"

"Let's take a look," Harlow said, pulling it open and peering inside with Nick by her shoulder.

"Okay, I can work with this," Nick said, reaching in and pulling out some items, then heading toward the pantry for spices and onions and a few other items. Harlow watched in amazement as Nick pulled out bowls from the cupboard and then mixed ingredients together.

"You can cook!" Harlow said. She couldn't take her eyes off Nick's arms. He'd rolled up his sleeves to sauté vegetables, which gave her a bird's-eye view of his muscles. Not to mention his rugged physique and nicely shaped butt. Search and rescue sure did a body good! How lucky was she to be on the sidelines for this incredible view?

"I can," Nick said, turning toward her and grinning. "I'm a dad. It would be pretty pathetic if I couldn't nourish my child. No offense."

"None taken," Harlow said. "Don't mind me. I'm just here taking notes. You could have a nice side hustle giving cooking lessons."

"Why, thank you," he said. "Cooking is something I've come to love. It can be exciting and unpredictable. Like right now, taking something from your fridge and transforming it into something delicious we can enjoy."

Harlow looked over at the pans on the stovetop. "Mmm. It smells amazing."

"Not bad, huh?" Nick asked, a satisfied smile etched on his face. "It's almost done. Can you grab some plates for us? And those rolls should be heated up in the toaster oven."

Thankfully she hadn't burned the rolls and she'd picked up a big Greek salad and dessert.

They ended up sitting on pillows on her living room floor and putting the food and their plates on the glass coffee table. Nick had whipped up a delicious stir-fried rice with vegetables using leftover white rice and other ingredients from her kitchen.

Harlow was impressed. Nick had taken her kitchen fiasco and turned it upside down.

"Thanks for rescuing me yet again," Harlow said. "That meal was on point."

"It was my pleasure. And this rescue was way less dramatic than the first one, although it did involve fire, which is pretty hair-raising." Nick wiggled his eyebrows.

"Good thing you're in search and rescue." Harlow

clutched her stomach as she burst into chuckles. At
least they could laugh about the fiery seafood paella
incident. "I've always known that my cooking was
bad, but I never thought I'd almost set my house
on fire," she said, shaking her head. "I'm constantly
surprising myself," she said as she got to her feet
and began collecting the dirty dishes.

"Let me help you," Nick offered, standing up.
Harlow waved him off.

"Absolutely not. You're my guest. I feel bad
enough that you had to put your chef's hat on
and cook for us," Harlow said as she headed off
toward the kitchen. After placing the dishes and
utensils in the dishwasher, Harlow pulled out the
box of cream puffs she'd ordered from Wicked Eats,
the bakery Stella had recommended. She grabbed
two small plates and headed back into the living
room.

As soon as Harlow entered the room she held up
the box from the bakery and said, "I come bearing
sweets." Nick was sitting with his back against the
sofa, his legs crossed in front of him. She loved the
fact that he was making himself at home.

"Oh, you discovered Mistletoe's best bakery.
Miles is crazy about the place. He can't get enough
of the marshmallow brownies," Nick said.

"Your son is a boy after my own heart," Harlow
said as she sat back down on the floor next to Nick.
Her arm brushed against his. "I love brownies."
Harlow opened up the box and placed the cream

puffs on the two plates. Neither one of them hesitated to dig in to the treats. Harlow closed her eyes as the sweet taste hit her taste buds. Nick let out a moan as he took a bite.

"Miles is a great kid. He's far from perfect, don't get me wrong, but I'm one lucky dad." Nick's face lit up as he talked about his son. Little crinkles surrounded his eyes and they shone with happiness. His connection to his son was touching.

"He seems like an amazing kid. And quite a looker. You're going to have your hands full in a few years. All the girls will be knocking at your door."

"He's a mini-me of his mother. That's for sure." Nick's voice was bursting with pride.

Harlow was curious about Nick's late wife. It was slightly awkward, but she was going to seize this opportunity to ask the question. "Nick, can I ask how you lost your wife?"

"Of course." Harlow watched as Nick took a breath before he continued speaking. "She was killed in a car crash. A drunk driver ran a red light and Kara died on impact."

Harlow nearly gasped out loud. She had been expecting to hear about an illness like cancer or multiple sclerosis, but not anything this horrific.

Tears pooled in her eyes. "Oh, Nick. That's awful. I'm so sorry." Her voice was thick with emotion. Harlow couldn't imagine what Nick and Miles had gone through. The circumstances were tragic and senseless. She had sensed his strength in their previous encounters, but learning this information cemented that fact. Harlow reached out and gripped his hand, needing to show him her support.

"Me too. She deserved better. Kara should have died peacefully in her bed at ninety-nine years old."

"And Miles shouldn't have had his mother taken from him," Harlow added. Although Miles had been much younger than she and Malcolm had been when their dad passed away, Harlow still knew that losing a parent as a young child was a life-altering experience.

"Thanks for saying that. She was a fantastic mother. Speaking of which, how's your mom doing?" Nick asked. Harlow didn't get the feeling Nick was asking just to ask. He seemed to truly care about the situation.

"She's stable, which is comforting. Malcolm is in Cape Cod for a few days assessing the situation. That's what he does best." Harlow couldn't put into words how much better she felt having Malcolm at the helm of her mother's care.

"So how are things between you?" Nick asked, half filling their glasses with wine.

Harlow felt a smile tugging at her lips. "We're back on track. I've come to realize that I need Malcolm's support even when I think that I can handle things on my own."

"I get it. Luke and I are really close, but we're both naturally inclined to try and fight our battles on our own." Nick scoffed. "Both of us have learned that leaning on each other for support is always better in the end."

"Cheers to that," Harlow said, raising her glass of wine in the air. She'd noticed Nick had drunk only one glass of wine all evening, and it didn't take a genius to figure out why. He would be driving home this evening and he was drinking responsibly.

He reached over and brushed her curls away from her eyes. They were sitting so close to each other that she could see the small scar by his mouth, which only heightened his rugged appeal. Harlow's pulse quickened and she found herself leaning in toward him. Something in the depths of his eyes told her he was about to kiss her. Although she'd wanted this kiss since the first time she'd laid eyes on him, she asked herself if it was happening too soon.

Too late to backtrack now. Nick leaned over and brushed his mouth over hers. She immediately responded, returning the kiss with equal measure. The moment their lips met, she felt an electric pulse flaring between them. Heat and fire combined. Her mouth felt scorched by his as the kiss intensified. Nick's tongue pushed past her lips, sending tremors through her body.

Harlow reached up and placed her hand on Nick's face, caressing his skin with the slight stubble chafing against her palm. She was soaring, flying in orbit, so consumed by Nick's caress that she never wanted it to end. She felt Nick's strong hands as they brushed her hair away from her face and grazed the back of her neck. His touch caused goose bumps to pop up on her arms. All of her senses were on overdrive. She breathed in the scent of him—a woodsy masculine scent that embodied Nick. With his hands around her waist, she had the sensation of being anchored to him.

This kiss was not just a kiss. As far as first kisses went, this one was spectacular. Fiery yet tender. Scorching and passionate. She couldn't think of the last time she'd had a smooch session like this one.

Kissing had never been a big deal for her, but for some reason this felt huge. Harlow hadn't been kidding around when she'd told Nick that she wasn't looking for a relationship. Feeling these over-the-top sensations scared her.

After the kiss ended, Nick helped Harlow clear the table of the small plates, napkins, and glasses. Harlow took out the charred dish from the oven and placed it in the sink before running cold water over it.

"I'm pretty sure this is what sparked the fire," Nick said as he picked up an item at the bottom of the oven with a pair of tongs. Once she saw it, Harlow let out a gasp.

"Oh, jeez. That must have fallen off the tray when I heated up pizza the other day," she said, staring at the stray slice of pizza that was now burned to a crisp. No doubt Nick was thinking this was an airhead move on her part. She wouldn't disagree with him if he was.

"Mystery solved. Now you don't need to call a repairman. Winning," he said, putting the burned piece of pizza in the trash.

"That's a good thing for sure," Harlow said. Now that her student loans were being paid off, Harlow's money situation wasn't as tight, but she still wanted to build up her savings. This was the first time in her adult life when she'd been afforded that opportunity.

"I hate to kiss and run, but I should head home," Nick said. "I'm on call for the early shift."

"It's okay. I have to be at the clinic by seven." The early mornings were brutal to Harlow, who wasn't a morning person. Thankfully, she had to work the early shift only three times a week. Loving her job helped fight the early-morning fatigue, and seeing the lake first thing in the morning was a wonderful way to greet the day. Her lakeside home was continuing to grow on her. Having Nick over this evening had been a great idea. He was down-to-earth and extremely easy on the eyes. He exuded goodness, especially when he talked about his son. For a man who'd lost so much, he didn't appear to be jaded. Obviously she hadn't really scratched his surface, but from what she'd observed, Nick Keegan had it going on.

"Thanks for tonight. I had fun," Nick said, smiling down at her.

"Me too," Harlow said. And she meant it. Despite the dinner fiasco, hanging out with Nick had been wonderful, and she appreciated that he hadn't judged her for the burned takeout incident. It told her a lot about the man himself and how he walked through life.

Harlow walked him to the door. Her outside lights came to life, illuminating the lake area and casting a spectacular glow. She didn't know what it was about this place, but it gave her such a feeling of calm and serenity. Or was it Nick?

"Wow. You've got one of the best views in town," he said, looking out over the property. The stars twinkling above and a full moon shining provided the perfect backdrop for the lakeside property.

As Harlow watched the blaze of his taillights as he drove down the darkened road, she let out a contented sigh. Although she knew this connection couldn't really go anywhere due to her short-term stay in Mistletoe, Harlow wanted to spend more time exploring Nick Keegan. Surely there couldn't be any harm in that.

CHAPTER NINE

A flurry of snowflakes drifted down from the sky, creating a blanket of snow on the ground. Harlow hadn't expected to see any snow till at least November, but she'd been warned about the unpredictability of Maine weather. She was happy to be inside the Starlight Diner at the moment instead of trudging around in inclement weather. Even though the snow was a nuisance, it was really beautiful to look at. Seattle experienced only about five inches of snow per season, so the fluffy white stuff wasn't something she was used to.

She had met up with Stella and Lucy for lunch. The snow provided a distraction from the impending grilling from the sisters. Two days had passed since her date with Nick and she'd been thinking about it ever since.

"It's really coming down out there," Harlow said,

mesmerized by what was going on outside the diner window.

"Don't worry," Stella said. "It's not going to last for long and it doesn't seem to be sticking. Just a passing flurry."

"Enough about the weather! Come on, Harlow. Give us the dirt," Lucy said, placing her palm down on the table. "We need the details about your date with Nick. Did you guys have any smooch time?" Lucy appeared to be holding her breath, waiting for Harlow to answer her.

"Lucy! I really don't want to hear about Nick's sexy times. He's like a brother to me," Stella protested. "It's TMI."

"Well he's not *my* brother," Lucy said, rolling her eyes.

Harlow giggled. "All I'm going to say is that it was a nice evening full of lots of heat and fire." Harlow was making an inside joke about the oven fire, but she knew the ladies would assume something else.

"La la la! I didn't hear that," Stella said, covering her ears and shaking her head back and forth.

Lucy and Harlow chuckled at her. Stella made a shushing motion with her finger, then jerked her chin in her daughter's direction. Jade was sleeping peacefully beside her in the booth, snug in her carrier. Harlow was impressed by the way Stella incorporated her baby into all of her activities. Even though Jade was a sweetheart, being woken abruptly from her nap wouldn't be pretty.

Harlow quickly glanced at her watch. She was on a lunch break, so her time to dish with Lucy and Stella was limited. Their lunch locale—the Starlight Diner—was all kinds of adorable. It was an old-fashioned diner with banquettes, leather booths, and a brightly colored jukebox playing upbeat tunes. The waitresses wore classic T-shirts emblazoned with the diner's insignia. The restaurant exuded a cool vibe that reminded Harlow of an old-school diner her grandparents used to take her and Malcolm to in upstate New York.

Bonnie, their waitress, brought their food and drinks to the table. Harlow had selected a bacon cheeseburger with sweet potato fries. Lucy had gotten a burger with tater tots, while Stella had ordered a steak and salad.

Harlow took a long sip of her chocolate shake, shivering as the frozen drink gave her slight brain freeze. "Thanks for inviting me to lunch, ladies," she said when she came up for air. "I love this place."

"It's our go-to lunch spot," Lucy said, biting into her burger. She grinned. "Always has been, ever since we were kids."

Harlow couldn't imagine living in the same small town she'd grown up in, yet Stella, Lucy, Luke, and Nick all still lived in Mistletoe. Staying in her own hometown had been unthinkable after her father's sudden death and the scandal that came before it. Maybe she would never be able to understand the appeal of small towns due to her own horrible memories.

Lately, she couldn't outrun her painful childhood memories. They were everywhere. She was beginning to think that Mistletoe itself was a big reason all of these feelings were bubbling up. In many ways, the town reminded her of Chestnut Ridge. Both were small New England towns with plenty of charm and picturesque views. She wondered if she scratched the surface of Mistletoe whether ugly truths would be revealed, as they had been in Vermont.

"Harlow, we have a festival question for you," Stella said, interrupting her thoughts.

"Huh. Okay. Shoot! I don't really know much about the fall festival to be honest," Harlow said. "Nick and Miles told me a little bit about it, but it's all new to me."

"Would you be willing to help out with the pumpkin raffle?" Lucy asked. "We're short one person, and we thought you'd be perfect."

"Oh, no. I'm not really good at stuff like that." Ugh. The last thing Harlow wanted to do was put on a smiley face and schmooze with the townsfolk.

"What stuff?" Lucy asked.

"People. I generally don't like peopling." Harlow felt silly admitting that she didn't do well with small-town folks. Admitting it might make her sound like a snob.

"She's not kidding," Stella said with a laugh. "How could I have forgotten that little detail. You've always claimed not to be a people person."

"How is that possible? You're so charming," Lucy gushed. "Everyone will love you. You'll sell so many tickets."

"You're really laying it on thick," Harlow said, looking over at Stella, who began to chuckle.

"Come on, Harlow. All you have to do is show up, sit with us at a booth, and sell some raffle tickets. We'll have so much fun," Lucy continued. "Did I tell you that all proceeds benefit the Free Library of Mistletoe?"

Harlow knew that Lucy was head librarian at the library. She deeply cared about it and all of her beloved patrons. She wasn't surprised that Lucy was hustling to raise funds to support the local institution.

"No, you didn't, Lucy. But knowing that it supports your library, how can I say no?" Harlow watched as a huge grin broke out on Lucy's face. Stella sent Harlow an appreciative smile.

Lucy let out a squeal. "Yay, Harlow. We're going to raise so much money. I also recruited Dante, who might be our moneymaker." Lucy winked at Harlow. "He has a lot of fans in Mistletoe."

Stella leaned across the table. "All age groups fawn over him. From the elementary school crowd to the retirement home folks."

"Well, the Inferno is a household name," Harlow said, using the moniker Dante had been given by the public. She hadn't gotten over the fact that Lucy was married to the famous action star. Meeting him still felt surreal.

"He is," Lucy said, beaming. "Oh, and we've also signed up Nick and Luke. The ladies love the two of them, so they'll sell lots of tickets."

Harlow wasn't surprised to hear about Nick's appeal here in town. He was smart and sexy and really easy to talk to. And despite having been through a hellish loss, Nick had a great attitude about life. He was devoted to his son, and it was obvious everything he did was for Miles's benefit. There wasn't anything not to love about the man. She shook off the thought. There would be absolutely no falling for Nick Keegan!

Lucy turned to Harlow. "Now that we've settled the fall festival issue, give us the scoop about you and Nick." She held up her fingers. "Just a tiny morsel."

"Stop begging, Lucy," Stella scolded. "Leave Harlow alone."

"It's okay, Stella," Harlow said. "Lucy, I'm not one to kiss and tell." She put her finger on her chin. "But I will say that Nick's kisses made me weak in the knees." Harlow ducked her head.

Stella and Lucy instantly reacted by letting out screams that carried to other tables. Several customers turned in their direction with questioning gazes. Harlow squirmed in her seat.

"You two are such a bad influence on me," Harlow said, shaking her head. "I'm usually very private about my love life."

"Uh-oh. We woke Jade up," Stella said, reaching

down and rocking the carrier from side to side as her baby began making fussy sounds. Moments later, the cries stopped as Jade went back to sleep.

"She's such a good baby," Lucy said. "I really hope Dante and I get lucky with a sweet-natured infant who's easy to put down to sleep. She's like a baby doll, Stella. You take her everywhere and she just goes with the flow."

Stella chuckled. "She's pretty chill, but Jade has her moments. Come over to our house in the wee hours of the morning or when she has a diaper explosion. Just ask Luke. He'll tell you."

Harlow watched her two friends dishing over the wonders of babies, all the while asking herself how she felt about infants in general. The idea of having a little one scared Harlow. She wasn't anywhere near ready to have a baby. Harlow wasn't even sure if she had a single maternal bone in her body. Jade was a cutie, though. But looking at her didn't swarm Harlow with maternal feelings. She didn't know why, but she felt slightly deflated. Maybe it meant she wasn't cut out for motherhood. Or the traditional storybook ending most women envisioned for themselves.

Perhaps it was a good thing that she'd come to this realization about herself. Knowing she wasn't looking for hearth, home, and a house full of babies would make life easier for her. She wouldn't have to go through all the rituals and jumping through hoops. If she wanted to see someone, she'd keep things light and casual. Like with Nick. She would make it clear to him that her time in Mistletoe had an expiration stamp on it and she wasn't looking to settle down in a cottage by the lake.

That way, she figured, neither one of them would get their feelings hurt. When she left Mistletoe, she would be just as single and fancy-free as when she had arrived.

* * *

By the time Harlow got back to Paws, several patients were seated in the waiting room. She'd barely taken her allotted forty-five minutes for lunch, yet she still felt guilty about the backlog. Had an emergency cropped up while she was gone?

So far she found herself enjoying the practice, the other vets and the support staff. The pace was steady yet not overwhelming, which was different from back home. She felt as if she was actually getting to know the owners and their pets on a more intimate level. Most of the clients had been coming to Paws for quite some time, so there was a strong comfort level and connection. If she was being honest with herself, back in Seattle there had been a high turn-over in clients. Because of veterinary shortages in Maine, she truly felt needed here.

Harlow discreetly approached her coworker Jon Silver at the front desk. He had worked at Paws for more than a decade, serving as the clinic's eyes and ears. He was super friendly and knowledgeable. With his buzz cut, bow ties, and blue glasses, Jon was the type of person who marched to the beat of his own drum.

"Hi, Harlow. How was lunch? What did you think of the Starlight?" Jon asked, his features animated as he spoke.

"Hey, Jon. The diner might be my favorite new spot. I loved it." She looked around the crowded room. "What's going on here?"

"There was an emergency with Violet Stewart's dog," Jon said, lowering his voice. "Another pup attacked her, and she was slashed to ribbons. Dr. Hart's been in with her for over an hour." Julian was one of the other veterinarians, a top-notch professional who was at the top of his craft.

"That's terrible. Have the next patient sent into room four. I'll be right there," Harlow said, reaching for the file Jon held out to her.

"So glad to have you here, Harlow," Jon said with a nod. "We needed another vet like nobody's business. Mistletoe has a lot of pet owners."

"Happy to help out," Harlow said. From what she'd seen, Paws did a bristling business. That's what every veterinarian wanted to see. It meant Paws was growing. Harlow's dream was to open up her own vet clinic, so she was taking notes on how to be successful.

A few minutes later, Harlow entered the examination room, pet file in hand. A petite, auburn-haired woman stood holding a black-and-white bulldog in her arms.

"Hi, there. I'm Doctor Jones," Harlow said, holding out her hand. "Are you Gillian Robinson?"

Gillian flipped back her auburn hair and said, "Yes, I'm Gillian."

Harlow put her hand down by her side when the woman didn't shake it. *Okay.* Clearly, she wasn't interested in the pleasantries.

"What's going on with Elvis?" Harlow asked, quickly referencing the notes in Elvis's file. "Why don't you put him down on the exam table," Harlow said, gesturing toward the table.

"Elvis has been a bit...hyper," Gillian said, placing the pup down. "He's also panting quite a bit."

"You told the receptionist that he's had some diarrhea and vomiting. When did that start?"

"Yesterday." Gillian shrugged. "He may or may not have eaten chocolate." Something in Gillian's tone came across as cavalier.

"May have? You're not sure?" Harlow asked. She was trying not to sound too shocked, but it was always surprising when owners didn't seem to realize the dangers of toxic substances.

"I'm ninety-nine percent certain he got into my stash of Godiva chocolates," Gillian said.

Godiva chocolates? It was a miracle Elvis was still breathing.

"And when do you think he consumed the chocolates?" Harlow asked. Most likely it hadn't been today, since Elvis's symptoms had started yesterday. But she still needed to ask.

"Yesterday, I think. I'm not too sure. The chocolates were on my bedside table." Gillian shook her hand at Elvis. "Naughty boy, getting onto Mommy's bed."

Yesterday! Gillian really should have called the office much earlier. Chocolate is toxic for dogs, and Harlow had seen dogs who passed away after consuming it. Gillian didn't realize how fortunate she'd been. Harlow examined the dog, palpating his stomach to check for any signs of pain in Elvis's abdomen. She also checked his heart rate, which appeared normal.

"He's not exhibiting any troubling signs at the moment. I think he's going to be all right, since it's been twenty-four hours since he consumed the chocolates. Chocolate has theobromine as an ingredient, which dogs can't metabolize," Harlow explained. "There's no point in giving him medicine now, since the time for that remedy has pretty much passed."

"Oh no. That's a bummer," Gillian said, looking away to scroll on her phone.

Stifling a sigh, Harlow reached into the drawer and pulled out a pamphlet for her.

"Here's a list of substances that are toxic to dogs. Chocolate. Grapes. Many others. You really should keep these items away from Elvis. It could be fatal for him." Harlow held out the information to

Gillian, who gingerly took it. "You really were very fortunate. You might not be so lucky next time."

"Thanks," the woman said curtly. "As you said, he'll be fine."

Harlow hated Gillian's indifferent tone. As an advocate for dogs, she could accept an owner making a mistake, but Gillian didn't seem as if she'd learned anything from the incident. Harlow had to wonder if her client even understood the gravity of the situation. Obviously, she loved Elvis, otherwise why would she have rushed over to Paws to have him checked out? As the appointment ended, Harlow sent Gillian to the waiting room so she could check out with Jon.

Moments later, Harlow was in the break room doing battle with a difficult Keurig machine. She began muttering to herself. Harlow banged her coffee cup down on the counter with more force than necessary. The noise echoed in the stillness of the small room. She was still feeling annoyed, thinking about poor Elvis and his owner.

"Are you all right? What happened? Tell me quickly while I get some coffee in these veins. I skipped lunch today, and I'm in need of a pick-me-up." Whitney Carr, the owner of Paws, had entered the room without Harlow's being aware of it. Whitney was down-to-earth and personable. Tall and statuesque, Whitney was a former beauty queen turned veterinarian. Harlow quickly got her up to speed on Gillian and Elvis.

"I know owners make mistakes. Who doesn't? We're all human." Harlow ran a hand through her curls. "But something about her attitude rubbed me the wrong way."

Whitney nodded as she fiddled with the Keurig machine. "She's been a dog owner long enough to be aware of those risks." Whitney frowned. "I seem to remember Elvis eating a toxic plant a few years ago. He was super lucky to make it."

"You've got to be kidding me!" Harlow slapped her palm to her forehead. "Unbelievable. Well, I did give her some literature about toxic items for dogs, so hopefully she'll read up on it and be more careful."

"Let's hope so," Whitney said, pressing the coffee machine's go button and filling Harlow's mug to the brim. She handed it over to Harlow with a grin.

"Oh, thank you," Harlow said. "I've been dying for some java, and I couldn't get the machine to work. You're a lifesaver." Harlow took a sip and let out a sigh of contentment.

"My pleasure," Whitney replied as she prepared her own cup of coffee. "So, Harlow, how are you acclimating to life in Mistletoe?"

"I'm doing well. Having Stella as a friend helps a lot. She's been showing me around and introducing me to folks." Harlow softly chuckled. "Lucy even roped me into helping out with the fall festival. It sounds like I'll be selling raffle tickets."

"That's awfully nice of you to pitch in," Whitney

said. "Paws is closing at noon that day, so I volunteered with my son, Jamie, at the pumpkin-carving booth."

"Sounds messy." All Harlow could imagine was the gooey insides of a pumpkin, seeds and all. Baked pumpkin seeds were yummy, but she could do without the rest.

"Oh it is," Whitney said, rubbing her hands together and letting out a wild cackle. "But that's the beauty of it. We'll be getting our hands dirty, all for a good cause. This particular booth is going to support our pet rescue initiative, which I would love for you to be part of."

"That's wonderful. I'd love to help out with that. It's something I'm really interested in." Pet rescue had always been at the forefront of Harlow's advocacy for dogs. Back in Seattle, she'd been part of a team of veterinarians who had found forever homes for rescue pups. Making matches between owners and pets had been one of the most rewarding aspects of her career.

"So...I don't want to overstep," Whitney said, eyes twinkling, "but I heard you and Nick Keegan are seeing each other. Not that you care what I think, but I fully approve."

Harlow froze. People were already gossiping about her and Nick? They'd had only one date, and it had taken place behind closed doors. *How in the world had this rumor gotten started? And how quickly could she extinguish it?* This was just another reminder that folks in small towns thrived on rumors.

Hmm. If something was true, then it wasn't a rumor. It was pretty much fact. Could she really be upset about the townsfolk whispering about her and Nick? He had been a widower for years now and was a beloved figure in Mistletoe. People in small towns loved to run their mouths.

Maybe she needed to take a step back and try her best to be objective instead of allowing the past to cloud her judgment.

She was new in a small town where everyone had known one another for most of their lives. Harlow was like fresh meat to chew on. Understandable, but she had zero interest in being fodder for the town gossip mill. Harlow knew all too well that this type of thing could get out of hand. When she was twelve, her father had been caught up in a small-town embezzlement scandal that had cost him his reputation and, ultimately, his life. Her family had been left in ruins.

"I didn't mean to make you uneasy, Harlow," Whitney said, touching her arm in a comforting gesture. "Nick is a great guy. He's actually one of my favorite people."

"We've had only one dinner," Harlow admitted. "I'm not sure that rises to the level of dating."

"Doesn't it?" Whitney asked. "I guess you have to ask yourself...do you want to see him again? Because if the answer is yes, that might mean you're open to dating Nick. Or at least exploring the possibilities."

With a grin, Whitney was gone, leaving Harlow with a lot to think about. Nick Keegan was a hot commodity in this sleepy little New England town. If she and Nick became an item, she knew with a deep certainty that tongues would be wagging all over Mistletoe. Would she be able to handle that type of scrutiny? Did she even want to have her name on people's tongues?

Harlow had to figure out if seeing Nick would be worth the aggravation of being put under a microscope and, as a result, having to face painful childhood memories. In a few days she would be able to test the waters with Nick at the fall event. She was looking forward to seeing him again. Maybe even stealing a kiss or two. Harlow couldn't ignore the butterflies flying around in her stomach at the mere thought of coming face-to-face with Nick again. He was the type of man she hadn't even known she needed in her life.

Uh-oh. She might be too far in with Nick to be able to easily find her way out.

CHAPTER TEN

Nick wasn't surprised to see that everyone in Mistletoe had come out of the woodwork to attend the fall festival. His own anticipation of the event took him back to his childhood. He, Luke, Dante, and a few other friends had always gone together as a posse, and they'd looked forward to the event for weeks. His stomach grumbled as the smell of fried dough wafted through the air. He breathed in deeply. Grilled hot dogs and apple cider doughnuts. Lobster rolls and grilled corn. Nick couldn't wait to get his hands on some food.

Autumn was his favorite time of year—the stunning fall foliage, the crisp smell in the air, apple picking, and pumpkins on every porch stoop. Halloween was his absolute favorite holiday. And since Miles hated Snickers and Reese's, Nick claimed all of them for himself. Life had gotten so busy lately with barely any downtime for himself. There were always people in need of being rescued, and since he was a senior team leader, more times than not, he was the one who received the call for high-stakes rescues. Add in Miles's activities and schoolwork, as well as family obligations, and Nick was over-extended. Today would serve as a nice break for him from the daily grind.

His parents met him at the festival, so they could walk around with their grandson while Nick manned the raffle table.

"See ya later, gator," Miles said as they parted ways, high-fiving Nick.

"In a while crocodile. Come see me at the raffle table if you run out of things to do," Nick said. He handed Miles a twenty-dollar bill. "Don't spend it all on candy apples."

"I'll try to swing by. I'm meeting up with my crew over at the hay rides," Miles said. "Peace out."

His parents exchanged a confused look and fol-lowed behind Miles. They were probably wondering where little Miles had gone. Nick didn't know whether to laugh or cry. *His crew? Peace out?* All of a sudden his little boy was growing up. His next birthday he'd be double digits. *Where had the time gone? Wasn't it just yesterday when Miles had learned to crawl?*

Nick swallowed past the huge lump in his throat as he watched his son walk away.

As he walked toward the designated meetup spot,

Nick stopped on numerous occasions to greet friends and town acquaintances. Nick knew his hometown was far from perfect, but the community had rallied behind him after Kara's accident. He wasn't sure if he would have made it through those dark days without the phone calls, casseroles, and endless support. Nick would never forget those acts of kindness. They were imprinted on his soul.

He spotted Harlow before he even noticed the booth. She stood out, with her dark curly hair and mahogany-colored skin. The crimson corduroy jacket she wore looked nice against her brown complexion. Dark jeans hugged her curves nicely. He dragged his gaze away from her for a moment, raising his hand in greeting to Stella, Luke, Dante, and Lucy. The closer he got to Harlow, the more fast and furiously his heart began to pound within his chest. *Easy there.* It was way too soon to fall for Harlow. Sure, she was easy on the eyes and a breath of fresh air, but he didn't know her very well. He'd only begun to peel back her layers.

"Hey, guys," Nick said as he walked up. He had to remind himself not to stare at Harlow. Nick didn't want to scare her off. She was probably used to men fawning all over her, and he didn't want to be like every other guy. Maybe he was overthinking things, but he wanted her to view him in a positive light.

"Nick! Thanks for coming out," Stella said, placing her arms around his neck and kissing his cheek. Luke reached out and bumped fists with him.

"Hi, Nick." Harlow's honeyed voice washed over him like a warm spring rain. He'd missed her. Feeling this way surprised him, because his life was very focused on a small group of people with Miles at the center. This was the first time in years anyone had been added to his circle.

"Harlow. It's good to see you," Nick said, leaning in for a hug. A floral smell hovered around her like a halo. Nick breathed it in. "You smell nice." *Had he just said that? Did it sound creepy? Ugh. Maybe he really was out of practice with women.*

"Thanks. I've been using this fragrance for forever."

Phew. She was smiling at him and seemingly pleased with his compliment. Maybe he still had it after all. He was a grown-ass man who had been through the worst life could throw at a person, yet at this very moment he felt like a teenager.

"I've been meaning to call you," Nick said. "Things have been pretty hectic, but I owe you a dinner."

Harlow laughed out loud. "I think it's me who owes you a dinner, Nick. Mine was disastrous."

The food may have been rotten, but the company had been exceptional.

"Truth is, I can't think of the last time I had so much fun with someone," Nick confessed.

Something flickered in Harlow's eyes that told Nick she felt the same way he did. She opened her mouth to say something just as Lucy began clapping to get their attention, breaking up the moment between them. "Okay, we're about to start selling the tickets. Here's the list of items they can win and pricing for the tickets. Ten winning items in all, with the grand prize being a weekend for two in Vail."

Luke let out a whistle. "Nice! I've never been to Vail."

"Well, buy some tickets," Stella said. "You gotta be in it to win it."

"If you buy a raffle ticket, selfies with a purchase," Dante called out. He flashed his million-dollar movie-star grin at the crowd.

People began flocking toward him and pulling out their cash. "Line up, people. Don't worry. Everyone will get a turn with the Inferno," Lucy called out.

"Dante's killing it," Nick said as he eyeballed the golden boy of Mistletoe working the crowd.

"Using that Hollywood charm!" Luke chimed in, nodding his head approvingly.

"You're not doing too bad yourselves," Harlow said. "Mistletoe's eye candy."

* * *

"You think I'm eye candy?" Nick asked in a low voice. Harlow had blurted out the words without thinking. Now she felt her cheeks getting flushed. She'd basically let on how much she was into him without saying it directly.

"I said what I said," she answered. "Stop fishing for compliments."

Nick chuckled. "Give me a break. I live with a nine-year-old. It's pretty rare to hear nice things about myself."

Harlow rolled her eyes. "Cry me a river, Keegan."

"Definitely Maine's finest," Stella said, beaming at her husband.

"We need to give Dante some competition," Luke said. "I'm a former Navy SEAL. He's bringing out my competitive spirit."

"You could take your shirts off and show some abs," Harlow suggested. She was only half kidding. She had a feeling Nick, with his search and rescue exploits, was hiding a serious six-pack under his sweater. She wouldn't be opposed to seeing his abs.

"I have my dignity," Luke quipped.

"Barely," Nick responded, earning himself a jab in the side from Luke.

"You think it would work?" Nick asked, slowly peeling off his jacket.

"Take it off. Take it off!" Stella, Lucy, and Harlow began to chant.

"Troublemaker," Nick said, looking straight at Harlow and wiggling his eyebrows.

"Always," Harlow answered, winking at Nick.

"I can't," Nick said with a shake of his head. "This is a family event. I might never be able to live it down if I go there."

Harlow, Lucy, and Stella let out groans of dis-appointment.

"What a tease," Harlow muttered, her lips twitch-ing at the bemused look Nick sent her. She hoped he knew that she was teasing him. Nick had the most playful facial expressions.

"You're right," Lucy said. "It's PG. Family ori-ented. Your abs might send the women of Mistletoe into a complete and utter frenzy."

Nick rolled his eyes at Lucy's comment, but Harlow totally agreed with her. Nick and Luke shirt-less might be too hot for the crowd to handle!

Luke dipped his head down and kissed his wife. "Thanks for the vote of confidence, babe."

"It's too risky for me," Nick said, quirking his mouth. "If Miles heard about me doing a Magic Mike routine at the fall festival, he might disown me. No kid his age wants his dad to act up in public," Nick said. Harlow thought it was sweet how Nick always seemed to put Miles first. That was parent-hood, she realized. Putting someone else's needs before your own.

"Ain't that the truth," Harlow said. "If my dad had done something like that I would have freaked out." She hardly ever talked about her dad, so it was a little surprising to think of him in this moment. Lately, memories of him were popping up at un-foreseen times. Jack Jones had been everything to Harlow, and she was beginning to realize he still was. Stuffing his memory away hadn't made those

feelings any less powerful and poignant. She was
stunned by the realization that she could handle the
memories of him. She wouldn't shatter.

"Were the two of you close? I know you said he
passed away when you were a kid."

Nick's question gave her pause. She didn't like to
think about her childhood and all of the good times
she'd shared with her father. Doing so made the loss
of him even sharper. She'd been his princess and
he'd been her king. In her eyes, he'd been magical.
To this day, she could still remember the way his
hand had felt in hers as they walked along the beach.
And sometimes he would come to her in dreams,
talking to her in his deep baritone voice. Showering
her with his love. Waking up to the knowledge that
she'd been dreaming was always heartbreaking.

Harlow nodded. "Yeah, we were very close. You
could say I was a daddy's girl. Wherever he was
I wanted to be there right beside him." The words
caught in her throat and she found herself blinking
back tears. "I need a minute, Nick." She walked
a few feet away and stepped behind the gazebo to
collect herself. The last thing she wanted was for the
entire town to witness her raw emotion.

"That's your problem. You stuff everything down."
Malcolm's voice buzzed in her ears. He'd said those
words to her time and again. Harlow knew it was
true. She had learned the trick of packing her feelings away as a child, and so far, she hadn't been
able to let it go. Hiding felt much safer than showing

her fears and insecurities. Maybe if she picked apart the past she could finally move on. But that took courage she wasn't sure she had.

"Are you all right?" Nick's voice washed over her. Harlow turned around to see Nick standing a few feet away. He'd come to find her, which was a sweet gesture. Harlow had a hard time looking him in the eye. Staring into his warm brown eyes might just break her down even further. There was something about this man that made her want to lean on him.

Ugh. That wasn't like her at all. Harlow prided herself on standing on her own two feet. Malcolm was the only person she truly turned to for support.

Nick stepped closer, then handed her a tissue. Harlow took it and gently dabbed at her eyes, sniffling to try and stem the tide of tears.

"I'm sorry. I don't know where that came from," she confessed.

Nick reached out and wiped tears away from her face with his thumb. His eyes brimmed with compassion. "I'm the last person you have to explain it to. I understand completely. Grief can rise up out of nowhere and take us by surprise."

Harlow took a deep breath and stood tall, jutting her shoulders back. She needed to get it together and sell some raffle tickets. "Thank you. I'm ready to get back to it now." She clapped her hands together. "Let's go sell some of these raffle tickets before Lucy fires us."

Nick leaned in toward her, whispering in her ear, "Okay, but no matter what you say, I'm not taking off my shirt."

A laugh escaped her lips. "So we're going to have to use our personalities to move these tickets."

"It seems so," Nick said with a wink.

"Game on!" Harlow held up her palm and high-fived Nick.

"Ain't nothing but a thing, chicken wing," Nick said as they headed back to the table. Harlow appreciated the fact that Lucy, Stella, Luke, and Dante didn't even glance in her direction. They must have witnessed her raw emotion and were giving her the grace to rejoin them without having to feel self-conscious.

Working alongside Nick kept her laughing all day long. When he wasn't cracking her up with celebrity impersonations, he was giving her the low-down on all the characters in town. According to Nick, Mistletoe was a hotbed of juicy gossip and small-town intrigue.

"If you run into Violet Stewart, be prepared to hear about the founding fathers of Mistletoe. She's a town historian of sorts and she loves to talk everyone's ear off about her research." The grin on Nick's face was contagious. Harlow found herself grinning in response. Or maybe it was the man himself who made her want to smile.

"Point taken," Harlow said. Ten minutes later, when Violet stopped by the booth, Harlow made sure not to engage her in a lengthy conversation. Nick stood by and watched with a huge smirk on his face. She almost lost it when he started making funny faces to distract her.

Harlow avoided eye contact with Nick while she listened to Violet talk about a famous pirate who operated out of Mistletoe in the 1600s. Harlow ended up selling her a bunch of tickets. She was proud of herself for not cracking up over Nick's antics.

As soon as Violet walked away, Gillian stepped up to the booth. Perhaps this would be an opportunity to smooth things over between them. Harlow had sensed that Gillian wasn't happy with their interaction at Paws. She always wanted clients to be comfortable, so it was worthwhile to be extra pleasant.

"Hi, Gillian. How many raffle tickets do you want to buy?" Harlow flashed the woman her most brilliant smile, hoping to cut through the tension from the other day.

Gillian kept her gaze focused on Nick, not bothering to even glance at Harlow. The woman was acting as if she hadn't heard a single word she'd said. As if Harlow were invisible.

"Twenty dollars' worth, please," she said to Nick. Her face was lit up with a huge smile.

With a confused look on his face, Nick took her money and doled out the tickets. "Here you go. All proceeds to benefit the Free Library of Mistletoe."

"Thanks, Nick. Good luck with the raffle," she

said in a sweet tone. To Harlow's ears she sounded overly cheery, as if she was putting on an act. Gillian turned on her heel without sparing Harlow a glance. She walked a few feet away, where she met up with a few friends. As Harlow watched, Gillian leaned in and spoke to the ladies, then looked in her direction. When the other ladies' gazes also landed on Harlow she knew without a shadow of a doubt that she was the topic of their whispers.

Immediately, her body stiffened up. Harlow felt her cheeks burning. Gillian wasn't being subtle at all. She'd deliberately ignored Harlow, pretending not to hear her. Then she'd made Harlow the object of her chatter.

"What's up with her?" Nick asked, turning toward Harlow with a furrowed brow.

Harlow shrugged. "I'm not sure. She came into Paws the other day with a pet emergency. Her pup, Elvis, ate chocolate, which is deadly for dogs. I don't think she appreciated my input, which was basically education on substances that are toxic to canines."

Nick shook his head. "She was being rude to say the least. You treated her dog, so the least she could do was be cordial. I don't want you to get the wrong impression of folks here in Mistletoe. Let me go set her straight."

"No!" she said sharply, grabbing hold of his arm before he could talk to Gillian.

"Are you sure? I have no problem with handling

the situation for you. I've known her since we were kids, so I've seen Gillian in action plenty of times and I know how to deal with her."

"Nick, it's a sweet offer, but not necessary. If I'm going to hold my head up high in Mistletoe, I can't have you fighting my battles for me." Nick's wanting to protect her made Harlow feel all warm and fuzzy inside, which wasn't her style at all. For the first time she thought about what it might be like to have a partner who helped her make it through the rough times. She couldn't imagine Nick ever letting his woman flounder. He'd be there for her, without a doubt.

He let out a sigh. "You're right. If you want to know the truth, she's always been a bit of a mean girl. Just tread carefully with Gillian." He wrinkled his nose. "She doesn't always play nice."

Harlow had known a lot of mean girls in high school. She'd handled them back then, and if necessary, she would deal with Gillian now. What bothered her was the fact that she'd been openly whispering about her in a group setting. *What could Gillian possibly be saying about her?* She barely knew the woman. And why had she snubbed her as if they were enemies? None of it made any sense. Harlow had only been doing her job by warning her about Elvis's consuming toxic foods. That was what veterinarians did. What was her problem?

"She doesn't have to like me or be my friend, but I'd like to keep things civil between us since she's a client at Paws. I'll do my part. I can only hope she returns the favor."

"I know you will," Nick said, sending her an encouraging smile. "I bet this will all blow over by next week. Probably just a misunderstanding that needs to be straightened out."

Harlow hoped Nick was correct. But something didn't feel right in her bones. She had an innate ability to read people, and Gillian was emitting bad vibes.

Nick's cell phone buzzed. "Excuse me for a moment," he said, answering the call. His features were animated as he talked. He was waving his arms around and walking in a circular motion. His dark brows were drawn together. It didn't take a genius to figure out something was wrong. Moments later, Nick ended the call and turned back toward her.

"I hate to ditch you, Harlow, but I have urgent business. A six-year-old is missing in the lake region in Darien. I'm being called in to work the case." Worry lines framed his eyes.

"Of course. That sounds terrifying." She couldn't imagine how the parents must feel about their missing child being out there, alone and in peril. "I hope you find the child."

"Me too. This is a parent's worst nightmare." Harlow could see the tension etched on his face. A vein was throbbing above his eye. She would guess adrenaline was racing through his veins right about now. Someone's life hung in the balance, and Nick bore the weight of that responsibility along with his search and rescue team.

She wrapped her arms around her middle. Just learning about the missing child caused a sick feeling to wash over her.

"Hey. Before I forget, would you like to go trick-or-treating with us? We can grab pizza or I can make dinner before we head out. Your choice."

Harlow didn't have to think about Nick's invite for long. She loved Halloween. It had been one of the highlights of a chaotic childhood. "Only if I can wear my *Black Panther* outfit."

"I like your style," Nick said, nodding his head approvingly. "Miles and I are still trying to figure out our outfits, but we're getting close to making a decision."

"Let me know if you need to brainstorm. I've had a lifetime of planning outfits for me and Malcolm. Minnie and Mickey. Raggedy Ann and Andy."

Nick made a face. "No offense, but there's no way I'm choosing either of those. No self-respecting dad would even suggest it." A small smile twitched at the sides of his mouth.

Harlow perched a hand on her hip. "Hey! That's not nice. We won actual Halloween costume contests back in the day with those outfits."

Nick scoffed. "Okay, I'll take your word for it. I'll call you about Halloween." Nick looked at his watch and said, "I've got to go. Have fun. And if Gillian even looks at you cross-eyed, toss a glass of water on her so she melts." Nick's lips were twitching with merriment. He waved at her before turning to leave.

"Be safe," Harlow called out after him, fully aware of the dangers Nick faced in his job.

Harlow couldn't take her eyes off him as he strode away from her. Have mercy! Nick looked just as good walking away as he did heading toward her. The attraction she felt toward him made her heart skitter inside her chest. She wanted more time with this man—more kisses and conversation, more laughter and cooking. More of everything! Nick Keegan had her full and complete interest right now and she couldn't wait to explore all of the possibilities.

CHAPTER ELEVEN

The town of Darien was an upscale community with stunning mountain views and beautiful lakeside properties. A local campground was a popular destination for tourists, especially in the summer months. Skyler Jakes, the missing six-year-old, lived in town and had gone missing at a birthday party at the lake. According to the hosts, the kids had been playing hide-and-seek.

"Who has a birthday party for a six-year-old at a lake?" a scowling Luke asked Nick as they gathered at the search and rescue command center for a short water break and to get new intel from the team. Luke had also received the call to report to work due to the urgent crisis. Working together was always a rush, but today felt different. A heavy cloud hung over the assignment. They'd been out in the woods for hours, with no luck in finding Skyler.

Nick had been asking himself the same question. Six-year-olds and water didn't always mesh, especially in this type of setting. "I'm not getting a good vibe with this one. The water aspect concerns me."

"They're going to bring in some divers tomorrow." Luke's expression was shuttered, but Nick knew his brother's emotions would match his own on this search.

Nick winced at the thought that Skyler might have ventured into the lake. This was the most difficult part of his job. Seeing a child in harm's way was agonizing, and not being able to rescue the child in a timely manner would be the worst possible outcome. "Temps are going to drop this evening, which could make it difficult for Skyler. If we don't find her, she's going to have a rough night."

"Right," Luke said. "And from what her parents said, she was wearing a thick sweater but no coat." Nick let out a groan. Any time a child was involved, he took it personally. Skyler was just a few years younger than Miles. He couldn't imagine what he would do if Miles was missing. He'd move heaven and earth to locate him, which is what he planned to do for Skyler.

Nick pulled out a map of the lake area and spread it out on the table. "Okay, help me look, Luke. What aren't we seeing about the area?" He pointed at the forested area that they'd searched earlier. "The sweep of this portion was comprehensive. Of course, we could have missed her, but I don't think so."

Luke studied the map. "Most of the houses are on the other side of the lake. That area was also checked."

"And the forested area is closest to the party location. This is tricky terrain. Skyler would be hard to spot by helicopter," Nick noted. He clenched his jaw. "I think this is where she is," Nick said, pointing toward a wooded area close to where she'd last been spotted. "It makes sense that she's somewhere in the woods, since she seemed to vanish so fast from the lake area. A wooded area would hide her from sight as soon as she stepped into the forest."

They continued to scrutinize the map. Neither one of them wanted to think about the fact that she might have gone into the lake. They weren't going to even consider it as long as other possibilities existed.

"Is there any location in this specific area that might provide shelter?" Nick asked. Troubleshooting with Luke helped Nick see the big picture. Kids loved to hide. Alone and scared, a child might seek to hunker down.

"Here," Luke said, pointing to a spot a few miles away from the last location where she'd been spotted. "What's this?"

Nick squinted. "It looks like some sort of structure. If they were playing hide-and-seek, she might have gotten lost and taken shelter there."

Luke nodded. "Makes sense to me. Are you thinking what I'm thinking?" he asked, glancing at his watch. "It's going to get dark in an hour or so, which means the search will be called off until morning."

"We should head out now," Nick said, standing up. "We'll have to haul ass to get to that area by dark. Ready?"

Luke flexed his biceps. "I'm always ready."

Normally Nick would make some sort of joke about Luke's comment, but at the moment he deeply appreciated the fact that they were in this together. The other members of the search and rescue team were amazing, but there was no one who he was in sync with like Luke. Their way of thinking was the same, as well as their tenacity and dedication. If anyone was capable of seeing this rescue through with him, it was Luke.

As they headed out, a few team members crossed paths with them and decided to join them. Rocky Donato and Danielle Parks were among the best of his team. Nick had worked with Danielle on several occasions, and although Rocky was relatively new, he'd impressed Nick with his diligence and follow-through.

Nick and Luke had mapped out a path through the woods, with the end goal of scouting out the perimeter by the edifice. Throughout their trek they called out to Skyler, pausing along the way to listen for any sounds of activity. The forest was still other than birds and animals scurrying around. Darkness was setting in with the sun quickly fading from the sky. A feeling of frustration rose up inside of him. *Lord, let us find her!* He wasn't a man who prayed a lot, but now was one of those desperate moments.

"Look up ahead!" Danielle called out, pointing at something in the distance.

Nick followed her gaze, his adrenaline pumping as he spotted the small log cabin. Most likely it had been set up for Girl Scout troops or other organizations for overnight stays. As they got closer, Nick observed that it was in disrepair, as if the structure hadn't been utilized in the past decade or so.

"Why don't Danielle and I check out the surrounding area while the two of you go inside," Rocky suggested, taking out his tactical solar flashlight. The sun was dipping below the horizon at a rapid rate. Darkness would soon envelop them, making everything more complicated.

"Sounds good," Nick said as he looked around the property before heading inside with Luke. "Skyler. Are you in here?" he called out.

"Skyler," Luke said in a cheery voice. "Don't be afraid. We're part of the search and rescue team."

They were met with silence. Nick wanted to let out a scream of frustration. He'd been so certain Skyler might be here in this dwelling. Maybe he'd been wrong.

Nick heard a rustling sound just as a little blond head popped out of the closet. Suddenly, he felt as if a hundred-pound weight had been lifted off his chest.

"Skyler?" Nick asked, getting down on his haunches so he wouldn't look so scary to a six-year-old. He knew his height could be intimidating.

She nodded her head but didn't speak or move toward him. Green eyes looked back at him with a mixture of fear and awe.

Luke stood in the doorway, keeping his distance so Nick could coax her out of her hiding spot. Although Skyler looked a bit disheveled, he was happy to see she seemed to be doing well otherwise.

"My name is Nick and I came here to find you, Skyler. That's my brother, Luke. It's our job to help people. I know you must be scared, but I'd like to take you back to your family. They're anxious to see you."

"Are you my friend?" Skyler asked, cocking her head to the side.

"I'd like to be," Nick said. "I have a son a few years older than you. You've been very brave, Skyler, but you're not alone anymore. We've got you." He reached into his backpack and pulled out a granola bar and a bottled water. "You must be hungry. It's past your dinnertime, I'm guessing. These are really good. My son likes them so much he takes them to school every day."

Skyler came running toward him, throwing herself against his chest and wrapping her arms around his neck. She was holding on to him so tightly, Nick couldn't breathe properly. But it was okay with him. She was safe! Her family would sleep well tonight knowing their baby girl was out of harm's way.

"I am really hungry," she said, pulling away from him and reaching out for the granola bar. "And thirsty."

Nick smiled as he handed her the bar and then twisted open the top of the bottled water. "Here you go, Skyler."

"I'll go tell Danielle and Rocky the good news, then I'll reach out to the rest of the search team," Luke said as he rushed out of the room.

This, Nick thought, *was his purpose in life other than being Miles's dad.* Being a helper. Rushing in when others rushed away from danger. In this moment, he was proud of his chosen profession. Grateful for his team. And for Luke. They'd made this rescue possible by working together as a united front. No egos. No posturing. Just hard work and a common purpose.

He couldn't even put into words what it had been like to lock eyes on Skyler for the first time, filled with the knowledge that she was safe and sound.

Nick's chest tightened. Today would go down in the record books as a very good day. He would sleep well tonight.

* * *

Later that night, Harlow's cell phone began to buzz just as she was settling in for the night. She was

pretty exhausted after a full day at the town event.
After Nick's departure, she had continued to sell
raffle tickets before hanging out with Lucy and
Stella and walking around the event. They had introduced her to a lot of residents who seemed happy to
have a new veterinarian in town. She'd even carved
a pumpkin and bobbed for apples. The best part was
being introduced to an abundance of dogs who had
accompanied their owners to the fair. Someone had
even brought their teacup pig along.

The fall festival had been fun, but not having
Nick around had been a bit of a disappointment. She
was beginning to look forward to the moments they
shared. Talking. Laughing. Kissing. He was the full
package.

Nick's name popped up on her screen, almost as
if she'd made it happen just by thinking about him.
She felt a smile tugging at her lips as she answered
the call.

"Hey, Nick! I didn't think I'd be hearing from you
tonight." Harlow had imagined he would be tied up
on his search and rescue assignment. She hoped this
signified a positive update about the missing girl.

"Sorry to call so late, but I wanted to share
the good news." He paused for a moment. "We
found her. We located Skyler in the woods." Nick's
enthusiasm radiated through the phone.

Harlow let out a scream. "Oops. Sorry to yell in
your ear, but that's incredible news." She was stoked
for him. He worked in an amazing profession where

burnout was high and successes should always be celebrated.

Nick let out a chuckle. "No worries. We've been celebrating on this end for hours."

"Her parents must have been so happy. And grateful."

"I don't think I'll ever forget watching that reunion play out for as long as I live." His voice was thick with emotion. "Truthfully, I wasn't sure about this one. I hoped. I prayed. But I also steeled myself against a possible bad outcome. To have it all come together like this...there's really no words to express how I feel."

"I'm so happy for Skyler and her family. And you and your team, of course. I wouldn't be at all surprised if Skyler's family makes you an honorary member."

"They don't need to do that. Something tells me I'll be checking in on that girl until she heads off to college."

"I'm sure she'll love that. No doubt you're her hero."

"And she's mine, for finding shelter and staying calm." She heard him let out a long sigh on the other end. "Well, thanks for sharing in my excitement. Night, Harlow."

"Night, Nick. Sleep well," Harlow said before hanging up.

As she climbed between the sheets, thoughts of Nick bombarded her. He was such a good guy. If he had a flaw, she hadn't yet seen it. Sweet. Kind. All kinds of gorgeous. Funny. And he saved people's lives for a living.

Harlow couldn't play it cool any longer. She was seriously crushing on Nick Keegan. And even though she was really good at putting up obstacles in relationships, she couldn't think of a single reason that she shouldn't have a wild fling with him during her stint in Mistletoe. Nothing serious. No falling in love. Just pure, footloose and fancy-free fun.

* * *

The next week flew by, with Halloween arriving just as Nick and Miles figured out their costumes. Nick was excited about his favorite holiday of the year, but more than anything he was looking forward to seeing Harlow again. He and Harlow had texted and talked on the phone a few times, which made Nick feel as if he was getting to know her bit by bit. She was funny and engaging. Nick liked her. This feeling of wanting to get under a woman's skin and learn everything there was to know about her was unfamiliar to Nick. He'd known his wife since they were kids, so their relationship had been a gradual process. With Harlow, Nick felt as if he was doing a deep dive off a cliff.

He kept going back to the way they'd kissed at her house. Nick hadn't felt a spark like that in years. He'd worried that he might never again feel that push and pull of heat and attraction, never connect with a woman who made him ache to be with her. Harlow made him want things he'd begun to believe were in his rearview mirror. Walks on the beach. A stroll in the moonlight. Holding hands. Dancing in the rain.

The sound of his doorbell interrupted his thoughts and he called out to Miles. Harlow needed to see their outfits together in order to get the full effect. Miles came running down the hall, which normally Nick would chide him for, but he was going to let it go just this time.

"Harlow's here," Nick said. "Let's see what she thinks about our costumes."

"She's going to love 'em," Miles said, rubbing his hands together. "We are killing it."

Nick opened the front door. Harlow was standing on his doorstep looking sexy as all get-out. He thought he might have to pick his jaw up off the floor. She was dressed as a female Black Panther superhero, wearing a tight black leather bodysuit with African accessories sewn into the fabric. For a moment, he wondered if he might be drooling.

"Wow." The single word fell out of his mouth.

"You like?" Harlow asked as she twirled around.

"Like doesn't even cover it," Nick said in a low voice as he checked her out. The costume hid absolutely nothing about her shape. She had curves for days.

"You look awesome, Doc Harlow. I think that's

what he's trying to say," Miles said, shaking his head at Nick as if he was pitiful. *Maybe he was,* Nick thought, chuckling.

"Holy Batman and Robin. You two look fantastic," Harlow said as Nick waved her inside. Miles had dressed up as Batman while Nick was playing the sidekick role of Robin.

"Thanks," Miles said. "I think Batman is definitely underrated in the superhero universe. And Robin always had his back."

"Well, I think you two look dope," Harlow said. "I'm no expert on superheroes, but I know what looks on point. If there was a best costume contest, the two of you would win it, hands down." Harlow flashed him a thumbs-up sign. Miles smiled shyly up at her. He wasn't used to hanging out with Nick's female friends, so this was all new to him.

"Your home is beautiful," Harlow said, looking around his foyer. Nick was happy with his humble abode. For him, the most important part of it was making it cozy and warm for his son. And filled with love.

"Thanks. We've been really happy here. Right Miles?" he asked, clapping his arm around his son.

"Yep," Miles said with a nod. "I'm going to finish my vocabulary words before we head out. I told some friends we would meet up with them over by Maple Street," Miles said before dashing upstairs with Zeus at his heels.

Maple Street? Friends? Trick-or-treating had

always been the two of them, with Stella and Tess occasionally coming along with them. Even when Kara had been alive she'd stayed back at the house giving out the candy. Luke had been overseas doing Navy SEAL heroics for most of the Halloweens in Miles's life.

"He's all about the friends these days. I guess I'm chopped liver," Nick said. His son was growing way too fast for his liking. Pretty soon he was going to be heading out to meet up with friends on his own. No more park meetups or playdates orchestrated by the adults in their lives. Unexpectedly, Nick found himself battling feelings of loss.

"Come on, Nick. Surely you remember being his age. Friends were everything. But deep in our hearts, we loved our families to the moon and back." She locked eyes with Nick. "I'm sure that's how Miles feels about you. I can see it written all over his sweet face."

"Just for making me feel better, how about a glass of wine while we wait for Miles?" Nick led her down the hall toward his kitchen. He pulled out a bottle of wine from his wine fridge, then took down two goblets from the cupboard. Harlow sat down at his kitchen counter and he slid a glass toward her before taking a seat.

This was nice, he realized. Life had gotten so busy he'd forgotten about chill moments like this one. Nick wanted more of this. More adult conversation. More relaxation. More Harlow.

"Hey, I didn't want to say anything in front of Miles," Harlow said, placing her goblet down on the counter, "but the biopsy results came back."

His heart sank. Zeus was Miles's bestie. The dog was even beginning to grow on Nick. When he wasn't acting like a maniac, the pup was pretty good company. Zeus had learned to track Nick down in the house at dinnertime. He had to admit it was pretty adorable.

"Uh-oh. I don't like the look on your face. Should I be worried?" Nick asked. He was dreading the answer. Bad news was something he'd learned to fear.

"It turns out that it's liposarcoma."

"Which means what? I've never heard of that."

"It is cancerous," Harlow said in a calm voice, "but I believe we can successfully remove it. Most liposarcomas don't spread to other parts of the body, which is good."

Nick ran a shaky hand over his face. "Wow. I wasn't expecting you to say that."

"I know," she said, reaching out to squeeze his hand. "No owner anticipates hearing bad news about their pet, but in Zeus's case this isn't a dire prognosis. Thanks to Miles, by the way, for speaking up. By saying something he may have saved Zeus's life."

"What do I tell him?" Nick asked. "I don't want him to freak out or be scared."

"Let him know what a good job he did by pointing

out the tumor. It was diagnosed at an early stage, which is promising. I'm confident we can remove it with clean margins."

Nick ran a hand over his face. "My kid has had his fair share of loss. One of the things I've been trying to instill in him is that his world is a safe place."

"I know, Nick," Harlow said, her voice oozing sympathy. "Just reassure him that Zeus is strong. I really think he's going to be fine, but he's going to need some tests and surgery. You can't sugarcoat that aspect, but you can tell him that this isn't the end for Zeus. He's going to be around for a very long time. If you want, I can be there when you tell him."

Nick's heart lurched. "That's a sweet offer, which I'm going to gratefully accept. Miles will have a million questions that I can't answer."

"I'm more than happy to be there for both of you," Harlow murmured, reaching out and touching his arm.

Nick hadn't realized how much hearing those words would affect him. To have Harlow offer her support to him and Miles was touching. Having Harlow in his world was opening him up to all the empty places in his life—spaces she was rapidly filling up. There were voids in his life he tended to ignore, because they reminded him of all he'd lost. But maybe now he was finding something new.

"Thank you, Harlow," Nick said. "You explained everything in a way that gives us hope. Believe it or

not, I can't imagine our household without Zeus."
His throat felt thick with emotion. "I appreciate you
saying you'll be there for us. It means a lot to me."

Their eyes met and Harlow shifted in her chair,
moving closer toward him. His eyes went straight to
her lips—her bow-shaped, extremely kissable lips.
He leaned in just as Harlow did. He placed his lips
over hers, feeling an instant rush as their lips met.
How had he forgotten how good this felt? Harlow
wrapped her arms around his neck and pulled him
closer, if that was even possible. He explored her
mouth with his tongue as the kiss intensified from
tenderness to molten lava. Nick wanted this kiss to
go on forever and ever. Time seemed to stop as they
explored each other—hands, lips, tongues, necks.

The sound of Miles's footsteps rushing down the
stairs put a halt to the kiss. "Van's at the door. I'll let
him in," he called out, making a racket as he raced
to the front door.

They slowly pulled away. For a moment, they
simply stared into each other's eyes, savoring the
moment. *To be continued.* The words buzzed in
his ear. Nick had every intention of kissing Harlow
again, and the next time it happened, he promised
himself, there wouldn't be any interruptions.

* * *

Kissing Nick was just as good as Harlow remembered. His lips tasted fruity from the wine they'd

been enjoying. Sweet and tangy. It had turned into a full-on make-out session, which had taken her by surprise. She felt a bit sheepish, because Miles had almost caught them in the act. She didn't know what the rules were for getting romantic with a single dad. Did Miles realize they were sort of dating? Seeing each other? Harlow still couldn't figure out how to label her relationship with Nick. Would Miles even care? For all she knew he would be protective of his dad because they'd been a dynamic duo for so many years.

"Let's go, Dad. I need to fill this up." Miles held out up an empty pillowcase as he stepped over the threshold. He didn't seem to have any clue as to what he'd interrupted. Nick and Harlow exchanged a glance.

"Ready to get your trick-or-treat on?" Nick asked, reaching for her hand as she got down from the stool.

She grinned up at him. "I sure am. I've been looking forward to this ever since you invited me," Harlow said. Suddenly she felt like a little kid again. A joyful sensation swept through her. It was a rare moment when Harlow felt carefree. Being in Nick's presence made her feel lighter and more relaxed. An air of calm surrounded him. Maybe it was contagious.

As they walked toward the Maple Street neighborhood to meet up with Miles's pals, Nick reached for Harlow's hand and entwined it with his. She loved the way his hand felt in hers. It had been a long time since she'd held hands with someone special. Years, if she was being totally honest with herself.

This felt good. Better than good, as a matter of fact. Nick's hand felt right in hers and she knew she'd never experienced an awareness like this before.

Harlow enjoyed seeing the wide range of costumes. Ballerinas. SpongeBob. Barbie. Pirates and Tinkerbells. And of course, an abundance of superheroes.

"Hey, Miles. Don't forget that your old man will be taking your extras. Snickers and Reese's," Nick said. He rubbed his stomach and made a funny face.

"Not so fast. I love Reese's too," Harlow said, reaching into Miles's sack and pulling out a few of the peanut butter cups. She let out a wild cackle at the shocked expression on Nick's face.

"Hey. No fair," Nick said, frowning at her. "I called dibs first."

"You snooze, you lose," she said, taunting him by waving the peanut butter cups in front of his face.

"Oh, you're playing a dangerous game, Doc." Nick advanced toward her and tried to grab the candy from her. Harlow darted away from him until he placed his hands on her waist and spun her around to face him. At the moment there was only about an inch separating their bodies. Having his hands on her waist was an intimate sensation. She could almost feel a heat radiating from him.

"How about we share?" Harlow asked as she held up a Reese's as a peace offering.

"Deal," Nick said as she tore away the wrapper and split the peanut butter cup in half. "Open up," she said as Nick parted his lips and she slid the chocolate in his mouth. He instantly closed his eyes and let out a satisfied sound. Sharing the Reese's felt like an intimate act between her and Nick. As he looked on, Harlow bit into the chocolate, savoring every ounce of it.

"You two are so weird," Miles said with a shake of his head. "Peanut butter and chocolate are not as good as Sour Patch Kids or M&M'S."

"Is that so?" Harlow asked. "Well, good thing we're here to eat all the yucky candy."

"Right," Nick said. "Keep it coming, Miles. We're not candy snobs."

"Oh, there's Tess," Miles said, racing toward his friend. They linked arms and went toward another house along with Miles's other pals.

Harlow was having fun. Wearing the Black Panther costume allowed her to be more outgoing and adventurous than usual. Because of the chill in the air, she'd brought along a black cape to keep her warm. Nick was cracking her up talking about how afraid he was of scary movies and Miles was running ahead with his friends to ring doorbells. He had already collected a massive amount of candy. She couldn't imagine how he was going to eat it all.

"Come on, tell me *Carrie* isn't terrifying?" Nick

asked as Miles walked toward a house. "This girl killed an entire room of prom guests. And *The Exorcist*." He shuddered. "That one gave me nightmares. Head swiveling and talking in tongues." Nick made an exaggerated face. "And don't get me started on *Transylvania*."

"Nick, isn't that a cartoon?" she asked, giggling. "I'm not sure even little kids think it's scary."

He made a funny face. "Don't judge. Cartoons can still be really frightening."

Harlow shook her head and let out a belly laugh. "If you're five."

Suddenly, Nick got really still like a statue. He let out what sounded like a growl. His eyes looked wild, and even though she'd thought for a split second that he was joking around with her, the air around him was charged.

"Miles, come back here," he shouted. Nick stormed across the lawn at a lightning-fast pace. One moment he'd been standing right beside her and in the next he was a man on a mission.

Harlow's gaze trailed after him as he took the candy from Miles and threw it down on the steps. Nick grabbed hold of Miles's arm and frog-marched him away from the house. Suddenly, all eyes in the crowd were focused on father and son.

Miles let out a squeal of outrage. "Dad! Why did you do that? They had the big candy bars."

"I don't care what they're giving away. Just go to the next house, okay?" Nick turned back toward the house and glared at the man standing in the doorway. Nick's stance reminded her of a boxer preparing for a fight. Miles stomped his foot and ran ahead, turning around to shoot Nick an angry look. But Nick didn't seem to notice. He was too busy staring down the man in the yellow house.

What in the world is going on? Had she missed something? Had the man tried to hurt Miles?

"Nick, what's wrong?" Harlow asked, her eyes glued to his frenzied expression.

Nick didn't seem to hear her. He was in a zone where he seemed to be focused on only one thing. "Nick! Are you all right? You're scaring me."

"It's him," Nick said, jerking his chin in the direction of the man doling out Halloween candy. "He's the man who killed my wife."

CHAPTER TWELVE

What the hell? Frank Baker, the man who had killed his wife, had been handing out candy to trick-or-treaters as if he had a right to be part of the Mistletoe community. And his own son had been at his door accepting the candy he was doling out! It was incredibly messed up.

Nick had seen everything through a red haze as he walked back to the house with Miles and Harlow. Miles had been upset with him about his outburst, but Nick hadn't wanted to tell him why he'd been so upset. Why should a nine-year-old have to hear such a terrible truth on a night meant for fun? He simply didn't have the words.

Nick paced back and forth across his hardwood floors in his living room. He hated this feeling of rage that he couldn't seem to extinguish. He wasn't a big fan of violence, but he'd been tempted to punch Baker in the face. He longed to make him suffer the way everyone who'd loved Kara had been tortured by her senseless death.

The light tread of footsteps sounded on the stairs, edging ever closer to his location. Seconds later, Harlow stood in the doorway. Even though he'd told her to go home, she hadn't listened to him. She had stuck around to make sure he was doing okay and to help out with Miles.

"Are you all right?" she asked, quickly closing the distance between them in a few strides.

He clenched his teeth. "Not really," he admitted. "Is Miles in bed?"

"Yeah. Zeus is sleeping at the foot of his bed. He went out like a light. Must've been all the carbs from today."

"Thanks for seeing to him and for dealing with Van. I'll explain things to Miles later." Nick said, "I'm sorry, Harlow. Tonight was supposed to be fun."

"You don't have to apologize for anything, Nick. Seeing him blindsided you. It's totally understandable."

Nick ran his hand over his face as he let out a ragged sigh. "I should have kept my cool. I hate that Miles saw me like that. He doesn't understand why I acted that way."

Harlow walked toward him and sank down on to his comfy couch. She patted the spot next to her. "Stop pacing, Nick. Come sit down. Seeing Baker was nightmarish. You had a human moment. It happens."

Nick sat down on the couch and Harlow pressed against him, then pulled him into a hug. "I felt you needed that. You're still shaking." Harlow reached for his hand and squeezed it tightly. "I know you're upset that Miles witnessed your reaction, but I think as long as you're straight with him, he'll be fine."

"What do I tell him? That's really heavy to lay on a kid." He wouldn't do it. Couldn't do it. His son had been through enough.

"So what have you told him so far? About Kara's death?"

Nick made a face. "Only that his mom died in a car crash." He hadn't had the heart to weigh his son down with the terrible knowledge that Nick carried around with him. A kid could understand an accident, but Miles wouldn't know how to process the fact that someone was responsible for taking his mother's life.

"Nick, you don't have to tell him everything, but I do think you should try to explain why you were so angry tonight. He'll get it."

Harlow was right. He didn't have to tell Miles everything about why he'd been so upset. But, in order to make sure his son wasn't fearful about the incident, Nick needed to be as straight with him as possible. "You're right. I'll definitely talk to him tomorrow. I want him to understand that even though I was angry I didn't let things get out of control."

"You did the right thing by walking away," Harlow said.

"This time," he said, gritting his teeth. "I've thought about paying him a visit to confront him. I've thought about doing a lot of things." How many times had he fantasized about tracking Baker down and dealing with him? It wasn't like him to be a vengeful person, but Nick was making an exception this time. He wanted Baker's world to fall down around him.

"You can't let this consume you. As awful as it is—"

"Awful doesn't even begin to describe it." He spit out the words. She didn't understand, hadn't walked in his shoes. How could she comprehend what he and Miles had been through? Although the ache of loss wasn't as razor sharp as it had once been, he still struggled with the notion that someone had ended Kara's life and taken her from them.

"Unless you've been through it, you wouldn't get it."

As soon as the words slid out of his mouth, Nick saw the shock on Harlow's face and the hurt brimming in her eyes. He hadn't meant to lash out at her, but all of his emotions were riding on the surface. He'd thought all of his anger had been extinguished, but with Baker's release, everything inside him had been stirred up again. Embers had blazed into an inferno.

"I do get it, Nick. Believe me, I do," she answered in a soft voice.

The look he sent her was one filled with disbelief. How could she know what he'd been through? How he'd suffered? How he had blamed himself for not dropping Miles at school that morning?

"I-I think it's time that I headed home," she said, jumping to her feet and grabbing her cape and purse. Her movements were full of purpose, as if she couldn't wait to get away from him.

"Harlow," he said, fumbling for a way to say he was sorry. He had snapped at her simply for trying to be a sounding board.

She turned back toward him. "Get some rest, Nick. I think you need to be alone right now." He could hear the discomfort in her voice. All because of him.

The thing was, Nick didn't want to be by himself. He'd done way too much of that over the past few years. But he'd made Harlow uncomfortable and she couldn't wait to leave his home. Before he could think of a way to get her to stay, Nick heard the click of the front door closing behind Harlow. She was gone.

Nick let out a groan. Harlow didn't deserve what he had just dished out. All of his anger should have been focused on Frank Baker and a justice system that didn't adequately punish perpetrators.

Harlow had just been in the direct line of fire this evening.

He'd screwed things up tonight, not just with Harlow, but with his son as well. *How in the world am I going to make things right?*

* * *

The next morning, Harlow woke up unsettled after a restless night of tossing and turning. The events of last night were still crystal-clear in her mind. She'd seen a side of Nick that had been in direct contrast to the man she knew. In those tense moments back at his house, Harlow hadn't recognized Nick. His laid-back personality was a hallmark of his character. But after seeing Frank Baker, he'd been agitated and seething with fury.

Of all people, Harlow should understand. Hadn't she harbored similar feelings after the false allegations lodged against her father and his fatal car wreck? The official cause of his death had been ruled accidental, but Harlow's mother had always been convinced he'd driven off the road on purpose. She and Malcolm had grown up believing their father had killed himself due to being branded a pariah in Chestnut Ridge. At this point, Harlow didn't know what to think. Could her mother have been wrong? Deep in her heart, she'd always resisted the notion that her father had deliberately crashed his car. Not for a second had she ever believed that the honorable man who'd raised her could have been a thief.

Once she'd arrived home last night she had called Malcolm. Harlow had been in need of a pick-me-up after the tense conversation with Nick. She kept asking herself if she'd mishandled the situation by saying the wrong things.

"What's wrong? I can hear it in your voice. Something's up," Malcolm had asked. "How was the trick-or-treating with Nick?"

A little sigh slipped past her lips. "It was the perfect night until Nick spotted the drunk driver who killed his wife. He was released from prison early and was actually handing out candy at a house," Harlow explained. She'd shivered just recalling the incident.

Malcolm let out a shocked sound on the other end. "That's horrific. Not only that she was the victim of a drunk-driving accident, but that Nick had to see the perp in Mistletoe." He let out a low whistle. "I can't blame him for losing his cool."

She let out a tutting sound. "I really feel for him. I'm hoping he isn't tempted to take matters into his own hands."

Harlow hated to imagine Nick acting as a vigilante. The very idea of it was terrifying. She was beginning to care a lot about Nick, even if her head was telling her to put the brakes on. *What if his anger got the best of him?*

No, he would never take things that far. Nick was

a strong man who wouldn't jeopardize his life with Miles by committing an act of violence. She felt pretty certain he would be able to take the high road, even if he was tempted to do otherwise.

"From the sounds of it, Nick has a good handle on things," Malcolm responded. "He was probably just blowing off steam. Who can blame him?"

"I know. It brought up a lot of memories, Malcolm," she confessed. Hearing about Kara's accident dredged up her own painful past. All these years later, and Harlow still wasn't sure if her family had ever dealt with their traumas. Everything had been buried after they packed up and left Chestnut Ridge.

"That's not surprising," her brother said. "I'm not sure we ever came to terms with what happened. To this day, we don't really have closure."

Harlow knew she hadn't. So much mystery had been shrouded around their father's fatal accident. Just before he died, he had been accused of embezzling from his medical practice. As a result of the allegations, they'd all been treated as outcasts in their hometown. He'd gone into a deep depression after being suspended by his practice, and when the accident had taken place, their mother was certain he'd veered his vehicle off the road on purpose. With their lives in ruins, their mother had packed them up and left Chestnut Ridge in their rearview mirror. It wasn't until years later that the true culprit had been caught and prosecuted. However, it had been much too late to give her father his dignity and reputation back.

Lately, Harlow had begun to wonder if their mother had been wrong. In her own grief, and still reeling from the allegations against her husband, she might have come to the wrong conclusion. Harlow's own accident had shown her how easily one could veer off a slick road. Maybe her father's death hadn't been deliberate. Perhaps the official cause of death had been accurate.

Closure. Malcolm was right. Harlow still carried around the weight of her childhood and the way her family had been treated like dirt in Chestnut Ridge. She'd been telling Nick the truth when she had told him she understood his pain. Like Nick, Harlow had been through trauma and she knew how easy it was to get consumed by it. Her past experiences were the very reason she couldn't allow herself to believe in happily ever after. In her experience, nothing good ever lasted for long.

And now she had to put her game face on as she started her day at Paws. *Good thing she loved her job.*

Throughout her career, Harlow had always had a nice rapport with her clients and the pets. Harlow had an innate love for animals that went all the way back to childhood. She had been the kid who'd tended to every broken-winged bird in the neighborhood. Not much had changed in that regard. Harlow still enjoyed patching up ailing animals.

This morning she had a new patient, a rabbit named Vera. Her owner, Stella's little sister, Tess, was waiting in the exam room with her mother. Harlow hadn't known Tess back in the day due to the large gap in ages between Tess and her older sisters. When Stella was a college co-ed at Spelman, Tess had been a baby. But, thanks to Stella's stories and hanging out with the tween on Halloween, Harlow had a good grasp on Tess's personality. It was obvious that she ran the Marshall roost and had her family wrapped around her little pinky finger.

Tess was a boss and didn't hesitate to spout her opinion on everything and anything.

"Hi, Harlow. It's nice to see you again," Mrs. Marshall said as Harlow walked into the room. With her bright smile and silver-tipped hair, Stella's mother was a beauty.

"Hey, Doc Harlow," Tess said in a chirpy voice. The young girl was beautiful, with warm brown skin, a button nose, and braided hair. *Maybe that was how she got away with bloody murder*, Harlow thought with a chuckle. According to Stella, Tess was a human wrecking ball at times with her sharp wit and candor.

"Hi there, Marshall family," Harlow greeted them. "Who do we have here?"

"This is Vera," Tess said. "The best bunny in the world."

"She's a beauty," Harlow said, admiring the white

Satin rabbit. "A lovely breed too. What's going on
with her?"

Tess made a sad face. "She's been acting funny.
She's been ravenously hungry and really tired. And
she doesn't want to play with me like she usually
does."

"Hmm, let me take a look," Harlow said, picking
Vera up and putting her on the exam table. Harlow
busied herself examining the rabbit as her owners
watched her every move. After a few minutes,
Harlow was done.

"Tess. Vera is going to have babies. She's pregnant," Harlow announced.

"Pregnant?" Mrs. Marshall asked while Tess let
out a gasp.

"How did that happen?" Tess asked, her mouth
hanging open.

Harlow tried not to laugh, but the sides of her lips
were twitching. The news had thrown Tess for a loop.
Harlow could see it stamped all over her face.

Harlow smiled. "I need to confirm with an ultrasound, so I'll get that started." She took Vera down
the hall, where she performed an ultrasound that
confirmed the rabbit's pregnancy. She walked back
to the exam room and handed Vera over to Tess.

"So? Is she preggers?" Tess asked bluntly.

"Yep. She sure is," Harlow confirmed with a
bob of her head. "Umm... congratulations." Harlow
wasn't sure if this was a good outcome or not for the
Marshalls. No one was smiling at the news.

Tess slapped her hand to her forehead. "What's in the water in Mistletoe? Stella just had a baby, Lucy's pregnant...and now Vera."

"How long until she delivers?" Mrs. Marshall asked. "I knew getting a rabbit was going to get complicated," she muttered.

"She's set to deliver within the week, I believe. Rabbits only gestate for roughly thirty-one days," Harlow explained. "Clearly this is coming as a surprise, so I'd like to offer my assistance finding homes for Vera's babies. I can put out some feelers, and Tess, you can make some fliers and hang them up around town." Harlow placed her arm around Mrs. Marshall, who seemed a bit shell-shocked. "Don't worry. People will be lining up for bunny babies."

"I sure hope so," she said, scrunching up her face.

"I like that idea. How many babies is she having?" Tess asked.

"I'm not sure, but typically rabbits deliver five or six, but it could be more or less." Harlow didn't want to frighten them by saying it could be fourteen or fifteen.

"I still don't understand how she wound up getting pregnant," Tess said in an awestruck voice.

"We'll talk about that later," Mrs. Marshall said. "Something tells me it's tied to that bunny playdate you had at your friend's house with her rabbit. Remember?" Tess's mouth formed an O shape as a lightbulb went off in her head.

"It was nice seeing both of you," Harlow said. "Keep me posted on Vera's delivery. And let me know if you need anything or have any further questions."

Harlow walked Tess and her mother to the front desk, where Jon could check them out.

"Harlow, someone is here to see you," Jon said with a smirk. Harlow followed his gaze, drinking in the sight of Nick wearing a navy blazer with a pair of dark jeans. Harlow sucked in a steadying breath at the sight of him. His brown skin gleamed as he advanced toward her, his stride full of swagger. All eyes in the waiting room were trained on Nick, who was clutching a vibrant bouquet of flowers in his hand. Something told her this detail would be all over town in no time flat.

He held the bouquet out to her. "These are for you."

"Thank you," she said, accepting the flowers. She was a bit speechless that Nick had shown up out of the blue at her place of business. Was this beautiful assortment of flowers his way of apologizing?

"Can we talk somewhere in private?" Nick asked, looking around him at all of the prying eyes. Clients weren't even pretending to mind their business. Everyone was all up in their conversation.

"Okay, people," Tess called out. "Nothing to see here. Just a smoking-hot guy bringing a girl he digs some flowers."

Harlow didn't know whether to laugh or cry at Tess's gumption. If she laughed, according to Stella, it would only encourage her little sister's boldness. The town of Mistletoe surely didn't need that. "Come on, Nick. Follow me," Harlow said, leading Nick toward her office. She could feel numerous pairs of eyes trailing after them. Once they were inside the small space, Harlow closed the door behind her.

"I know flowers aren't exactly a creative way of saying I'm sorry, but I figured it was better than chocolates," Nick said, looking sheepish as well as adorable.

"I love chocolate," Harlow said. "Especially Reese's."

Nick smacked his palm against his forehead. "Dang it! That would have been a much smoother move." He looked back at the door. "Is it too late for me to run out and get some?"

Harlow playfully swatted at Nick's chest. "That's not necessary, but it's a sweet thought. The flowers are stunning, and they'll really brighten up the place. My office is a bit on the drab side." Harlow had to remember to bring some decorations in to jazz up the place. She laid the flowers down on the counter and turned back to Nick. Harlow sensed he was itching to tell her something.

"Well, I came here to say I was out of line last night. You got the brunt of my anger, and I'm really sorry. That was pretty messed up." He crossed his arms around his chest and leaned back against a counter. "All this time I convinced myself that I was fine because I'd managed to make it past the grief stages. But learning that Baker was released early from prison, then seeing him handing Halloween candy to my son—" He let out a frustrated sound. "Last night gave me a lot of time to mull things over. I may have grieved my wife's death, but the way she died... the way she was taken from us... I'm still not over it. But I want to be."

Harlow got it. Nick's feelings mirrored her own. The past still had a grip on her, even though she yearned to move forward. Just because a person wanted to be over something, it didn't mean they were. Wasn't that her story?

"I know you do, Nick. And I totally understand why you were so upset last night. It must've felt like a violation to see him living in your community and being so close to Miles." Harlow shuddered. She was even more impressed that Nick hadn't confronted Baker. Walking away had probably cost him every ounce of restraint he possessed.

Nick moved toward her. "You do understand. I can see it in your eyes. I was wrong to shut you down last night. Want to tell me what's going on with you?" he asked, reaching out to touch her forehead. "These worry lines must have a story behind them."

"That's a story for another time, Nick. I've got to get back to work." For once Harlow wanted to be open with someone, to share her tangled past and peel back her own layers. Doing so would be scary, but maybe they could both help each other heal. Nick had opened up to her about Frank Baker, exposing all of his hurt and pain about the deadly crash. He was inspiring her to be more transparent and to unpack some of her own emotional baggage. No one had ever made her feel this way before.

"Okay, Harlow, but I still want to make you dinner. Guest's choice," Nick said. "Whatever you want. Thai. Italian. Soul food."

"After that meal you cooked at my place, I wouldn't miss out on another chance to sample your culinary genius. Whatever you make will be fine," Harlow said, flattered by the invitation. "Surprise me." A part of her had worried that their budding relationship would crack under the strain of last night. She should have known better. Nick was a good person who didn't mind admitting his mistakes. She could learn a thing or two from him.

Nick dipped his head down and pressed a swift kiss on her lips. Harlow reached up and smoothed her hand across his cheek, making contact with slight stubble as she did so. A woodsy masculine scent rose to her nostrils. All of her senses were on fire.

"I'm taking that as a challenge," Nick said as the kiss ended and they pulled apart. "I'll be in touch," he said before opening the door and striding down the hall and away from her.

Harlow touched her lips. They were still blazing from the kiss they'd just shared. Nick always managed to affect her equilibrium in the most intense way. She took a few moments to collect herself before going out front to call in her next client. This was what it felt like to be swept off one's feet. Nick had skills! She had to remind herself that it wasn't part of the plan to fall for Nick. Doing so might mess up her agenda—to do her time in Mistletoe, pay off her loans, and then get out of Dodge. Falling in love wasn't an option.

CHAPTER THIRTEEN

It was a beautiful fall day for exploring Mistletoe, Harlow realized as she cruised along the back roads to her destination. For years she had loved antiquing and finding vintage items. She had acquired quite a collection of jewelry, clothing, and small furniture pieces. Whitney had told her about this shop called Something Old on the Post Road, which was located about twenty minutes from her lake house. Harlow lowered the windows and cranked up the radio as the sunlight caressed her face.

Her GPS let her know she was approaching the destination on her left. Harlow scanned the area, immediately spotting a white farmhouse with a black-and-white sign announcing the business. A few doors down was a restaurant, a gallery, and a farmers' market.

"Sweet," Harlow murmured to herself as she

stepped out of her car and headed toward the vintage shop. Although it was a gorgeous day, there was a brisk wind that required the use of a denim jacket. As she stepped onto the wraparound porch, Harlow paused to admire the decor. Tinkling wind chimes hung from the rafters. Colorful Adirondack chairs decorated the space along with flowers in hanging pots. Harlow felt as if she had traveled back in time as she headed inside.

"Good morning," a robust voice called out. Within seconds an older woman with silver hair stepped forward. "Welcome to Something Old. I'm Agatha and this is my place." She stuck out her hand for Harlow to shake.

"Hi, Agatha. Nice to meet you. I'm Harlow," she said, sliding her hand into Agatha's.

Agatha's smile made it all the way to her sky-blue eyes. "The new vet in town, I presume," Agatha drawled. "A lot younger and prettier than I imagined," she said with a chuckle.

"How do you know who I am?" Harlow asked. She could feel her eyes widening in surprise. Small towns really did have big ears.

"I've lived in Mistletoe all my life, Harlow. Not much gets past me," Agatha said with a cackle. All of a sudden, Harlow felt movement against her leg. When she looked down, she saw an alabaster-white cat grazing against her and emitting loud meowing sounds.

"That's Sheba," Agatha said, bending over and

scooping up the Siamese cat. "My pretty baby. We've been together for ten years and counting."

"Hello, Sheba," Harlow cooed. "Aren't you a beauty?" Harlow peered into the cat's face, immediately noticing a red appearance to Sheba's eyes. She looked over at Agatha. "Does Sheba visit Paws regularly?"

"She hasn't been to the clinic for a while, if I'm being honest. Why? Is something wrong?" Agatha asked, sounding panicked.

"Not necessarily, but she does have a reddish appearance to her eyes, which should be checked out by professionals." Harlow could see Agatha's distress, so she wasn't going to tell her it could be glaucoma or tumors. Tests would have to be run, as well as a thorough exam, in order to make a diagnosis.

"I'll make an appointment right away. May I ask for you?" Her eyes were wide.

Harlow patted her shoulder. "Of course you can. I'd be honored," Harlow said. "I'll take good care of Sheba."

"I know you will, Harlow. I have a very good feeling about you." Agatha waved her hand around the shop. "Look around to your heart's content," Agatha said. "If you have any questions, I'll be at the front desk."

"Will do," Harlow said as she began to putter around the establishment. Whimsical items were in abundance—rhinestone-encrusted jewelry boxes, jazz-era clothing items, fine china, and classic movie posters. For the better part of an hour Harlow explored every nook and cranny of the shop. By the time she checked out, she'd found a pearl necklace, a rose-printed duvet, a pair of cowgirl boots, a red leather journal, and a stack of Nancy Drew books.

"Here you go," Agatha said, handing her a large bag filled with her items after Harlow had paid for them. "Don't forget to visit the farmers' market next door. Vic, the man who runs it, is my husband." She winked at Harlow. "We never got hitched, but we've been together for forty years the last time I checked."

"Good for you." Forty years was a lifetime as far as Harlow was concerned. "I'll make a point to stop by."

Harlow dropped off her bags at the car, then made a beeline to the farmers' market. A nice-sized crowd was milling about the area and bagging up produce to take home. An older man with white hair and whiskers approached her and introduced himself as Vic, proving to be just as adorable as his wife. Harlow made sure she selected a wide range of items. Apples. Pumpkins. Zucchini and squash. And her favorite—corn. She bought way more than she could consume, but she planned to bring some into the office for others to enjoy. Just as she was heading out with her bag of fresh produce, Agatha came rushing toward her.

"This is for you," Agatha said, handing her a large

bag bursting with items. Harlow could see ears of corn, a baguette, lettuce, a floral bouquet, and some other items peeking out.

"What? Are you serious?" Harlow asked. "This is so sweet of you."

Agatha beamed at her. "We have a tradition here in Mistletoe that goes way back. This is a welcome-to-Mistletoe gift. If you let it, this town will nourish you, body and soul."

"Thank you so much. I'm overwhelmed." Harlow blinked away the moisture pooling in her eyes.

Agatha patted her on the shoulder. "This town needs good-hearted folks who love animals. We're blessed to have you here."

"I hope to see you and Sheba soon," Harlow said, knowing she would follow up if she didn't see Sheba's name on the docket. After saying her good-byes to Agatha, she decided to grab a late lunch at the restaurant a few doors down. She put her bags in the car, then walked over. The tantalizing aroma of grilled food rose to her nostrils, causing her stomach to grumble. Harlow took a peek at the menu hanging by the entrance to the Blue Crab.

Harlow, sold on the lunch options, opted to sit out-side. By the time the waiter came to take her order, Harlow didn't even need to refer to the menu. She'd memorized her selection by heart. When her meal arrived, Harlow attacked it with gusto. She might have even let out a few moans of appreciation.

A girl could get used to this, she thought.

Sitting outside on the deck eating stuffed lobster with corn on the cob and a nice glass of wine was a heavenly experience. She took her time and savored the meal and the stunning view. When was the last time she'd treated herself to some me time? Exploring her surroundings had paid off big-time. Mistletoe had really shined today. As a result, she felt invigorated.

When the waiter came over to clear her table, Harlow couldn't stop raving about the lobster. "It might just be the best lobster I've ever eaten," Harlow gushed.

"If you enjoyed this lobster, you'll love the town lobster boil," the waiter said. "It's Mistletoe's fiftieth annual event and you won't want to miss it."

Harlow was sold on attending. If the lobster was even one third as good as the one she'd just eaten, she would be in crustacean heaven.

By the time Harlow headed back home, she was feeling as if all was right with her world. Mistletoe had surprised her by showing her new experiences that she'd thoroughly enjoyed. Maybe there was way more to this quaint town than she had been willing to admit.

* * *

A few days later Nick was finally enjoying a day off after working overtime on a rescue at Mount Snow. Nick, and a few of his colleagues, had been called in for support after an avalanche struck a ski area. The operation had been a success, with all four skiers being found alive. Due to their injuries, they had been transported to a local hospital, but they were all expected to make it. As always, Nick was thankful for a happy ending to the rescue. In moments like this one, Nick knew he was right where he needed to be. Things didn't always work out the way he wanted, but when the search and rescues were successful, his spirits couldn't be better.

He was still trying to connect with Harlow so he could cook for her at his house. His unrelenting schedule was a barrier to their next date, which was frustrating. Nick didn't want Harlow to think he wasn't interested. Nothing could be further from the truth. The dazzling woman was never far from his mind. The truth was, he was wild about her. Something inside him had clicked from the first moment he'd clapped eyes on Harlow trapped in her car.

It wasn't like him to fall so fast. Before now, the only other woman he'd had any serious feelings for had been his wife. He'd never imagined that he could begin to feel this way for anyone else. Nick had always thought of love as happening once in a lifetime, if a person was lucky. And it wasn't as if he was in love with her or anything, but he now knew it was quite possible.

At the moment he was preparing himself for a difficult discussion with Miles about what had taken place on Halloween. He'd avoided having this talk for as long as he possibly could. Despite feeling ill-equipped to discuss Kara's death, he knew that he needed to get the conversation going. Miles was only nine years old, but with Frank Baker now back in Mistletoe, it was likely he would hear about the car crash from someone else.

"Hey, buddy. Can you sit down for a few minutes?" Nick asked as Miles trudged into the kitchen wearing his Spider-Man pajamas and matching socks.

"Can I have my cereal first?" Miles asked, letting out a yawn.

"It'll just take a few minutes. I kind of need your full attention." Nick ran a shaky hand across his jaw as Miles sat down.

He leaned his elbows on the table and propped his face on his hands. "So, what's up? You have that this-is-an-important-talk look on your face."

Nick was torn between laughter and tears. He needed to straddle the line between the two so he didn't overwhelm Miles. Everyone thought he was incredibly resilient, but he was still a kid struggling with the loss of his mother. "I know you were confused with my behavior on Halloween."

"Yeah, you kind of lost it, Dad," Miles said, shaking his head. "You're usually much more chill. Honestly, I thought you were mad at me."

Nick leaned toward Miles and placed his hand on his shoulder. "No way. I was mad, but not at you. I got upset when I saw the man who was giving out candy at that house."

Miles's eyes widened. "Why? Did he do something to you?"

Nick steepled his hands in front of him. He swallowed past the thick lump in his throat. How could he tell Miles without freaking him out? "Yeah, Miles. Because of him, we lost Mommy. He was driving the car that caused the crash she died in."

A look of confusion crossed over Miles's face. "Why? What happened? Was he a bad driver?"

Suddenly, Nick had the sensation of a thousand-pound weight sitting on top of his chest. How was he going to find the words so Miles would understand?

"This is really heavy stuff. To be honest, I hate that I even have to bring it up, but you're a bit older now. I don't want you to find out from someone else at school. That wouldn't be right." Nick let out a ragged sigh. "Frank Baker went to jail for causing the car crash that took your mother from us. He shouldn't have gotten behind the wheel that day and I can't forgive him for being so selfish." Nick winced at the shocked look radiating from his son's eyes. Although he knew this moment had been inevitable, he couldn't rid himself of the feeling that he was taking away his innocence. "So when I saw him handing out Halloween candy, I just reacted. Seeing him in the flesh made me sick to my stomach."

"It's not fair!" Miles said in a raised voice. Miles rubbed at his eyes, which looked suspiciously moist. "He took her away from us. He's a bad man."

"No, it's not fair and it never will be," Nick acknowledged. "But I know that we can get through this together, Miles. I refuse to be angry anymore, because I've wasted so much time feeling that way. I won't give that to Frank Baker. And neither should you. We've already given him enough. I want to watch you play soccer and enjoy time with our family. I want to see you go to middle school and become the best version of yourself."

"Am I not already the best version of myself?" Miles asked, making a goofy face.

Nick laughed and reached out to tweak his chin. "You're pretty perfect, but there's still room to grow. For both of us."

"I know. I'm aiming to be taller and stronger than you and Uncle Luke," he said matter-of-factly. Right at that moment, he resembled Kara so much, with his big brown eyes and expressive face, that it caused a hitch in his heart. Having her mini-me around reminded him that Kara lived on through their son. No one could ever take that away from him.

"What do you want to do today?" Nick asked, veering away from the topic of Frank Baker. He didn't deserve to take up another moment of their time and attention. He'd told Miles the important stuff he wanted him to know. His son had handled it like a champ. For now, it was enough.

"Can we go over to Tess's house? Her rabbit had a litter of baby bunnies." Miles reached into the cabinet and pulled out a box of Cocoa Puffs and a big bowl before getting a carton of milk out of the fridge.

Nick held up his hands. "We just got Zeus." Zeus perked up his ears upon hearing his name. "We're not getting any bunnies. That's not happening." Just the thought of bringing a bunny into the household made him shudder.

Miles rolled his eyes. "I don't want a bunny, Dad. I've got my hands full with Zeus." Miles's morning routine of getting up early to walk Zeus and feed him was proving to be a challenge, but Nick had to hand it to his son. So far he was being very responsible caring for Zeus.

"I just want to see the litter. There are ten babies," Miles explained. "Can you believe that?"

"Ten!" Nick let out a whistle. "That's a lot of bunnies. What is Tess going to do with all of those rabbits?" He couldn't imagine having to find homes for ten bunnies.

"I have no idea." Miles shrugged and busied himself with eating his Cocoa Puffs. Pretty soon, all Nick heard was the clink of his spoon banging against the bottom of the bowl. "So, can we go over? Tess invited me."

Nick glanced at the clock on the wall. It wasn't even nine o'clock. "I'm going to finish my breakfast, then hop in the shower. Then we can go take a look at the bunnies."

Miles let out a celebratory shout. "Dad. I appreciate you," Miles said in a solemn voice.

"Ditto," Nick said, his heart melting. How lucky was he to have a son like Miles? One who could feel all the joy all around him and freely express his love without reservation. He often thought about the fact that life wasn't fair, but having Miles as a son served as a great equalizer.

By the time they arrived at the Marshalls' home, it was ten o'clock. There were numerous other vehicles parked in front of the house. Miles led the way to the backyard, where several people were gathered by the shed. Tess came running over as soon as she spotted them.

"Miles! Come see my baby bunnies. They're beautiful," Tess said, waving him over.

As Miles ran off to join Tess, Nick called out to him. "Miles. Why don't you find the perfect bunny for Uncle Luke?"

Miles turned back toward him and flashed him a thumbs-up. "Great idea."

Just the thought of Luke having to take care of a bunny made Nick laugh out loud. That would teach his brother to dump a dog on him.

Nick caught a glimpse of dark curls and a curvy figure in a red sweater and dark jeans. Harlow was here! Nick hadn't expected to run into her today.

Nick strolled over. "Hey, what are you doing here?" Harlow swung her gaze up, surprise registering on her face at the sight of him.

He leaned in to give Harlow a tight hug. His lips brushed against her cheek.

"I'm Vera's vet," Harlow answered. "The Marshalls called me when she went into labor and I've been checking in every day since then."

"Vera? Is that the bunny who gave birth to a small village of rabbits?" he asked, wrinkling his nose.

"Yes. It's a cute name, right?" Harlow asked. "I promised Tess I'd help her find families for the litter. Are you interested?"

Nick chuckled and held up his hands. "Absolutely not. We've got our hands full with Zeus."

"How's that going? Have you talked to Miles yet about his tumor?"

"No, not yet," Nick admitted, feeling guilty for putting it off. He hated sharing bad news, especially with his son. He'd already given him a heavy dose of reality by telling him about Frank Baker. At this rate Miles was going to age practically overnight.

"If the offer still stands, maybe you can be there to explain things and answer questions. And I can cook us a fabulous meal."

"Of course I'll talk to Miles about Zeus. Whatever you need," Harlow said with an enthusiastic nod.

"Can you manage tonight? Dinner at my place?" he asked, sending her an apologetic look. "I know it's last minute, but my work schedule has been brutal. I hardly know if I'm coming or going."

"I should play coy and say I have plans, but I really don't," Harlow said with a grin. "I'm still trying to get the lay of the land here in Mistletoe."

"Well, I hope it's growing on you," Nick said. "I'm sure you miss Seattle."

"I do, but being here puts me closer to Malcolm and my mom. That means a lot to me. And I must admit, the folks here have been really welcoming." The expression on Harlow's face reminded him of a little kid—full of wonder and awe.

"Not to mention the pets, right?" Nick teased. "I'm sure they love you too."

"I sure hope so," she said with a slight shrug. "Would you believe someone sent a homemade meal over to my house? I've never received a tuna casserole before. I haven't had one since I was a little kid." A wistful expression passed over her face. He didn't want to pry, but it seemed apparent that some things from her past were bubbling to the surface.

"I can't say I'm surprised," Nick said. "That's Mistletoe for you. And casseroles are a sign that the community is opening their arms to you."

A look of surprise crossed her face. He thought he spotted the beginnings of a smile tugging at her lips. "Seriously? I didn't expect that, especially not so soon. I thought I'd have to work hard to win the town over."

"There's no timetable on things like that," Nick said. "Just face it. You've made a big splash here in town."

She ducked her head and didn't answer. Harlow didn't seem to recognize her appeal. A small town like Mistletoe tended to welcome newcomers with enthusiasm, especially if they had a particular skill to share. Even though Harlow insisted she wasn't sticking around Maine, he also knew that Mistletoe had a way of getting under a person's skin. Before she knew it, Harlow would feel as if this town was her very own.

Nick hoped Harlow would stick around town and became a permanent fixture in Mistletoe. The thought took him by surprise, forcing him to realize that Harlow was way more important to him than he even wanted to acknowledge.

CHAPTER FOURTEEN

D o you understand, son?" Nick asked Miles, who appeared to be blinking back tears. With Harlow present, Nick had just explained to Miles about Zeus's medical situation. As far as Harlow could tell, Miles seemed to be taking the news fairly well. "Zeus's tumor is cancerous," Nick continued, "but Harlow thinks with treatment and lots of love, he's going to be just fine."

Miles looked back and forth between Harlow and Nick. "Is that true, Doc Harlow?" He looked down at Zeus, who was obediently sitting at his feet. "Is he going to be all right?"

She placed her hand on his shoulder and stared into worried brown eyes. "I can't predict the future, and it would be wrong of me to promise you a particular outcome, but I'm really optimistic about his chances of a full recovery."

A huge grin broke out over his face. He looked down at Zeus and began enthusiastically patting him. "Did you hear that, boy? You're going to be all right." Miles put his face against Zeus, who began to lick him as if he understood what was going on.

Harlow rarely was able to observe her clients in their own houses, so it felt refreshing to be able to witness this incredible moment between Miles and his beloved dog. There was no ignoring the fact that Miles was a little boy who had a lot of love to give.

While Nick was cooking dinner, Harlow sat at the kitchen table with Miles answering a host of questions about Zeus. Every time the dog heard his name, he looked at them with his ears standing up straight and his head cocked to the side. Harlow was captivated by Miles's depth and wisdom. He possessed an emotional intelligence that was impressive for someone his age.

Is Zeus going to need surgery?
Will he still have lots of energy?
Can you one hundred percent cure him?
What can I do to help?

Harlow had done her best to give it to him straight without scaring Miles. As a nine-year-old, it would be understandable if he continued to ask questions until the situation resolved itself.

"I'm very optimistic that Zeus will recover with

the proper treatment," Harlow reiterated. Miles listened with big eyes, even jotting her words down on a piece of paper.

Harlow had a hard time keeping her gaze from veering toward Nick as he whipped up dinner. He'd rolled his sleeves up to cook and his strong russet-colored arms were toned and muscular. Nick was wearing an apron emblazoned with the words WHAT'S COOKING, GOOD LOOKIN'? Harlow wasn't sure she'd seen anything quite as sexy.

The ding of the doorbell caused Miles to jump up and run to the front door. A few moments later, he came back into the kitchen holding up a brown paper bag. "It's my dinner delivery from the Funky Rooster." Miles rubbed his stomach. "Can I eat in the playroom, Dad? The football game is about to come on."

"As long as you clean up after yourself, I'm good with it," Nick said, looking over his shoulder at his son.

Miles grabbed a soda from the fridge and said, "Thanks! Catch you later. Enjoy your dinner."

"He's not eating with us?" Harlow asked after Miles left the kitchen. "I hope that's not on my account."

"No worries, Harlow. Miles loves chicken nuggets and fries. He begged me to let him order through DoorDash tonight." He locked eyes with Harlow. "He said that he didn't want to be a third wheel." Nick laughed. "I've got my hands full with that one."

"He's a really great kid, which I'm guessing you already know."

"I do," Nick said. "Not sure what I'd do without him."

Harlow walked over toward the stove. "So, what are you making? It smells amazing."

"Beef bourguignon. It's a French dish."

Harlow fluttered her eyelashes. "Ooh la la. Sounds fancy. But then again, I can't cook, so everything sounds fancy to me," she said with a chuckle.

"If you play your cards right," Nick said, flashing her a flirty grin, "I'll give you some lessons."

She waved him off. "I wouldn't do that to you. You'd die of frustration."

He shook his head and joined in on her laughter. They were at ease with each other, developing a natural rapport the more they were in each other's orbit.

A short while later, Nick announced that dinner was ready. He led her into the dining room, where he had set a beautiful table for them, with a red table runner stretched down the middle. He'd lit a few candles and scattered them around the table. Gold-and-cream plates were set out, along with two wine goblets and silver utensils.

"You didn't have to go to all of this trouble, Nick," she told him as soon as she sat down.

Harlow was secretly glad he had gone all out. She hadn't felt this special or cared for in a very long time. Most of the men she'd dated had been more concerned with what Harlow could do for them rather than making her feel special. No wonder she'd never really been in love.

His eyes twinkled. "Are you kidding me? Most nights I make mac 'n' cheese and grilled hot dogs or something else Miles enjoys. I actually feel like a grown-up tonight."

Harlow took a bite of the meal, letting out a hum of appreciation. "This is great. You really can cook your behind off."

"That's high praise," Nick said, grinning. "Save some room for dessert."

"You made dessert?" she asked, letting out a little moan. At this rate, Nick was going to spoil her for the mundane meals she'd been eating. Most nights she picked up takeout or heated up leftovers.

He shrugged. "Nothing too fancy, just a chocolate molten lava cake with raspberry sauce."

A sigh slipped past her lips. "Good thing I'm not watching my calories, because I'm going to eat every single morsel you put in front of me." She continued eating the beef bourguignon until her dish was empty. Harlow had literally cleaned her plate so it was gleaming. Nick glanced over at it and smiled.

"I'm glad you liked it. Julia Child's recipes never disappoint."

"It was really great," Harlow raved. "You're inspiring me to take cooking lessons. Or at least buy a decent cookbook."

"Well, I have loads of them if you ever want to

borrow any. I had to learn how to cook meals that Miles enjoyed, which is a bit different than the type of food I was used to making." He wrinkled his nose. "There were a few bumps along the way, but I really enjoy cooking. I actually make special dinners for my search and rescue teams a few times a year. They come over to my house and chow down."

Visions of stuffed lobster and chicken cordon bleu danced in her head. "They must love you for that! That's the kind of bonding experience with your colleagues I've always been hoping for." But had never found, she wanted to say.

"Whitney's a great boss and an even greater person. I think she would be receptive to hosting team bonding events."

"She's a class act. Maybe I'll suggest something like a painting night or wine tasting," Harlow said. The wheels were beginning to turn in her head. Getting to know her coworkers outside the office would help her acclimate to Mistletoe.

"So, I haven't met a lot of Black female veterinarians," Nick said matter-of-factly.

Nick was right. That had been her perspective growing up. "Historically speaking, no, there haven't been a lot. It was one of the reasons I wanted to pursue a veterinary career. But that's changing, especially with more opportunities to attend vet school and scholarships. It's really an expensive road to go down. Honestly, I doubted myself at the outset, but I pushed through and got my degree."

"From what they say, it's harder to get into vet school than law school."

"So they say," Harlow answered. "There are only thirty-two vet schools in the United States, so it's difficult to get admitted. The process is pretty much jumping through hoops."

Nick raised his glass and held it out. "But you did it. Cheers!"

Harlow clinked glasses with him. "And cheers for this meal. It's melting in my mouth. How in the world did you pull this off? French cuisine is difficult to master."

"Have you actually tried?" Nick wiggled his eyebrows at her. Harlow didn't even mind the fact that he was making fun of her inability to cook.

"Absolutely not. The closest I came was taking French for a year in high school. All I remember is oui and bonjour." Harlow shook her head. "Although I would love to go to Paris one day."

"When I was in college, I spent a semester in Provence. I worked at a French restaurant and shadowed a Michelin-star chef in his kitchen. He taught me to love cooking." He winked at her. "Not to mention all the French swear words that I learned."

"Sounds like a life-changing experience." An image of a young Nick wearing a chef's hat and working in a fancy French restaurant flashed before her eyes. Nick Keegan had lived an interesting life before settling down in Mistletoe, Maine.

"It was," Nick said, lifting his wineglass and

taking a lengthy sip. "Cooking centers me. It's one of the constants in my world. That probably sounds strange, but I can always count on the fact that if I follow the recipe I'm going to end up with a good meal, whether it's baked ziti for Miles or something more elevated. There are no curve-balls."

"That totally makes sense." Especially for some-one like Nick, who'd been blindsided by things out of his control. She still found it intriguing that he put himself in such high-stakes rescue situations after losing his wife so tragically.

All of a sudden, Miles ran into the dining room. "Dad! You have to come quick. The game is tied and it's going into overtime. You don't want to miss this!" Just as fast as he'd appeared, Miles was gone in a flash. The sound of his bare feet smacking against the flooring rang out down the hall.

Nick put his head in his hands and shook his head, then swung his gaze up. "I'm sorry about that. Miles and I practiced him not interrupting our dinner, so I think his excitement about the football game took over."

"It's fine. Why don't we join him? I don't need to be alone with you in order to get to know you better."

Nick's eyes widened. "You don't mind?"

"Absolutely not. Honestly, just watching you and Miles together gives me a really good idea on who you are, not just as a man, but as a father. If someone doesn't want to spend time around your magnificent kid, that's a huge red flag."

"That's a good point," Nick said. "This dating as a single dad is all new to me, so I'm learning as I go. But you're right about Miles. Anyone who doesn't want to get to know him is missing out."

Harlow didn't want to miss out on getting to know this special kid. She found herself wanting to know Miles as deeply as she desired to know Nick.

"Let's go join him," Harlow suggested. "I didn't say anything before, but I'm a huge fan of the Seattle Seahawks and I'm itching to see the score."

"You're not just being nice, are you?"

She let out a laugh. "No! I swear. I'm stoked to watch the game with the two of you. No offense, but I'm going to be cheering for the Seahawks."

"Hey, you're pretty amazing," Nick said as he stood up and came around to her side of the table, reaching for her hand. Harlow felt all tingly inside at the skin-to-skin contact. She wasn't sure it was a good thing to be so gaga over Nick. That's when things got complicated. Harlow didn't do complicated in relationships. She liked keeping things nice and easy. Malcolm always accused her of having surface relationships. In other words, no depth. What she was experiencing with Nick went a lot deeper than her previous connections.

"You're not half bad yourself," Harlow said, standing on her tiptoes so she could press her lips against his. Kissing Nick was an impulsive gesture, but as his lips expertly moved over hers, Harlow couldn't deny the burst of happiness exploding inside of her. This was different from anything she'd ever known. Nick was special. And when she was with him, Harlow felt worthy of something better than she'd ever imagined. Feeling this way was new to her, and it was scary opening herself up to all the possibilities. She wrapped her arms around Nick's neck and pulled him close as the kiss soared and deepened.

When it ended, Nick pressed a swift kiss on her temple. It seemed that she wasn't the only one who wanted their embrace to go on and on.

Harlow gave Nick a stern look and said, "Don't forget about that dessert you promised me. We can eat it while my Seahawks stomp on your Patriots."

"Aww, trash talk. I love it."

The sound of Nick's laughter filled her ears as they headed down the hall to join Miles in the TV room. This time it was Harlow who reached for Nick's hand, linking it with her own as they settled down on the couch. This was what she had never known in her life. A soft place to fall. A man who made her melt with his kisses. A man who wasn't afraid to be emotionally vulnerable.

If only for a little while, Harlow was going to lean into Nick and all he had to offer.

CHAPTER FIFTEEN

Miles Keegan considered himself to be a fairly lucky kid. He lived in a pretty cool town, he had a lot of good friends, and his dad was the absolute best. How many kids had dads who worked in search and rescue? None that he could think of. His dad was a real-life superhero.

The only part of his life that was sad involved his mother. She was dead. Sometimes he forgot how her voice had sounded or the way she'd worn her hair. He shut his eyes tightly in order to focus. Braids. She'd worn her hair in African braids a lot. Her eyes had been the prettiest brown he'd ever seen. As dark as chocolate. Twinkling like Christmas lights. That's what he remembered the most. The happiness.

Even though he was a little kid, Miles knew his dad was lonely. But ever since he'd met Doc

Harlow, something had changed. He smiled more. His dad seemed happier, which should make Miles happy. But he was starting to worry that soon it would be the two of them with him on the outside. He knew his dad loved him, but what if he started to love Harlow more? What would he do then?

Watching the football game with Harlow and his dad had been fun, especially since the Patriots won, but it also made him feel kind of funny when he saw them holding hands and making goo-goo eyes at each other. His tummy had done a few flips just watching them together.

Of all the kids he knew, Tess was the wisest. She was the perfect person to talk to about this situation. He was hoping she told him not to worry at all. Maybe they would break up soon. He felt guilty thinking this way, but he couldn't help himself. He was uneasy.

"So, how do you like your dad's new girlfriend?" Tess asked before biting into an Oreo.

"She seems nice." Miles shrugged. "But he hasn't called her his girlfriend."

"Yet," Tess said, smirking. "It's only a matter of time."

His heart sank. *So Tess saw it too.* His dad was smitten with Harlow. He wasn't really sure what the word meant, but Tess always used it when she talked about her sisters falling for their husbands.

"She really does seem nice," Tess said with a

smile. "And she's good friends with Stella." She grinned. "Then maybe they'll get married. And you'll have a mom again."

He bit his lip. A new mom? Doc Harlow married to his dad? This was all so confusing. A part of him was fine with his dad dating Harlow, while something inside his gut twisted just thinking about such a big change in his life.

"I'm just worried," Miles admitted. Tess was his friend and he wanted to be honest with her, but he didn't want to sound like a hater. In his heart, he wanted his dad to be happy, but the thought of not being his number-one person in the whole wide world made Miles feel sad. They were the dynamic duo. Two peas in a pod. Batman and Robin.

Tess frowned. "What are you frowning about? Isn't this what you wanted?"

Harlow seemed cool, but that didn't mean he wanted her to replace his mom. He didn't like how he was beginning to forget things about his mother. She'd been the most special mom in the entire world.

"I thought I did," he said, biting his lip. "But that was before—"

"Before you had to see it in action, right?" Tess asked. "Like all the hand holding and kissy faces. Trust me, I've seen it all." Tess rolled her eyes. "Between Lucy and Stella, I could write a romance novel at this point."

"Yeah, Doc Harlow was at our house the other

night. My dad made this special dinner for her. And we all watched the game, which was fun, but they flirted the whole time, which was so annoying."

"Been there, done that," Tess quipped. "And Lucy married Mr. Hollywood, so there's been lots of PDA."

"What's PDA?" Miles asked.

"Public displays of affection. Kissing. Hand holding. Making out." Tess shrugged. "The usual."

Miles scrunched up his face. *Yuck.* It was all gross to him. There wasn't a single girl on the planet he wanted to hold hands with or kiss. And he couldn't imagine that ever changing. "What can I do?" he asked with a groan. "It's all happening too fast." He held his face in his hands.

"You do have options." Tess wiggled her eyebrows.

"I do?" Miles asked. Leave it to Tess to have all the answers. It had been smart of him to have this conversation with her.

"Yep. If your dad thinks you don't like Harlow, then he won't date her," Tess said. "Easy-peasy."

She made it sound so simple, but Doc Harlow was nice. He would have to pretend, and he hated being fake.

"But I do like her," Miles protested. All of a sudden he felt guilty talking badly about Doc Harlow. She'd always been nice to him and she was taking care of Zeus's tumor. Plus, she'd answered a million of his questions about Zeus. But he hated this feeling that his dad was slipping away from him. He liked being with his dad, just the two of them.

"Technically, yes, but you don't like her being with your dad. Right?" Tess pressed. "Or did I read your situation wrong?"

Miles bowed his head. "No, you didn't. I just... can't lose my dad. And if he gets married, he might have a whole new family. I like being his only kid."

Tess rubbed her hands together. "Say no more, Miles. If you want to put a wrench in their relationship I've got a few ideas. Nothing too shady, but it'll get the job done."

For a moment Miles hesitated. Maybe he should just wait and see if they broke up on their own. Sometimes Tess came up with twisted plans. She'd really gotten him in trouble when she had involved him in the dognapping of her sister's dog, Coco Chanel. They had gotten busted by Uncle Luke at Miles's house. As punishment, he'd gotten grounded for a week. This was different though. He wasn't going to do anything to get in trouble.

"I'm listening," Miles said to Tess, who scooted closer to him and began to talk to him in a low voice as they put their heads together.

* * *

The ding of a text message woke up Harlow from a deep sleep a few minutes before her alarm was set to go off.

Happy Kiss a Pet Day!

Harlow smiled at Nick's greeting. She quickly sat up in bed and ran her fingers across the screen to text him back.

Uh-oh. I guess I'll be kissing a lot of animals at work today.

A few bubbles appeared on the screen and Harlow waited for Nick to respond. Seconds later his message popped up. Lucky them. 😊

Harlow responded with a blushing, smiley-faced emoji.

Have a good one! Hope to see you at Baxter's.

Harlow grinned at his text, then put the phone down as she stood up and began dressing for work. The casual dress code for veterinarians was a perk of the job, so she pulled on jeans and a long-sleeved shirt. Once she was at Paws she would put on her navy lab coat before she met with any clients. Harlow dug into a quick breakfast of oatmeal, coffee, and a blueberry muffin, then stashed a bottle of water and an energy bar in her purse for a quick snack at work.

Gorgeous fall foliage greeted her the moment she stepped outside. Oranges. Reds. Yellow and brown leaves. With the shimmering lake waters as a backdrop, the view resembled a picturesque postcard. Maine at its most glorious. Maybe small towns weren't as bad as she'd always imagined. With every passing day, Harlow was discovering that Mistletoe wasn't Chestnut Ridge. She was being welcomed so heartily by the residents. Other than Gillian, her clients had been amazing. And her experience the other day at the farmers' market had been incredible. She had visited enough of the United States to know that moments of true connection didn't happen in most places. She'd been seen by Agatha and welcomed and treasured. Every time she thought about that experience, a chill raced through her.

What if the folks in Chestnut Ridge had extended that type of grace to her family instead of treating them like pariahs? Kindness would have made all the difference in the world.

She couldn't be mad at this town for the things that had happened to her family in the past. So far Mistletoe was surprising her. There weren't any bogeymen waiting in the shadows to torment her. They were only in her head, shadows from the past. Maybe being in Maine would finally allow her to extinguish them.

Harlow was excited about this morning's meeting at Paws with Whitney. They would be discussing a rescue plan for dogs in need, which was near and dear to Harlow's heart. She was heading in a half hour early to lay her plan out for Whitney. She hoped she would be on board with the project. When Harlow walked into Paws, she stopped at the front desk to chat with Jon before heading to Whitney's office down the hall. Since no clients were in the waiting room, the clinic felt peaceful. The aroma of brewed coffee hung in the air, giving Harlow a pick-me-up without even having to drink a cup of java.

Harlow knocked on Whitney's partially open door. She instantly heard her boss inviting her in and she walked inside the small area, admiring the beautiful flowers on her desk and the animal paintings on her wall. The vibe matched the woman herself. Upbeat and colorful. As far as bosses went, Whitney was among the best she'd ever had. She allowed Harlow to chart her own course and to treat animals without being micromanaged. That hadn't always been the case with some of the practices where she had worked. Part of growing in her profession meant being able to work autonomously.

"Good morning, Harlow. Take a seat," Whitney said, raising her coffee cup to her lips. "Do you need to go grab a coffee?"

"Nope. That's how I started my morning. If I have another one I'll be bouncing off the ceiling," Harlow said with a laugh.

"Now, tell me about your dog rescue idea. I've been dying to hear all about it. It's an area I want Paws to expand on."

For the next fifteen minutes, Harlow laid out her idea of a dog rescue attached to Paws. She could hear the passion ringing out in her voice and she didn't even try to dial it back. She had been wanting to do something like this ever since she was a teenager. Even if Whitney turned her down, she was determined to get one going. Supporting rescue dogs was important to her. Because Bear was a rescue dog, Harlow held a special place in her heart for animals who needed a forever home. Many times over the course of her career Harlow had tried to set up animal rescues, with no success. Having the time and money to support the project had always been cited by her employers. Over the past few years, she'd learned a lot about writing grant proposals and figuring out the specific requirements. She might not be in Mistletoe a year from now, but she could still do some good while she was here.

"Ultimately this will be a good way to support rescue animals and connect them with their forever families. I know it's not an easy undertaking, but we could get resources from the state. For me, veterinary medicine isn't just about seeing clients. It's also about helping defenseless animals who don't have homes through no fault of their own."

Whitney had been listening intently and nodding throughout the presentation, which Harlow hoped was a good sign. "I love the idea of setting up a rescue, but I'm a bit confused, since you're only in Mistletoe for a year. Unless, of course, you've decided to stick around because you love us so much."

Harlow battled feelings of regret. She would love to see the dog rescue program flourish, but it just wasn't possible. "I know that I won't be here to run the program, but I'd still love to set it up for success and do something positive while I'm here. I'm enjoying Mistletoe way more than I imagined, but I still plan to go back to Seattle. I'm a city girl at heart," Harlow confessed. Now when she said those words Harlow didn't feel as convinced about her future plans.

Whitney's face revealed her surprise. "Really? You seem to have settled here in town like a natural."

Harlow didn't know how to respond to Whitney's comment. The truth was, she was way more invested in Mistletoe than she'd ever imagined. The town—and its residents—had grown on her in a way she'd never expected.

"Well, even though I won't be here to help out with the rescue program long-term, I can still set it up and get the ball rolling. With a grant for the program you can hire someone to run it."

Her boss nodded as she listened to what Harlow had to say. "I really want to make Paws more philanthropic and we've dabbled a bit in pet rescues, but I'd like you to write up a proposal so I can make a decision. We have some additional space to house the dogs in the building out back, but we'd need to make renovations. As you said, it won't be easy."

"I'll get right on it and explore some grant opportunities as well," Harlow said, as excitement bubbled up inside of her. Whitney sounded intrigued by the idea of the dog shelter; Harlow could work with that.

Whitney let out a beleaguered sigh. "On another

note, something has come up. I don't want you to worry, but I need to tell you that some rumors are swirling about the practice." Whitney's brow was furrowed and tiny lines surrounded her eyes. Harlow knew Whitney had just said not to worry, but she seemed concerned.

"What's going on?" she asked. Harlow had a niggling feeling in the pit of her stomach she couldn't ignore. Feeling ill at ease in certain situations was an unfortunate by-product of a tumultuous childhood. A part of her was always ready for something bad to happen. Even as an adult, it was terrible grappling with such anxiety.

"I don't know any specifics," Whitney said, "but our town gossip, Patsy Sampson, called the office earlier and canceled her appointment. She said she'd heard that one of our pets didn't get the best care here." Whitney made a loud tutting sound.

Harlow shook her head. "That doesn't sound right." She was racking her brain trying to remember if anything alarming had taken place. A surgery with bad results? A canceled appointment? "Do you think it has anything to do with me?" Since Harlow was relatively new at the practice, she couldn't help but worry she was somehow involved.

"Not at all. I completely trust your professionalism. I really wanted to give you a heads-up just in case you heard something or in the off chance this turns into something. I'm not taking it seriously, especially since no details were given."

For the rest of the day, Harlow couldn't stop thinking about Patsy Sampson canceling her appointment. Harlow had heard all about Patsy and her tendency to spread gossip all over town. Did the woman realize that she was potentially affecting their place of business and the reputations of the staff? It was reckless behavior that could hurt people.

Shake it off. It's probably nothing to worry about. Whitney was only giving her a FYI about a cranky client. Patsy was known for talking out of turn.

After getting off work, Harlow headed over to Baxter's pub. Stella had invited her to join a few friends at the establishment for a happy hour. Her friend had made a point to let her know that Nick would be there this evening. So far, she hadn't been out in a group setting in Mistletoe. She was looking forward to the social scene in town. Although she had never been one to stay out until the wee hours in Seattle, she loved the energy of people gathering for conversation, music, and fellowship. And with every new person she met in Mistletoe, Harlow began to feel more at home in her new surroundings.

Once she entered Baxter's, the sound of blues music immediately reached her ears. The rhythms were upbeat and pulsing, giving her a New Orleans vibe. Harlow knew instantly this was no recording. A live band was playing on the premises. She craned her neck and spotted the band on a small stage. Patrons were dancing on a makeshift dance floor and enjoying the music.

"Harlow!" Stella was calling her name and waving her over to a table where she and her friends were seated. "I'm so glad you came by," she said as Harlow reached the area.

"This place is great," Harlow gushed, looking around the establishment. She was secretly looking for Nick, who wasn't seated with the group. Luke was here. He greeted her with a warm smile and a hug. Troy, Dante's younger brother, was there along with his wife, Noelle. Stella introduced Harlow to all of her friends seated at the table.

"It's nice to meet you, Carolina. Eva," Harlow said. Both women were lovely. Carolina was petite and curvy with dark hair while Eva was a statuesque blonde.

"Eva owns the movie theater, Casablanca's," Lucy said. "When she came back to Mistletoe she renovated it into a classic theater that the entire town adores." Harlow had seen the building on Main Street and she'd been promising to treat herself to a day at the movies. Maybe she should invite Nick to join her. Miles too if he wanted to come.

"It was a labor of love," Eva said. "I'm wild about classic film stars like Dorothy Dandridge and Cary Grant."

"And Carolina works with me in the trenches at Mistletoe Elementary. She also teaches second grade," Stella explained.

"Stella's the sweet teacher while I'm the salty one," Carolina said, emitting a throaty laugh. They all laughed along with her. Carolina seemed bubbly and fun while Eva seemed to be kind and steady. They matched up exactly with the way Stella and Lucy had described them.

Suddenly, Nick was standing next to her, looking a bit tired but still eye-catching in his gray pullover and slacks. Usually he wore more casual clothes, so seeing him leveling up like this was a treat for the eyes. The scent of cedar rose to her nostrils, providing Harlow with an olfactory rush. She resisted the urge to press herself against his chest just so she could breathe him in.

"How was your day? Your lips must be exhausted," Nick teased. She liked the way he laughed, showcasing pearly white teeth and little indents at the side of his mouth. His brown skin was flawless. One of these days she was going to cave and ask him for his skincare secrets.

"It was hectic, what with smooching all those pets," she responded. "I was definitely in need of a night out, so coming to Baxter's was a nice way to unwind. The music alone is incredible."

"That band is called Switch," Nick said, jerking his chin in the direction of the stage, "and they've been playing here for at least ten years. They've gotten pretty famous but they still do gigs here."

"That's fantastic. Loyalty is everything." The older she got, the more she realized how important it was to be surrounded by people who had her back. On a few occasions, she'd been blindsided by so-called friends who didn't have a loyal bone in their body. Being back in Stella's company reminded her of what a good friend she'd always been. Supportive, kind, and loving. It was depressing to admit, but she didn't have a single friend like Stella back in Seattle.

"Let me get you a drink," Nick offered, leading her toward the bar. "What'll you have?"

"Sangria with lots of ice," Harlow said. "If they don't have it, a wine spritzer."

A few minutes later Nick held two drinks in his hand—a beer for himself and a sangria for her. He led the way back to their table. Most of the group had headed over to the dance floor, which gave Harlow and Nick some privacy in a crowded setting.

"So, how are you?" She reached out and smoothed worry lines from his forehead. "You look like you've been through it."

"I can't complain," he said with a shrug. "Feeling wrung out is part of the job. Not just physically, but emotionally as well."

Harlow took a sip of her drink. "Actually, you can complain. I'm listening if you need to talk or vent. You work in a high-stakes job, Nick. Self-care is important." Nick was all smiles and easy charm on the outside, but the loss of his wife and raising a child by himself, as well as the demands of his profession, could put his mental health at risk.

Nick nodded at her. "I appreciate your mentioning that. I'm really in tune with taking care of myself and

I make sure to immerse myself in things that bring me joy. Music, books, exercise. And lately, a certain curly-haired beauty who keeps me on my toes."

Harlow was flattered. Nick was letting her know she was important to him, which knocked her off her feet. She honestly didn't know what to say. Right about now she would normally make a joke to deflect from the comment. But the snappy comeback died on her lips. She didn't want to shut this moment down for anything in this world.

Instead, she murmured, "That's nice to hear." She couldn't pretend that she didn't get a little kick out of hearing Nick say kind things about her. His sweet words made her feel a little giddy. Or maybe it was the sangria. Harlow hoped it was the fruity wine rather than Nick himself.

She already knew she was falling for Nick's considerable charms. It was happening so fast, she could barely think straight. Frankly, she wanted to suspend time so her head could catch up with her heart. She refused to be led by raw emotion.

Slow down, she warned herself. You didn't come to Maine to fall for a gorgeous single dad. *Stick to the plan, Harlow. Stay footloose and fancy-free.*

CHAPTER SIXTEEN

Harlow liked seeing this relaxed version of Nick. Although he was normally a chill guy, there was an ease about him tonight being in these surroundings with all of his friends.

She watched as Nick took another swig of his beer, finishing it off in record time. He set the empty bottle down on the table, then splayed his hands out in front of him. "So, here's the deal. Luke and I worked together on a search team today. An older gentleman wandered away from his home in Deerfield, and we were tasked with locating him."

Harlow swallowed hard. "D-does he have dementia?" Thoughts of her mother being vulnerable and lost washed over her. Before she'd been placed in a facility, Harlow's mother had wandered from her condo numerous times. Each incident had been nightmarish. Even though Malcolm had been living with her, it had still been difficult to keep constant watch over her. In those frantic moments when they hadn't known if she was alive or dead, she and her brother had been desperate and full of fear. Harlow's heart went out to the family. She knew firsthand about guilt and fear while dealing with a loved one suffering from dementia.

Nick nodded. "Yeah and he'd been missing for hours. He's eighty years old. We ended up finding Walter down at the beach. He was running through the waves and crying like a newborn." Nick winced as if he were reliving the incident. "When I waded into the choppy water to get him, he held on to me like he wasn't ever going to let go. He was completely defenseless."

Harlow made a tutting sound. "Oh, Nick. That must've stayed with you well after the rescue." Nick had set the scene so vividly that Harlow saw it in her mind like a movie reel.

"He was so grateful that we found him. As were his family members. They'd been frantic." He rolled his shoulders. "Sometimes it just hits me hard when we come so close to losing someone."

"But you didn't. So celebrate that." She reached across the table and linked her fingers with his. Even though the pub was noisy and people were milling around, the moment between her and Nick felt intimate.

"You've got a point," Nick conceded. "I'm a big

believer in seizing the moments. I'm trying to teach Miles how important that is."

Seize the moment. Why not? She could look back on her time in Mistletoe and be able to savor all of her memories.

"Dance with me," Harlow said as she jumped up from her seat, grabbing Nick's hand and pulling him to a standing position.

"I don't know," he hedged, slightly resisting her tugging. "It's been a while. I might be a little rusty."

"Come on, Keegan," she pleaded. "Remember, you're celebrating. I'll help you dust off the cobwebs." Nick let out a full-throated laugh, tilting his head back a little as he did so. His unbridled laughter and easygoing personality served only to heighten her attraction to him. In her experience, most men who looked like Nick were stuck on themselves.

She tugged on Nick's hand and led him over to where everyone was dancing. Stella couldn't contain her huge grin as she watched their approach. Harlow made a mental note to tell her friend not to start dreaming about bridesmaid dresses and her relocating to Mistletoe. Ain't gonna happen.

Truthfully, she had a hard time envisioning Nick as a terrible dancer. He did everything with finesse. He even walked with a certain swagger. She didn't really care either way. Right now all she wanted to do was dance... with him.

Before she could even process it, Nick reached

out and whirled her around as he moved his hips and feet in time to the music. Harlow almost had to stop and catch her breath. His movements were graceful and razor sharp. She was going to have to step it up to keep pace with Nick.

"Rusty? Seriously? You were totally playing me, weren't you?" Harlow shook her head and laughed at the expression on Nick's face. He seemed extremely pleased with himself.

"Maybe," Nick said, smirking down at her. He placed his hands around her waist and pulled her against him. Harlow reached up and laced her arms around Nick's neck, enjoying the way their bodies fit together. Everything around them faded away as Nick held her in his arms and they swayed to the music. Harlow rested her head against his chest as the music soared and pulsed in her ears.

For now, she wasn't going to think about the future or worry about her blossoming feelings for Nick. Right now she was simply going to lean in and enjoy herself with this delicious man. Being in Nick's orbit felt like a little slice of heaven and she wasn't going to squander a single moment of this precious time.

* * *

By the time Baxter's closed and Nick walked Harlow to her vehicle, it was midnight. Somehow the night had flown by without his even realizing the hours rushing past them. Nick reached for Harlow's hand as they walked in lock step down a nearly deserted Main Street. The hush of an empty street combined with the soft glow of lampposts made Nick feel as if they might be the last two people on earth. A brilliant full moon hung in the sky, providing a romance-worthy backdrop.

"What's so funny?" Harlow asked, looking over at him as they walked. "Come on. Share the joke with me."

Nick hadn't even been aware that he'd been chuckling. "I was just thinking it's the type of quiet that one sees in a zombie-apocalypse movie right before all hell breaks loose."

Harlow's hearty laughter caused his stomach to do flip-flops. The sound of it was pure unbridled joy. "Now that you mention it," she said, "this does remind me of the setting of a zombie flick." She cast a furtive glance over her shoulder. "Any moment now we're going to be swarmed by them."

"I think as long as we stick together we'll be fine," Nick drawled. He squeezed her hand.

"Phew!" Harlow said, swiping her hand across her forehead. "This is me right here," she said, jerking her chin toward a Saab parked a few feet away. Nick felt a stab of disappointment that the night was coming to an end.

"I enjoyed myself tonight. Funny how sometimes we don't know how badly we need downtime and a night out," Nick said. Hanging out at Baxter's with

Harlow and his friends had served as the best type of medicine.

"Food for the soul," Harlow said, nodding in agreement.

"I'm having fun getting to know you. I like you a lot, Harlow Jones. Matter of fact, I like you more than I've liked anyone in a really long time." He didn't want to say anything over the top, but he wanted her to know where she stood with him. "I just thought you should know." He hoped his words hadn't sounded lame. He may not have been rusty at dancing, but he was a bit out of practice in the wooing department.

Nick grazed his thumb against her cheek. She was looking up at him, her brown eyes full of secrets he wanted so badly to uncover. He needed to know everything about her. What made her smile? What was her favorite book? What was her love language? Nick was eager to fill in all the blanks. He sensed there was something in her past that made her put up walls. He was hoping she would open up to him as they grew closer so there was nothing standing between them. He'd told her all about Kara and the accident for that very reason.

A hint of a smile danced around her lips. "I like you too, Keegan. Thank you for letting me into your world."

Bam! Her words hit him right in the center of his solar plexus. He dipped his head down and swept his lips across her own. Harlow met his kiss with unbridled enthusiasm. He slid his tongue past her lips as the kiss intensified. Nick ran his hands through her wavy hair, then pulled her even closer, anchoring her to him. She murmured his name against his lips, placing her hands solidly against his upper body. He had to wonder if she could feel his heart beating fast and furiously inside his chest. Her lips tasted fruity, like the sangria she'd consumed. His lips trailed to her neck, where he breathed in the floral scent of her. Her skin was as soft as butter. A little sigh slipped past her lips as he continued his exploration and rained kisses on her supple skin.

Sweetness!

"Night, Nick."

"Good night, Harlow. Get home safely. Text me when you get there."

"I will," she promised. With a wave she stepped into her vehicle and within seconds roared off with her taillights blazing in her wake. Nick stood on the sidewalk for a moment and watched her drive away. Wanting to know she'd made it home safe and sound was tied up in his wife's fatal accident. He took nothing for granted now. Nick didn't believe he ever would.

As he drove home his head was filled with thoughts of the stunning veterinarian. Their good-night kiss had left him wanting more. All night long, Luke had been sending him looks loaded with hidden meaning. He'd tried to ignore it, but he knew his brother was curious about his relationship with Harlow. He wasn't sure he could call it a relationship yet. *What was the etiquette for such things?* He had no idea. Being out of the dating game for so long had a few drawbacks. Whatever was brewing between them didn't feel casual to him. He'd realized a long time ago that he wasn't the type of man to fall headlong into love, but he also knew his heart didn't usually thump so wildly in the presence of a female. He was catching feelings for Harlow at an incredibly fast rate, and there wasn't a way to backtrack his way out of this.

Harlow was different. She made him feel all the possibilities stretched out before them. It was exciting just thinking about it. The holidays were rapidly approaching. He and Miles always spent them with his parents, but this year Luke, Stella, and Jade would be there, along with Lucy, Dante, and their families. What was two more people to add to the mix? He would invite Harlow and Malcolm, making it a grand celebration of the holidays.

Was it too soon to call her his girlfriend? He let out a deep-throated chuckle. He hadn't felt this uncertain since his teenage years. Pretty soon he was going to break out in pimples and make plans to ask Harlow to prom. All of this was both thrilling and nerve-racking at the same time.

Once he reached home he glanced at his cell phone, smiling at the message he'd received from Harlow.

I'm at home, snug as a bug in a rug. And I
can see the moon from my skylight. Sigh.

A sense of relief washed over him at the knowledge that she'd gotten home safely. Now he wouldn't
have to worry or wonder. He could rest easy once
his head hit the pillow. It was yet another sign that
he was beginning to care deeply about Harlow.

Nick let himself into the house and walked toward
the lit-up kitchen. Van was sitting at the kitchen
table with his books spread out on the table in front
of him. As a biology major, Van was one of the most
dedicated students Nick had ever known. He was a
huge asset in their lives. Nick was forever grateful
that Van was Miles's caregiver.

"Hey, Van. How's it going?" Nick asked, reaching into the fridge for a cold water.

"Miles went down for the night around nine
o'clock. I helped him with math and a book report."
He pointed toward the fridge. "There's a field trip
slip for you to sign. They're going to the aquarium.

"Just a heads-up. Miles asked a million questions
about where you were tonight," Van said with a
shrug. "He seemed really hung up on it. A bit
unusual for him."

Nick knit his brows together. "Really? I told
him exactly where I was going. Did he say that he
missed me?" Miles was used to Nick staying home
most nights so perhaps he'd just been curious about
his whereabouts. Maybe Nick needed to talk to him

about grown folks requiring adult time just like kids needed to be around other children.

"Honestly, I think he was more interested in who you were doing it with," Van said with a raised eyebrow. "I'm just giving you some intel. He wouldn't let up until he put his pjs on and went to bed. I think he might be questioning some things about you and Harlow."

Nick shook his head. Maybe he'd read his son wrong. Perhaps he'd been fishing about Harlow for a reason. It was a bit perplexing, because Miles had never seemed to care about any of the other dates he'd been on. Not that he'd ever spent much time with a particular woman. Hmm. Could it be that Miles sensed this time was different? That his dad was navigating in a different manner with Harlow? For so long now, it had been the two of them against the world. Miles was bound to feel insecure if he sensed their dynamic was shifting.

"Thanks for the heads-up, Van. I'll talk to him tomorrow. Feel free to crash in the spare bedroom if you don't want to drive back to campus this late," Nick offered. He would feel much better knowing Van wasn't out on the roads so late.

Van stretched and let out a yawn. "I might just take you up on that offer. I'm pretty beat. Thanks, Nick."

"Anytime," Nick said, clapping Van on the shoulder as he walked past him. "Thanks for always taking such great care of Miles. You're a huge part of our lives."

"He makes it easy. Sometimes it feels like I'm getting paid to watch my little brother," Van noted with a smile.

Van had become an honorary member of the Keegan family due to the close bonds they all shared. Having Van as a caregiver made it possible for Nick to work in his chosen profession while providing Miles with stability and a loving environment at all times. Nick knew single parents who struggled to find good care. He could never take Van for granted.

"Because you're family, Van. Always will be. I'm turning in. Night."

Nick headed upstairs where he paused briefly on the way to quietly open the door to his son's bedroom. The soft glow of a night-light cast a warm glimmer over the room. He looked over at Miles, bundled up under his Spider-Man sheets and matching comforter. All was right in his world just knowing his son was safe and sound. Nick would make sure to check in with Miles based on his conversation with Van. If something was troubling Miles, Nick wanted to know, so he could allay his fears. As happy as he felt about life right now, Nick wanted Miles to be content as well.

His life was moving in a good direction, Nick realized. After so much pain and heartbreak, the sun was finally breaking through the clouds. He would never forget his life with Kara or what she meant to him as his first love and the mother of his child, but he was at a point where making room in his heart for another woman felt right. Not just another woman. Harlow.

It had to be Harlow.

* * *

The following morning Harlow woke up at the crack of dawn feeling invigorated. Last night at Baxter's had been a perfect evening out. She ran her finger over her lips as thoughts of kissing Nick flashed in her mind. He was both tender and passionate, making her feel wanted in a way she hadn't experienced in a long time. And not just in a physical way. Unlike other men she'd been involved with, Nick was exploring all aspects of her. He seemed curious about her as a person, wanting to know what made her tick. There was absolutely nothing superficial about the man. Nick radiated sincerity.

As soon as Harlow arrived at Paws, she was up to her elbows in work, all the way up until lunchtime, when she could finally breathe. She'd been bringing Bear into work with her for the last few weeks, and on impulse, Harlow decided to take him for a little drive around town so they could both get a dose of fresh air.

Once she got Bear settled in the back seat, which allowed him to stretch out, they took off toward the center of town. Harlow smiled as she watched Bear in her rearview mirror. He loved the sensation of wind whipping through his shaggy mane. A creature of habit, he always put his entire head out the window so he could enjoy the view. As people drove past them, Bear garnered a lot of smiles and friendly waves. Everyone loved an adorable Sheltie.

"You're so popular, Bear," she called out to him, which earned her a quizzical look from the pup. "Who's a pretty boy?" she asked in a crooning tone. Once she reached the grassy area in the town square Harlow pulled over and parked. She reached for Bear's toys, then attached his leash to his collar. Harlow got out of the Saab and opened up the back door for Bear. Her dog didn't hesitate to jump down onto the sidewalk, his tail wagging happily behind him.

"Let's go play," Harlow said, throwing the tennis ball on the grass. Bear followed the trajectory of the tennis ball and chased after it, his large body lumbering across the green. Bear fetched the ball and trotted back to her, breathing heavily as he reached her side. The exercise was good for him, since he was technically a few pounds overweight and he spent his days in her office sleeping.

"Good boy," she said, leaning down and patting Bear before throwing the ball again. Without skipping a beat, Bear ran off after the tennis ball. Bear was a sweetheart of a dog who always sought to make Harlow happy. Her pet was a people pleaser.

A few moments later, Harlow heard a slight commotion across the street. She turned toward the area, where a young boy in a wheelchair cradled a small dog in his arms as his older female companion looked on. The pup was letting out mournful cries that sounded as if the dog was in pain.

"Come on, Bear," Harlow said, picking up the dog's leash and crossing the street with the Sheltie by her side. As she got closer, the noises coming from the dog intensified.

"Hey there. Is everything all right?" Harlow asked the attractive woman with the short bob.

"Honestly, we're not entirely sure," the woman said with a frown.

"We found him behind the trash bin," the boy said, pointing at a spot nearby. "He doesn't have a collar or a name tag."

"You're the new vet, aren't you?" the woman asked, smiling. "I've seen you around town a few times. I should have introduced myself."

"Yes, I'm Harlow Jones. No worries about not introducing yourself earlier. We were bound to meet sooner or later in a town this small," she said with a laugh, getting a good feeling from the lady. Friendly faces were in abundance in this small New England town. Thankfully, it offset the whispers about her.

"Nice to meet you, Harlow. I'm Mimi West and this is my grandson, Jimmy."

Jimmy looked away from the dog and nodded his head at her. He was a sweet-looking boy with a nice smile. The way he was holding the pup was filled with care and tenderness.

Mimi West. Dante's mother and Lucy's mother-in-law. Her friend had spoken about what a warm and wonderful presence Mimi was in her life. Considering her son was a world-famous movie star, Harlow was impressed by her low-key vibe.

Harlow leaned over so she could get a better look at the canine. "Do you mind if I hold her? I want to quickly check things out," Harlow said.

"Go ahead," Mimi said. "We just happened to be walking by when we heard her whimpering." Harlow instructed Bear to lie down before she lifted the dog off Jimmy's lap. She began examining the dog—a small female poodle—quickly finding a gash in her side.

"Oh, I see why you're crying sweet girl. This must hurt something awful," Harlow crooned, lightly pressing the surrounding area to see how deep the wound was.

"Sorry," Mimi said apologetically. "We didn't even notice the cut." She made a tutting sound and put her hand on Jimmy's shoulder. "Poor little thing."

"You probably didn't notice because of her thick fur and the fact that it's really not oozing a lot of blood. Don't beat yourselves up about it. By finding her when you did, your actions saved her life."

Jimmy's worried expression eased up a bit.

The tooting of a horn drew their attention to the road. Nick was driving by and he slowed down to ask, "Is everything okay?"

Such was life in small towns. Mistletoe was such a small community, it was no great surprise that Nick would be in the vicinity.

Harlow beckoned him over and he quickly parked his vehicle and jogged over.

"We have a hurt dog on our hands," Harlow explained. "Mimi and Jimmy rescued her. She has a pretty deep laceration that needs attention."

"Any idea who he belongs to?" Nick asked, reaching out and patting the poodle on the temple. "Looks like there are no tags."

"He's a she," Harlow said, making a face at Nick.

"Noted," Nick said with smirk. "Does she have any identification?"

"There are no tags at all," Mimi confirmed. "And I've been racking my brain trying to recall if I've ever seen this poodle before, but I honestly don't think I recognize her."

"What's going to happen to her if we can't find her owners?" Jimmy asked, a look of worry stamped on his face. From what Harlow had observed, Jimmy was a compassionate kid who couldn't just carry on with his life without knowing the poodle's fate.

"Well, first I'm going to take her over to Paws and patch her up. She needs wound care and maybe a dose of antibiotics. Stitches for sure," Harlow explained. "We'll do our best to find her owners." Harlow meant what she'd just said about locating the poodle's family, but she had a funny feeling someone might have abandoned the dog. There was absolutely no sign that anyone was looking for the dog. Most owners would be frantically searching if a small dog had gotten lost in a downtown area. She might be wrong about the situation, but Harlow had seen this before in her Seattle practice.

"I can help," Jimmy volunteered. "I'm going to ask my mom and Troy if I can take her home with us if she's up for adoption."

"Slow down there, buddy," Mimi said, her eyes widening. "I'm not sure if your parents will agree with that plan. And whatever you do, please don't say I encouraged you."

Nick let out a bark of laughter that earned him a scowl from Mimi. "I'm not kidding. Noelle and Troy plan on having more kids one day, and I don't want to be the grandma who gave them a dog they didn't want."

"But Grandma, everyone will grow to love her," Jimmy said in a pleading tone. Harlow could barely look at him without melting. Who could resist that gorgeous little face? She sensed he could really pile it on when he wanted to in order to get his way.

Good for him! She imagined life wasn't easy for him being in a wheelchair, but he seemed to be well-adjusted.

"Yeah, sometimes dogs just come out of nowhere and become a part of a household," Nick said with a grimace. Harlow stifled a chuckle. Nick had been an unwilling dog parent, but she believed he truly loved Zeus.

"Don't encourage him," Mimi urged in a loud whisper. In response, Nick held up his hands and focused his attention on Bear. Nick crouched down and began to enthusiastically rub the dog's belly.

"Why don't I take him to the clinic now? I'll be in touch to give you an update if you like," Harlow suggested. She looked down at Bear, who was enjoying the fact that Nick was lavishing him with attention. The two of them were getting along so well. She was a huge believer in taking stock of the way a man treated animals. If Bear loved him, that was surely a good sign. Not that she needed her dog's approval, but it cemented what she already knew.

Nick was one in a million.

"Why don't I take Bear to my house?" Nick suggested. "He can have a doggy play date with Zeus while you deal with the mystery poodle. They'll love it."

Had she heard him right? No one except Malcolm had ever offered to watch Bear for her. "Are you sure? He's really well behaved, but I don't want you to get bogged down in double dog duty."

"It'll be fine. Miles will love it," Nick said as he reached for Bear's leash. "I think Bear will too." Nick's grin was contagious. Harlow felt as if a brilliant sun was shining down on her. "How about it?"

"Y-yes. Of course. I appreciate it," Harlow said, fumbling with her words. "I can swing by right after work to get him."

"Sure thing. You might as well stay for dinner. We're having shrimp and grits with cheesy biscuits," Nick said, turning as he led Bear away with him. She hadn't even had time to respond to his dinner invitation. Saying anything other than yes wasn't even a possibility. Spending time with Nick was one of her favorite ways to unwind.

Harlow couldn't ignore Mimi's curious gaze. "He's something else, isn't he?" the older woman asked as Harlow turned toward her. "Fine as wine and an amazing chef to boot."

"Yes," Harlow acknowledged with a nod. "He sure is."

"Some might say he's a keeper," Mimi added with a wink. She turned toward Jimmy and said, "Say goodbye to Doc Harlow. We've got to head home."

Harlow said her goodbyes and quickly crossed the road so she could load the poodle in the front passenger seat beside her. That way she could keep a close eye on her patient during the ride to Paws. By now the pup's cries had died down a bit and she'd curled herself up in Harlow's cozy sweater for comfort. A wave of protectiveness washed over her as she gazed at the poodle. She hadn't asked to be injured and abandoned. All dogs really wanted was to love and be loved.

Her heart was pumping wildly at Nick's heartfelt gesture. Taking Bear off her hands for the afternoon was boyfriend stuff. Even though her intention from the get-go had been to keep things casual with Nick, it just so happened that she'd stumbled into a relationship. A full-fledged, honest-to-goodness relationship. She agreed wholeheartedly with Mimi. Nick Keegan was a keeper, and she had no idea what to do about it.

CHAPTER SEVENTEEN

Nick knew he must be wild about Harlow to offer himself up as a host for a doggy play-date. It wasn't in his wheelhouse at all, but he was glad he'd made the offer. The two dogs had run him ragged by late afternoon, when Miles had taken over and given him a well-deserved break from the mayhem.

He wasn't actually a dog person. But Zeus had grown on him at such a rapid rate that it was hard for him to remember a time when he hadn't considered him as the pet of his heart. Bear was an incredible dog who listened to commands and emitted a very relaxed vibe. However, putting the two canines together in their fenced-in yard had led to wild dog energy and utter pandemonium. Miles had been on cloud nine, running around the backyard and playing games with the dogs.

Once he came inside, Miles dropped a bombshell on him.

"Maybe we should get another dog, Dad. Zeus needs the company." Miles had looked up at him with big brown eyes full of manipulation.

Another dog? Did Miles have any idea how close he'd been to not having a dog at all? His son's suggestion was so ludicrous that Nick nearly laughed in his face. He quickly realized his son was serious. How could he let him down gently?

"Read my lips. Absolutely not!" Nick tried not to roll his eyes at Miles. Adopting Zeus had been a miracle. His son really shouldn't push it. Two dogs would be beyond his abilities. He was still trying to wrap his head around how he'd become a dog owner in the first place.

"If you're so into dogs, I'm sure Harlow would let you help out over at Paws from time to time," Nick suggested. "Maybe you could fill water bowls or hand out treats."

"I'm only nine, Dad," Miles said with an eye roll. "They don't let kids my age do anything."

When the doorbell, rang Nick quickly made his way to the front door to welcome Harlow. She was standing on his doorstep with a box of baked goods in her hands. Dressed in a red turtleneck dress and black low-heeled boots, she looked amazing. She'd ditched her veterinarian's jacket for something far more fashionable. He felt flattered that she'd taken the time to look nice for him.

"Wicked Eats? Again?" he asked, eyeing the pink-and-white box. "You sure know how to make an entrance."

"What can I say? I'm addicted to the place. Trying that bakery out may be the best advice I've ever gotten in my life. I'm now their biggest fan," Harlow explained.

He rubbed his hands together. "I can't wait to see what's inside."

"You'll have to wait for dessert," Harlow said, stepping inside. "No peeking."

"You're going to earn major cool points with Miles. He loves anything sweet."

He led Harlow to the living room, where she immediately greeted Miles with a huge grin. "Hey there. How's it going, Miles?"

"Oh. *You're* here," Miles said with a scowl. For a split second Nick wished he could sink through the floorboards. His son was acting like a little punk.

"Hey!" Nick said sharply. "Wait a minute. Where are your manners? Look Harlow in the eye and say hello. Nicely," he said through clenched teeth.

"Hello," Miles said, dragging his gaze up. His lip was stuck out in an unnatural position. There wasn't an ounce of warmth on his face.

"Hi there, buddy. Thanks for hosting Bear today. I'm sure he loved it," Harlow said in a sweet tone.

His son shrugged. "It wasn't my idea. Dad made me."

Harlow darted a glance at Nick and raised her brow, as if asking him a question. She definitely knew Miles was acting strange. Where was the boy who'd hung on Harlow's every word about Zeus's treatment? Nick resisted the impulse to grab his son by the collar of his shirt and yank him from the room. Instead, he counted to ten in his head and tried his best to stay cool.

"Are you going home soon?" Miles asked Harlow. "It's almost dinnertime and I'm hungry."

"Miles!" Nick said in a raised voice. "You know Harlow is staying for dinner. We talked about it earlier. You're supposed to be taking the dogs for a walk around the block."

"Aww, man. Why do I have to do it?" Miles asked with a loud groan.

"Why don't you go upstairs and cool down?" Nick suggested. "And while you're up there, find your manners. You're being rude."

Miles made sure to make a lot of noise as he headed upstairs. Nick couldn't remember ever feeling so ashamed of his son. He had no idea what to say to Harlow.

"I'm so sorry about that," he apologized. He couldn't imagine anything more awkward than this very moment. He'd wanted Harlow to feel welcome in his home. Clearly, his son hadn't been on the same page.

Harlow couldn't hide being taken aback by Miles's attitude. Nick felt even more ashamed of his son.

"Did I do something wrong?" she asked. "He was really giving me the cold shoulder."

Nick let out a groan. "I have no idea what's going on with him, but you haven't done a single thing wrong. I'm sorry if Miles made you feel that way. Kids can be fickle." And rude as hell, he wanted to add.

Nick felt deeply embarrassed by his son's behavior. It wasn't like him to be so downright rude and lacking in the social graces. He was a good kid and super friendly. Nick hoped he hadn't hurt Harlow's feelings.

All of a sudden, he realized that he'd completely forgotten to follow up with Miles after his night out at Baxter's. Van had made it clear that something had been bothering his son. He'd gotten so wrapped up in daily life matters—getting Miles off to school, paying bills, grocery shopping, heading to work—that he'd forgotten to talk to him about it. It was moments like this when Nick felt like a complete failure as a dad. Miles deserved better.

"Are you all right?" Harlow asked. "You look a bit frazzled. If tonight doesn't work for dinner that's totally fine. I have a Lean Cuisine in my freezer," she said with a laugh.

"No way. I've been looking forward to spending time with you." He would talk to Miles later and focus on an evening with Harlow in the meantime.

"And showing off your kitchen skills?" she asked in a teasing voice.

"I can deliver way better than a Lean Cuisine," he drawled. "Not that there's anything wrong with frozen meals." He motioned for her to follow him. "Come on in the kitchen. Your first lesson awaits."

"Are the dogs okay?" she asked.

"They've been fed and watered. They're outside in the yard, if you want to check on Bear. Our yard is fenced in," Nick answered. "Miles is going to take them for a short walk in a few moments while we cook."

"Are you sure he's up to it?" Harlow asked. "I don't want to pile on any additional stress."

Nick let out a ragged sigh that seemed to come from deep within. "I know he was acting bratty, but he's super responsible and a huge dog lover. Bear will be in good hands with him. I promise."

"I trust you," Harlow said as she walked into the kitchen behind him. "Sorry for asking, but for all intents and purposes, Bear is my emotional support dog. Although I technically rescued him from a shelter, Bear saved me in every possible way. He's gotten me through some stressful moments. I can't imagine what I'd do without him."

"No need to apologize. Bear is a part of your family. I get it," Nick said. "Don't tell anyone, but I'm starting to feel that way about Zeus," he said, lowering his voice to a whisper.

Harlow nodded. "I kind of figured that out on my own. Face it, Nick. Zeus has you wrapped around his little paw."

Nick let out a groan. He'd never wanted to be a dog person. "So what happened to our poodle friend? Any intel on her owners?"

Harlow leaned back against the kitchen counter and crossed her legs. "I stitched her up and gave her some antibiotics. We weren't able to track down the owners. I honestly don't think we ever will." A distressed sound escaped her lips. "I think she was deliberately left on the street. And there's no telling how she sustained that injury."

"That's pretty awful. What will happen to her? Paws isn't a rescue."

A grin broke out over Harlow's face. "Well, for the next few days she's going to be staying with Jimmy." Harlow chuckled. "He's a persistent one. He showed up at Paws with his parents to check in on Thelma."

"Thelma?" Nick asked. "Wait. Did I miss something?"

Harlow laughed. "Not only did Jimmy name her on the spot, but he made his intentions to adopt her pretty clear. I have to say, Jimmy's love for Thelma threw me for a loop. I want to start up an official dog rescue here in town. Now I'm more determined than ever to open one up and help abandoned dogs."

"I think a dog rescue would be great for Mistletoe. There's a lot of Jimmy's out there." Nick took two wineglasses from the cupboard and placed them down on the table. "Wine or iced tea?" he asked.

"I'll take the wine now and maybe the iced tea later," Harlow answered. Within seconds he'd filled her glass.

He began taking ingredients out of the fridge— shrimp, lemons, shallots, garlic, cheddar cheese, and milk. "So tell me. What inspired you to become a veterinarian? Do you have some sad animal story from childhood?"

Harlow chuckled. The sound of her laugher was a relief. The awkwardness of Miles's behavior had lingered in the air between them. He was happy to see that Harlow was able to shake it off. "No poignant stories. It was the opposite, in fact. Taking care of animals was a way of feeling good about myself when I was growing up. Malcolm was a brilliant artist, but I didn't have a lane to run in. There wasn't anything I was particularly good at." A smile stretched across her face. "However, I was fascinated by patching up turtles and broken-winged birds. Animals were my passion, and I began to realize that it could become my future. I walked neighbors' dogs for free until I realized that I was missing out on a golden opportunity to make major bank."

"Sounds like you were an enterprising young girl," Nick said. "I'm impressed."

"Tossing it back to you. What made you go into search and rescue?" Harlow asked, taking a lengthy sip of her wine.

He took out a cutting board and began slicing

and dicing. "I've never liked sitting on the sidelines. Back when I was in fifth grade a kid in my class went missing. Tommy Hicks. The entire town was in a panic. We all saw ourselves in him and imagined being snatched up by some mysterious visitor to Mistletoe."

"Of course," Harlow said dryly. "Blame the outsider."

Nick rolled his eyes. "Well, the entire town formed a search team in order to find Tommy before he met with a terrible fate."

Harlow wrinkled her nose. "Does this story have a happy ending?" she asked. She seemed to be hanging on to his every word.

He felt a smile twitching at his lips. "This is the good part. Turns out Tommy wasn't missing at all. He was hiding in his family's attic the whole time. He was a little bit of a drama queen. He'd gotten in trouble at school, and he thought by going missing it would divert attention from his antics."

Harlow burst out laughing. "Wow. That's unbelievable. I'm guessing this stunt got him in way more trouble than whatever he'd originally done."

"Not really," Nick said, quirking his mouth. "Everyone was so happy he hadn't been snatched that he got a pass for everything."

Harlow's jaw dropped. "Seriously? That is so wrong."

"Tell me about it. But, seeing everyone band together in a crisis really lit a fire in me. For the first time in my life, I was able to see how a community works together for the common good. Corny, right?"

"Not at all. It sounds like the Mistletoe I'm experiencing." She bit her lip. "I'm ashamed to admit that small towns haven't always been my thing."

"And why is that?" Nick asked, pausing in his cutting duties to learn more about this fascinating woman.

"Let me help," Harlow offered, reaching for the knife and the cutting board. "I can't cook, but I can chop." Nick slid the vegetables over to Harlow, who immediately began to slice and dice.

She shook her head, causing dark tendrils to swirl around her shoulders. "I don't want to get too heavy tonight. My family wasn't exactly treated well in Chestnut Ridge. We ended up leaving after my father died. Let's just say I don't look too fondly on that period of my life. It was pretty painful."

Nick didn't want to press any further. Clearly Harlow was carrying around some issues related to her childhood and her father's death. If he pushed, she might shut down on him, and that was the last thing Nick wanted. He wanted every moment spent with Harlow to shine.

"By the way, how's your mom doing?" Nick asked.

Harlow looked down at the board, focusing on her cutting job. "She's been better, honestly. I really need to visit her soon and see for myself how she is.

I get daily reports from the facility, but it's not the same as seeing her face-to-face and looking in her eyes. Maybe I'm afraid that I won't be able to see myself reflected there anymore. That look of recognition is fading, Nick, and it's heart-wrenching to experience." She swung her gaze up, and he could see moisture pooling in her eyes. "My mom was the best storyteller. She used to tell Malcolm and me all about her grandparents and her childhood on Cape Cod. After my father died, she made a point to tell us about their courtship and all the sweet moments they had shared. I keep thinking how cruel it is that she doesn't have those memories to sustain her."

"I'm so sorry," Nick said. "It isn't fair."

"It isn't," she said with a shake of her head.

"Don't wait, Harlow. You don't want to ever regret not seeing her as much as you possibly can, especially if time is of the essence." He held up his hands. "That's my piece of advice for the day."

"Thanks, Nick. I appreciate it. I'm going to make plans to fly to Cape Cod soon." She placed the knife down on the chopping board. "It's time for me to face the situation head-on instead of burying my head in the sand." She locked gazes with him across the kitchen island. "I've got to put on my big-girl panties and woman up."

Nick nodded. He knew all too well about facing things that overwhelmed him. His own life had been full of such moments in the aftermath of Kara's death. If Harlow needed support, then Nick wouldn't hesitate to be there for her. He had no clue what their official status was, but there was no doubt in his mind how he felt about her. And maybe he didn't have any sense at all, because these feelings should terrify him rather than make him more excited about life than he'd been in a very long time.

CHAPTER EIGHTEEN

Harlow didn't want to jinx anything, but life in Mistletoe was good. Everything was shaping up quite nicely. She loved her workplace, the Paws staff was amazing, and with a few exceptions, the residents had rolled out the welcome mat for her. She had a core group of friends, which seemed to be growing every day. And she was with Nick. Sweet, delicious Nick. How had she gotten so lucky as to meet a man who cooked like a master chef, looked like he could be in print ads, and was caring and thoughtful? He was also a good kisser. Last night, they had stepped out on Nick's back porch to gaze at a sky full of stars. Before too long they'd landed in each other's arms with her lips on fire from Nick's kisses.

On her way home she'd thought about what it might be like to be a permanent fixture in Nick's life. That would mean sticking around Mistletoe, but that didn't seem out of the question any longer. She didn't harbor any illusions about becoming Mrs. Nick Keegan, but the moments spent in his company were precious to her. He was the real deal, and she liked seeing herself through his eyes. Nick always made it very clear that he thought she was special.

Hanging out with Nick at his place had been pretty amazing. She did wonder about Miles and his behavior toward her. Although she hadn't let on to Nick, his rejection had hurt her feelings. He was such a big part of Nick's life. If Miles hated her, it was hard to imagine that her relationship with Nick could continue. She wished that she could pin down what she'd done to alienate him.

As she sat in her kitchen nook and looked out the window across the lake while eating her breakfast omelet, Harlow's mind began to whirl. She was going to call the airlines this morning and book a flight to Cape Cod. She would reach out to her brother in the hopes that he could join her on the trip. Some might say she used Malcolm as a buffer in certain situations, but he was her human security blanket. Ever since they were kids, she'd leaned on him. Sometimes she thought it was a twin thing.

Harlow checked her watch and decided to take a quick walk around the lake before it was time to head to work. Once she was bundled up in her warmest fall coat, Harlow headed outside. The sun was poking out behind the clouds. She lifted her face up toward the sky and spread her arms wide. *This is the life.* A charming home by the lake. Working at a thriving practice. Nick. Most of all Nick. She couldn't remember a time in her life when she had felt so content. So fulfilled.

Could these feelings last? In her experience, good times were as fleeting as a summer rainstorm. But maybe for once she needed to believe that she was worthy of all this. She couldn't always walk around with a dark cloud hanging over her head. Harlow knew she needed to be in a more positive head space so she could accept the blessings in her path.

Do better! Be better! It'll pay off in the end, a voice whispered in her ear.

With a sigh, she turned her back on the lake and headed inside the house, where she took a quick shower and got dressed for work. On her way to the clinic, Harlow stopped at the floral shop to pick up flowers. Sunflowers would look beautiful at the front desk.

"Good morning, Jon," she said, breezing into the office as if she didn't have a care in the world. She held out the flowers to him. "These are for you. A nice dose of autumn for your workspace."

"Thank you, Autumn." Jon gave her a huge smile as he took the flowers from her.

"There's someone here to see you," he said, nodding toward the waiting room area. Harlow turned her head and laid eyes on Miles, sitting in a nearby chair. "Miles! What are you doing here?" She looked around the room for Nick. Perhaps there had been an emergency with Zeus.

"Is your dad here?" she asked. If so, where was he hiding?

Miles stood up and approached her. "No, he's at work. Can I talk to you in private?"

Private? What in the world was going on?

"Sure," she said, leading the way to her office. Once they stepped inside, she closed the door behind them. "Shouldn't you be in school right about now?"

"This won't take long. Van drove me here, so he's going to get me to school in time for homeroom meeting," Miles said before taking a huge breath.

"Okay, shoot. I'm all ears," Harlow said, waiting for Miles to start talking.

"Are you going to marry my dad?" Miles asked. His lips were trembling and the expression on his face was a panicked one. Harlow wanted to burst out laughing, but she sensed this wasn't funny to Miles.

"Miles, I just met your dad. We're getting to know each other right now, so no, we aren't making plans to get married," Harlow explained.

Miles let out a sigh of relief. His entire body language shifted from tension to a more relaxed posture. "I was planning to break the two of you up," he blurted out. "That's why I was so mean to you the night you came to our house."

"Oh," Harlow said, taken aback by Miles's admission. "Is there a reason you don't want us together?"

Miles looked down and fumbled with his fingers. "I like it being the two of us. I don't want that to go away." Miles began to sniffle. "And I don't want my mom to be forgotten."

Harlow reached out and grasped his hand. "None of that is going to happen. Your father loves you to the moon and back. You're his favorite person on earth. And with regards to your mom, I know what it's like to lose a parent at a young age. I lost my dad when I was a few years older than you."

Miles's eyes bulged. "Really? You did?"

Harlow nodded. "Yes. And I know how much it hurts. Trust me, Miles, you can keep her memory alive just by talking about her. By loving her."

"I don't talk about her sometimes, because I don't want my dad to be sad."

"Oh, I'm sure he would love to hear you talk about her, Miles. Remember, he loves her too."

A few seconds passed by without either one of them uttering a word. Harlow believed Miles was taking in everything she'd said to him.

"I'm really sorry I was plotting against you," he said with a sheepish expression. He shifted from one foot to the other. "I wasn't very good at it because I like you, Doc Harlow. It didn't feel right to treat you badly."

"And I like you too, Miles. I want to be friends, okay? If there's ever a time when you feel uncomfortable about me and your dad, make sure to speak up. Talk to your dad. He's a good listener."

"I will, but can we just keep this between us for now?" He looked at her with pleading eyes.

"For now," she said, "but you need to tell him sooner rather than later." She looked at her watch. "You really need to scoot or you're going to be late for school. And I have a patient arriving soon."

"Thanks for hearing me out. I feel a lot better now," Miles said with a grin.

Harlow walked Miles back toward the waiting room, where they said their goodbyes before Miles raced out the door. She walked back to reception to pick up her schedule for the day. Surprisingly, Jon didn't greet her in his usual effusive manner. Instead he made a motion for her to step closer toward his desk. She immediately wondered what was going on when she saw him furtively glancing around as if worried he might be overheard.

"Harlow. Heads up," Jon said in a low, conspiratorial voice. "One of our clients is making trouble for you."

A chill ran down her spine as she absorbed his words. *Trouble?* Jon could be a bit dramatic, but he wasn't the type to make something up out of thin air.

"What are you talking about?" she asked, dreading his response.

"Thanks to Gillian, the town rumor mill is swirling, saying you mistreated her dog."

"That's ridiculous." Surely no one would believe such lies. Harlow's heart began to thump wildly in her chest. Sadly, the past had taught her that sometimes falsehoods were believed. Her entire career could implode if false stories were circulated.

"I know it's ludicrous, but some of your clients have requested another vet." Jon discreetly pointed in the direction of Andy and Darlene Rubin, a couple who owned three spirited pugs. They were sitting a few feet away from the front desk, studiously avoiding eye contact with her.

"Talk to Whitney," Jon urged. He slid a piece of paper toward her. "These are your appointments for today." Was that a look of sympathy on his face?

"Thanks," Harlow answered, glancing down at the slip. Four clients! Normally she had four times that amount. She was being canceled left and right. What did this mean for her reputation as a veterinarian?

Needing answers, she headed straight to Whitney's office, pausing briefly to knock upon the partially open door. She poked her head in just as Whitney called out for her to come in. Whitney was sitting on the edge of her desk, looking deep in thought. As soon as she spotted Harlow she ushered her in, then made a point to firmly shut the door behind her.

"Harlow. I've been waiting to speak to you." Whitney's expression was shuttered, which was unusual for the bubbly veterinarian. Whitney was the lifeblood in the practice, mainly due to her ebullient personality and her mentoring the staff. Even if Jon hadn't alerted her to the fact that something was going on, Whitney's demeanor would have tipped her off.

"Hey, Whit. I just talked to Jon. What's going on?" Harlow asked, willing herself to stop shaking. Nerves had taken over, and she'd never been any good at calming herself down.

Whitney huffed out a breath. "A whole lot of foolishness," she said, sounding annoyed. "I never imagined it would come to this, but Gillian and a few others in town are circulating rumors about Elvis not receiving proper care here at the clinic. I'm really surprised that we actually have clients calling to cancel or switch up appointments. They're messing with our livelihoods."

Harlow placed a hand over her chest. Whitney's concern about the situation ratcheted up her own. "This is about me isn't it? I was the one who checked out Elvis, so it falls on me."

"You did nothing wrong," Whitney said, reaching over to pat her hand. "Elvis's owner put him in danger, not you. This is about pettiness and unfounded gossip, not your professionalism."

"Thank you for saying that," Harlow said. Whitney's words made her feel slightly better about the situation. It didn't sound like her job was in jeopardy at the moment.

"We're just going to take a pause on the dog rescue until all of this dies down. It's not the right time to launch this program." Whitney bit the end of her pencil. "I know it must be disappointing, Harlow, and I'm sorry for that."

"But what if the gossip doesn't die down?" Her heart was hammering wildly in her chest. For a moment she was completely breathless. The dog rescue meant so much to her, and now it was being sidelined. For what? Gillian didn't even know Harlow. Was she trying to even the score because Harlow had tried to educate her about toxic substances for dogs? None of it made sense. But as Harlow well knew, not everything always added up. People could be cruel.

Whitney held up her hand. "Harlow, you know I don't give any credence to this ridiculous rumor, but the timing is off. This rescue was your idea, so ideally you'd be the one to get it up and running. I think it's important for us to hold off for a little bit, but I'm in no way suggesting any wrongdoing." An understanding look washed over Whitney's face.

Harlow's entire body felt cold. Never in her professional life had her abilities been questioned. Not a single client had ever accused her of mistreatment of an animal. And now her appointments were being canceled. This could also have repercussions on the dog rescue and their funding opportunities.

"Just breathe, Harlow. I promise you this will all get sorted out."

She nodded her head and got up to leave Whitney's office. Although she knew her boss meant well, she didn't believe her. Things didn't always get straightened out. Sometimes people were forced to walk around with a scarlet letter emblazoned on their chests for all to see.

Hot tears stung her eyes as she entered her own office and closed the door behind her. Harlow refused to cry. She wouldn't give these people the satisfaction of crumbling. She had worked so hard over the years to develop a professional relationship and hone her skills as a vet. Coming to Mistletoe was supposed to have been an answer to her prayers for financial relief from her student loans. Relocating from the West Coast had been a big decision. Being here had been an act of faith, which she'd never been very good at. She had seized this opportunity in the hopes of creating a better life for herself.

Just when she'd started to fall in love with this quaint little community, the rug had been pulled out from underneath her. And now, her career and reputation was going to crash and burn, all thanks to the petty gossips in Mistletoe, Maine.

CHAPTER NINETEEN

Where *was Harlow?* Nick looked at his watch and paced back and forth in front of Casablanca's. He checked his phone to see if she'd left a message. Nope. Nothing. At this rate they weren't going to make the movie. There was a big retrospective of Spike Lee's films and tonight's offering, *She's Gotta Have It*, was one of his all-time favorites. The movie was set to start in five minutes.

He hoped nothing was wrong. Harlow wasn't the type to blow off meeting up with him. Just when he was beginning to get really concerned, Harlow drove up and parked in a spot right in front of the theater. He walked over to meet her, calling out to her when she was a few feet away.

"Hey, if we don't hurry we're going to miss the opening scene. I already bought the tickets, so we just need to score some snacks. I don't know about you but popcorn with lots of butter is my go-to."

As soon as Harlow reached his side, he knew immediately something wasn't right. Her beautiful features were drawn tight with stress and an emotion he couldn't identify.

"What's wrong? You look like someone just stole your last Reese's."

Harlow didn't laugh at his Reese's joke, which was another sign that she wasn't in the best of moods.

"Nick, I don't think I can sit through a movie tonight," Harlow admitted. "I'm so sorry to bail on you." Nick reached out and tipped her chin up. He could see fear and anxiety swirling around in her brown eyes. All he wanted to do right now was make her feel better.

"It's okay. We can see a movie anytime. Tell me what's going on, Harlow."

"I-I can't believe it," she said, shaking her head.

Harlow's lips were trembling. Her beautiful brown skin appeared slightly ashen. Nick immediately knew something was deeply affecting her. Whatever was going on seemed serious enough to rattle her to the core. She seemed lost. Harlow opened her mouth to speak, but no words came out. She was clearly frightened, which gutted him. His immediate reaction was to hold her and offer comfort.

Nick reached out and pulled her into his arms.

His first thought was that something had happened to her mother or Malcolm. "What is it?" Nick asked. He needed to know what had shaken her up so badly.

"Something terrible has happened." She let out a ragged sigh that made her body shake. "People are gossiping about my veterinary care. I'm not sure what's going on, but Whitney told me rumors are going around that I was negligent in my treatment of a client's animal."

"Who's saying this stuff?" he growled. His main objective was to protect her and nip this ridiculous mess in the bud. Nick knew gossip flew on the wind in Mistletoe, but this was despicable.

"People think I neglected Elvis. Thanks to Gillian, half the town doesn't want me to treat their pets. I had only four appointments today," she said, her voice cracking. "Most of them were swapped out or canceled."

"I'm so sorry," Nick said, placing his palm on her cheek. "I know this must be awful."

"That doesn't even begin to describe it," she said angrily. "I'm barely holding on at the moment."

He sensed she was holding back a tsunami of emotion swirling around inside her. Her jaw was clenched, and she was blinking back tears. She appeared extremely shaky. "Truthfully, all I want to do right now is pack up all my belongings and head back to Seattle, where things like this don't happen."

* * *

Nick's expression changed after her outburst. He was now frowning at her, which made her feel even more teary eyed. Why didn't he understand how she felt? She was experiencing an all too familiar sense of déjà vu. She had seen this scenario play out with her father. Although she'd been only a child, Harlow had vivid memories of the town scandal and its aftermath. Getting out of Dodge seemed like a decent option for her.

"Harlow, you can't be serious. You're not a quitter. You came to Maine so your student loan debt would be paid off. That will all be made null and void if you leave."

She bristled as soon as the word *quitter* came out of his mouth. Never in her entire life had she been associated with that word. It hadn't been in her vocabulary. In fact, she'd always been a go-getter, someone who had worked extra hard to succeed in life. She had pushed past her childhood traumas to achieve excellence. It hurt to know he didn't see all of that in her.

She took slow breaths before speaking. Blowing up at Nick wouldn't be fair. None of this was his fault. "It wouldn't be quitting, Nick. Sometimes it's smart to cut your losses," she muttered.

He scoffed. "You have clients here in Mistletoe who count on you. And friends who adore you." He stroked his jaw. "Not to mention a handsome single father who literally saved your life. He's pretty invested in your staying put."

Hearing Nick say her presence here in Mistletoe was important to him caused little flutters low in her abdomen. Knowing she was wanted and needed by Nick meant everything to her. But it still didn't erase all of the angst she was experiencing. Try as she might, these particular feelings wouldn't allow themselves to be stuffed down into a deep black hole.

"What's the point in staying if my reputation is going to get trashed?" she asked, throwing her hands up in the air. "I'm a good vet, Nick. I've never had so much as a whisper about my level of care or professionalism. Not once. And now, in a matter of weeks, my reputation has been tarnished."

"It's a little bit dented at the moment, but not broken. I'm curious to hear what Whitney's take was on all of this?"

"She basically said that it will all blow over and that she trusts me."

"Whitney's the real deal. She's not just blowing smoke. We'll get to the bottom of all this. I promise."

Although his words should have calmed her down, they had the opposite effect on her. Why wasn't he more upset on her behalf? Rumors like this were career suicide.

"I'm not sure you realize how devastating this is for me. I've worked for years to become a vet. I sacrificed. I studied. I scrimped to pay tuition. I'm in debt up to my ears, which is why I'm here in the first place. I have no idea how to stem the tide of this."

Nick reached for her hand. "Harlow, I've got your back. So will Stella and Luke. Whitney too. The truth has a way of rising to the surface."

Nick's words sounded like white noise. He didn't seem to get it. This was her whole career on the line. This entire mess was dredging up painful memories of the embezzlement accusations lobbied against her father. She'd been twelve years old when the cruel whispers about her father had rocked their small New England town. Because of lies, her family had lost everything they held dear. Harlow couldn't help but think history was repeating itself.

All of a sudden, she couldn't hold it in any longer. "I'm angry, Nick. Pissed off. As my mother used to say, I'm fit to be tied." Harlow clenched her hands at her sides. Her head pounded and she wanted to smash something to smithereens. "I've tried my entire life to avoid being in this position. Trust me, I've seen this stuff up close and personal. My father was a victim of these types of vicious whispers. Smears."

Nick's eyes widened. "This must bring up painful memories. What exactly went down with your dad?"

Harlow's entire body was trembling. All she could think about was her mother warning her and

Malcolm against small towns like Chestnut Ridge.
Petty people stirred up lies and gossip just for kicks.
Lives were ruined in the process. Why hadn't she
heeded the warning? She should have stayed back
in Seattle, where she belonged. She'd made herself
vulnerable by believing that she could become a part
of this community.

"My father's professional reputation was ruined
when he was falsely accused of stealing large sums
of money from his medical group. Those allegations
completely shattered him and destroyed everything
he'd worked so hard to achieve." She choked back
a sob. "In the end, those lies cost him his life in a
car crash."

* * *

Harlow's words cut to his core. He could hear the
hurt and pain laced in what she'd just told him. This
was too deep of a conversation for them to be having
in front of Casablanca's in a public area. Anyone
passing by could overhear snippets of their discussion. He didn't want that for Harlow. He knew how
deeply she valued her privacy. Rumors were already
flying around, and he didn't want this to spiral any
further out of control.

"Let's go somewhere quiet and sit down to talk
this over," Nick suggested. "We could grab something to eat at the Starlight Diner."

"I'm not hungry. To be honest, I just want to head

home and get under the covers. I won't be very good company tonight."

Nick wanted so badly to comfort her. He dipped his head down and brushed his lips against her temple, then swept some tendrils of hair away from her forehead. "You only have to ask if you want some company. I'd love to join you." Snuggling with Harlow under the covers sounded amazing, but instinct told him she wasn't in the mood for any type of intimacy. She was hurting and seeing her so broken caused him pain.

"I'm just not up to it," she admitted, looking at him with moist eyes. "I really want to be by myself. I'm sorry, Nick."

"I understand," Nick said, trying not to sound too disappointed. This wasn't about his feelings. This moment was about lifting up Harlow and making sure she felt supported so she didn't bolt back to Seattle and leave Mistletoe behind in her rearview mirror. The thought of her leaving...it wasn't something he wanted to think about at all.

"I hate this!" she said, fists clenched at her side as if she were about to fight someone. "I have no control over what's happening. I'm not used to feeling so useless."

"I know what that's like," he said. "Sometimes life hands us situations that we think might break us. But they don't, Harlow. This won't break you unless you let it."

For a few beats, silence stretched out between

them. Harlow just stared at him without saying a word. He wasn't sure she had really heard him. Her eyes looked a little vacant.

"Night, Nick," Harlow finally said, walking off toward her car. Nick had missed the opportunity to kiss her good night, but she had walked away with a determined stride that let him know she wanted to be by herself. Even though he didn't want her to be alone, Nick knew that he needed to give her space.

Nick let out a hiss of air as he watched her drive off. *What was going on?* Nick personally hadn't heard any nasty gossip about Harlow or Paws. But he wasn't part of the rumor mill in town. With his busy schedule, he was rarely in Mistletoe during weekdays, while weekends were spent with Miles, Harlow, and his family. In general, he tended to run in the opposite direction if people were talking smack about others. Now, as a result, he was completely out of the Mistletoe loop.

Who did he know here in town who was privy to town rumors? Tess Marshall, Miles's buddy, was a serious ear hustler. She was constantly getting in trouble for spreading gossip and eavesdropping on adult conversations. But he couldn't drag a little girl into this mess. Stella and Lucy wouldn't appreciate him involving their little sister.

Stella! As a second-grade teacher, his sister-in-law came into contact with all kinds of people. Co-workers. Parents. Delivery people. Photographers.

She had a pulse line on what was going on in Mistletoe. Nick made the short walk toward his car and hopped inside. Feeling like a man on a mission, he dialed Luke's number and asked if he could swing by.

"Of course you can. Jade's waking and sleeping hours are all mixed up, so there's no telling when she'll go down for the night." He let out a chuckle, letting Nick know he was taking it all in stride.

"Thanks, bro," Nick said. "I'll be there in ten."

On the drive over Nick thought about Harlow's situation. He hoped that he hadn't minimized her concerns. She'd been so upset and on edge. Although he had known there had been issues surrounding her childhood, he'd been blown away by what she had revealed to him about her father. Of course Harlow distrusted small towns after what she'd experienced! He didn't blame her one bit after what her family had been through.

But Nick knew this town like the back of his hand. He'd lived with the people of Mistletoe his entire life. Yes, gossips lived here and sometimes things got out of control, but he refused to believe that they were evil or had intended to ruin Harlow's life. This, like most issues, could be straightened out. Harlow had a chip on her shoulder about small towns due to her father's experiences, so she was bringing a lot of baggage into the situation. Maybe if he could get to the root of the innuendoes, he could help calm things down before they spiraled out of control.

Luke opened his front door the moment Nick's feet hit the front steps.

"I thought you had a date tonight with Harlow," Luke said as Nick stepped over the threshold. Nick took a moment to breathe in the scent of spiced apples. Nick and Stella's place always exuded a warm and cozy vibe. Located right on Blackberry Beach, the cottage had belonged to Stella before she and Luke were married. Stella had purchased the beachfront property as a fixer upper and shed blood, sweat, and tears renovating the place. Their family of three was perfectly content in the cheerful, airy abode with a view of the ocean that stretched out before them for miles.

"Our movie night didn't go as expected," Nick said with a ragged sigh. "Which is why I'm here. It seems that the rumor mill has been whirling about Harlow." Luke led him into the kitchen, where Stella was attempting to feed a rebellious Jade. Nick couldn't hide his grin as he watched his niece spatter her food around.

"Hey, Nick," Stella said, pausing in her duties to greet him. Nick, poised to duck any incoming splats of mashed peas and carrots, bent down and kissed Stella on the cheek.

"Hey there, Stella. What's good?" Nick asked, resting his hand on her shoulder.

"Not this one, if I'm being honest," Stella admitted, jutting her chin in the direction of her daughter. "She's determined to fight me tonight."

"Hey there," Luke said. "Be easy on our princess. It's tough being little."

Nick avoided loudly sucking his teeth. Jade had already figured out how to wrap her Navy SEAL dad around her tiny little finger. And she hadn't even turned one yet. This didn't bode well for the future. Stella was definitely going to be playing the bad cop role.

"Jade, be a good girl and eat your dinner," Stella crooned just as she was hit with another splash of food. She took a napkin and slowly wiped her face as Jade grinned.

"So, are the rumors about you and Harlow?" Luke asked with a smirk and a shrug. "I could have told you that weeks ago."

"Not exactly," Nick admitted, earning himself curious gazes from both Stella and Luke. "This is really messed up, but Harlow seems to be the topic of a nasty rumor. People are saying she's not to be trusted as a vet and that she caused harm to one of the animals in her care."

"That's really awful," Luke said, running his hand across his jaw. "I know Mistletoe loves to generate juicy stories, but that's really toxic stuff. At least with me and Stella, it was fairly harmless." Luke and Stella had engaged in a fake dating scenario in order to prevent town matchmakers from trying to fix them up on dates. Tongues had wagged all over town about their relationship, which had blossomed into a genuine love story.

"I, for one, know how painful gossip can be. When Rafe ended our engagement, the town rumor mill went into overdrive." She lifted the baby out of her high chair. "People can be so cruel. They forget that living, breathing people get hurt in the process."

"You hit the nail on the head, Stella. Harlow is really a mess over this," Nick said, clenching his jaw. "She even made a passing reference to leaving town, although I think she was probably just venting. She's got a lot to lose if she bails on her agreement with the state of Maine."

Stella looked sheepish as she jiggled Jade on her hip. "Lucy and I did hear some chatter, but we shut it down really fast. We weren't going to let anyone get away with spreading gossip around town about Harlow." She rubbed noses with Jade. "Isn't that right, little mama?"

"What were they saying?" Nick asked. He bit down on his back teeth, steeling himself against hearing petty rumors about someone he cared about. Harlow wasn't the only one feeling pain about the situation. He'd always been proud of his hometown, but it was difficult under the current circumstances. No one had the right to smear someone's name and jeopardize their career in the process.

"It was ridiculous!" Stella said, letting out a sound of disgust. "Honestly, I didn't even think it was important enough to repeat to you or Harlow, because it's so petty. Patsy was running her mouth and warning people not to make an appointment with the new veterinarian in town."

"Did she say why?" Luke asked, taking the words right out of Nick's mouth. Was she actually being accused of something or was it just random negativity?

"Something about an animal almost dying in her care," Stella continued.

"That never happened." Nick spit out the words. His frustration was threatening to boil over. Harlow had been right.

"Take it easy. We know that," Luke said. "At this point, let's focus on figuring out how to make things better for Harlow."

"I don't even know how to begin, guys. How do you put the genie back in the bottle?" He ran a weary hand over his face. "She's already losing clients. It's hitting right at the heart of who she is. She would never mistreat an animal, or anyone for that matter."

Stella handed the baby over to Luke, then came to stand by Nick. She pulled him in for a hug, then placed her head against his chest. "I don't know either, but Luke and I are both team Harlow, so we're in this with you, Nick. Now I'm going to put my child to bed, so you two can brainstorm."

"I know she'll appreciate the support," Nick said. "She doesn't deserve this."

Stella plucked Jade out of Luke's arms and padded down the hall toward the nursery.

"So, is it official between the two of you?" Luke asked. "You seem...smitten."

Nick let out a snort. "Smitten? You sound like somebody from the roaring twenties."

Luke chuckled. "Don't change the subject. I haven't seen you like this since...well, you know. Since Kara."

Nick nodded. His brother was right. He had never expected to find someone else who made him feel all the emotions he'd felt with his wife. Hope. Nervousness. Joy. Fear. Butterflies in his belly. He knew what it meant. Nick was in too deep now to find his way out.

"I'm happy with what we're building. It's all happening really fast, but it feels right. When we're together, we vibe so well."

"There's no timetable on love," Luke said in a singsong tone.

Nick reached over and punched his arm. "Will you quit it with the sappy sayings? You sound like a greeting card."

"Seriously, Harlow seems to make you happy. And I haven't seen that in a really long time, so congratulations. Are you falling in love, bro?" Luke leaned across the counter, waiting for Nick's answer.

Nick tapped his fingers on the granite counter. He'd known for a while, but he had pushed it to the back of his mind. He was ready for it, had hoped for it over the past year when he knew he'd made it past the worst of his grief. But he wasn't ready to share it with anyone but Harlow. She needed to know how he felt before anyone else.

"Let's just say I'm catching feelings for her," Nick said. He could feel a smile stretching across his face. This is how Harlow made him feel. As if his feet weren't touching the ground. As if anything was possible.

"And now you sound like a Hallmark card," Luke said, chuckling. Nick joined in along with him. Despite the heaviness of their discussion, he and Luke shared a camaraderie that soothed them even in difficult circumstances.

Luke put a finger to his lips, shushing him. "We don't want to wake the baby. If we do, Stella's going to let us have it."

Seeing Luke being such a responsible dad floored him. Funny how one's life could turn on a dime. Not too long ago, Luke's life had been in jeopardy after an explosion in Afghanistan. His brother had been retired as a SEAL due to a leg injury, but he'd gained a family of his own as a result. Nick was grateful for second chances. He was hoping life handed him one as well.

Luke was right. Love was his only excuse for being sappy. He was over the moon about Harlow, and he was pretty sure his brother could see it written all over him. He wasn't really doing much to hide it.

Nick wanted to make things right for Harlow

and show her that Mistletoe wasn't going to hang
her out to dry. He wanted Harlow to know that he
understood how much these rumors had affected her.
Nick needed her to understand that she wasn't in this
alone. Not by a long shot.

Once the issues were resolved surrounding the
gossip about Harlow, Nick planned to tell her how
he felt about her. And hopefully, with any kind of
luck, her feelings mirrored his own.

CHAPTER TWENTY

The following morning, Harlow was driving her rental car along the coastal road to the Bay Shore Rehabilitation Center. Skies were blue and the wind was crisp. She'd needed some time away from Mistletoe, so she could clear her head from all the ugliness swirling around the smear campaign against her, and visiting her mother was way overdue. Pretending that her mother wasn't losing her fight against dementia served no purpose other than to shield Harlow from being hurt. In the end, she would have to face it and absorb the pain. All she could do now was show her unconditional love and support.

She had the weekend off from work and this morning she'd taken a flight from Maine to Cape Cod in order to see her mother. Maybe she was being paranoid, but she was beginning to wonder if

Whitney was going to let her go from Paws. After all, who could blame her? She'd been in town for only a few months and she was bringing the practice's reputation down. The thought of all the whispers and cancellations made her shudder. Knowing she'd been targeted with false rumors was frustrating and hurtful.

And she couldn't help but feel frustrated by Nick's cavalier attitude toward the slow destruction of her career and reputation. It hurt to think he didn't care or that he was more invested in the town of Mistletoe than in her. She let out a groan. Why had she gotten so tangled up with Nick? From the very beginning, she'd known falling for him wouldn't serve her long-term interests.

On the bright side, Malcolm was driving up from Boston to join her for the visit.

She felt more confident because they would be making this visit together. Harlow didn't scare easily, but her mother's rapid decline terrified her. Dementia was a frightening, debilitating disease that had come out of nowhere and stolen her mother from her and Malcolm.

Although her childhood had been painful at times, there had been joyful moments mixed in with the bad. Her mother didn't remember those times. Every now and again, Deidre had moments of clarity when she mentioned Harlow's father and precious memories spent at carnivals and birthday parties, summer vacations and campouts. But Harlow never knew what she was going to experience with her mother, and given her deterioration, it was unlikely she would even recognize her children. No matter what, Harlow still wanted to wrap her arms tightly around her mother and never let go. At her core, she still felt like a little kid who needed her mom.

Fall in Cape Cod was much quieter than spring and summer. All the tourists and warm-weather seekers had gone elsewhere. The vibe was subdued, but incredibly picturesque.

As soon as her plane landed, Harlow had reached out to Malcolm, who was scheduled to arrive at Bay Shore shortly after her. Harlow wanted her and Malcolm to head into the facility together. She knew it was silly, but she didn't want to see her mother by herself. At moments like this, Harlow leaned on Malcolm for strength.

Harlow battled nerves as they headed inside and were led to the activity room, where residents were gathered. A quick look around the space revealed a variety of activities, such as puzzles, bingo, coloring, and reading. Malcolm gently elbowed her and said, "There she is. Over by the window." Harlow's gaze followed Malcolm's. She felt a hitch in her heart at the sight of her mother gazing through the bay window at the ocean in the distance. She'd always loved the sea, which was one of the reasons they'd chosen Bay Shore. It was Harlow's fervent hope that her mother knew she was by the ocean and that it gave her comfort.

"Come on, Harlow," Malcolm said, grabbing her by the hand and leading the way toward their mother.

Deidre Jones was dressed in a pale pink sweater that Harlow had bought her as a birthday present last year. The color looked gorgeous against her mother's cocoa-colored skin. Despite everything, she was still beautiful, with her high cheekbones and striking features. Just looking at her face in profile brought tears to Harlow's eyes. Malcolm, seeing her emotion, squeezed her hand.

"Mom," Malcolm said as a greeting once they'd reached her side. He gently touched her shoulder. "Mom. It's Malcolm and Harlow." She continued to gaze out the window without turning her head toward them.

"Hi, Mom," Harlow said in a louder voice than her brother had used, since she hadn't reacted to Malcolm's voice. Nothing but a blank gaze.

Mom, please. I know you're in there somewhere. Look at me. Say my name.

"Hi there. Are you guys okay over here?" Harlow and Malcolm both turned in the direction of the honey-coated voice. Claire Beck, the head of the unit, was standing behind them. Claire was a dedicated staffer who always made herself available to her and Malcolm for phone calls or Zoom meetings so they could get regular updates.

"Hey, Claire," Harlow said, greeting the staff member. "How's she doing?"

"Today hasn't been the best for Deidre," Claire answered as she reached out and lightly patted their mother on the shoulder. "Given the rapid progression of her disease, it's to be expected, but I know it can be difficult to see."

"So she's not talking today?" Malcolm asked.

"Not much," Claire answered, sounding regretful. "Occasionally, we'll get one-word responses, but it's doubtful you'll get a conversation. It's just the progression of the disease. I know that's hard to hear."

Harlow's heart began to hammer wildly in her chest. Her palms got sweaty and she knew her pulse was racing. Her mother was fading away from them and there was absolutely nothing they could do to fix things. She hated feeling powerless. She had worked so hard with her education and professional career to never feel that way again, yet here she was in this vulnerable position.

"Malcolm, I'm sorry. I need some air." Without waiting for his reply, she walked back toward the entrance and pushed past the front doors. A blast of cold air greeted her, and she drew a shaky breath. All she could think of was escape. With staggering steps, she made it back to her rental car, pulled the door open, and got in the driver's seat.

Why did it feel as if a hundred-pound weight was sitting on her chest?

A few seconds later her car door was wrenched open and Malcolm slid into the passenger seat. "Harlow, are you okay? You're scaring me!"

"I-I can't breathe," she said, placing a hand on her chest.

"If you can talk, you can breathe," Malcolm said, placing his arm around her. "I think you might be having a panic attack. Just take small little breaths until you feel better."

Harlow closed her eyes and began breathing in and out. Malcolm placed his hand on her back and patted it gently as she tried to calm down. After a difficult few minutes she began to feel better.

"I think I'm good now," she said, turning toward Malcolm. She felt guilty about the terrified look on his face.

"What just happened?" he asked.

"I don't know exactly, but seeing Mom like that...it felt as if the walls were closing in on us." She swiped away tears from her cheeks. "This has never happened before."

"You used to have panic attacks when we were little."

Harlow frowned. How had she forgotten that? The first time, she'd thought she was dying. After a while she'd outgrown them and put them behind her. This one had come out of nowhere, completely taking her by surprise.

Malcolm touched her wrist. "It's not too shocking, given all the stress you're under."

She looked out the window, focusing on a flock of seagulls that were gathered on the beach. For so long she had bottled up her emotions. Now everything was pouring out of her and she couldn't stem the tide. "I wish that I could tell her about Paws and my student loans being paid off by the state of Maine. I wish that I could look into her eyes and know that she recognizes me. I always made not visiting about the distance, but I think the truth is that I was too scared to face her being sick." Harlow put her face in her hands and sobbed. She wasn't a crier. She'd never been comfortable wearing her emotions on the outside. But lately that had transformed. She was having trouble holding everything in.

"Hey! You can still tell her those things," Malcolm said in a soft voice. "And you're facing all of this right now. You're not running from it."

"But will she hear me? Can she understand?" Harlow asked, sniffling.

"I believe she does, Harlow. Just talk to her, all right? Whatever you have to say, don't hold it in. She's still in there. She's still our mom."

"It's scary to think that we've already lost her."

"But we haven't. And I refuse to let you mourn her before it's time."

As usual, Malcolm saw things way clearer than she was able to. He always got to the heart of the matter in no time at all. Harlow sucked in a fortifying breath and said, "You're right. I've got to put my big-girl panties on and deal with it like a grown-up."

A few minutes later, Harlow went back inside with Malcolm and sat down next to her mother.

"Mom, I brought you something," Harlow said, reaching into her pocket and pulling out a bottle of perfume. "I thought you might like to wear this. Chanel No. 5 has always been your favorite." Harlow sprayed a little on her finger before reaching out and spreading it on her mother's wrist. Instead of pulling away, she let Harlow touch her. Harlow then raised her mom's wrist to her nose so she could smell the fragrance.

"Guess what?" she asked in a chipper tone. "I'm working at a new veterinarian clinic called Paws. It's a great practice in Mistletoe, Maine. And I'm really loving it. I didn't think I'd fall in love with Mistletoe, but it's so charming. And everyone is really nice." She made a face, then corrected herself. "Well, not everyone. There's this one nasty woman who decided to smear my name by bad-mouthing my veterinary skills." Just talking about the situation made her feel anxious.

Malcolm leaned over and squeezed her hand. "Take a deep breath," he whispered. As usual, her brother was right. She needed to breathe.

She inhaled deeply and then exhaled through her nose before continuing. "But don't worry, I'm not going to let lies tear me down. I've worked too hard to get where I am," she continued. "I met someone. His name is Nick and he's one of the good guys. He rescues people for a living." She let out a chuckle. "Honestly, he rescued me when I first arrived in Maine. He's a single dad, and he has the most adorable son named Miles." She touched her mother's hand. Harlow didn't want to frighten her, but she needed the contact. She ached to be held by her. When she was little, her mother used to sit her between her legs and braid her hair. What she wouldn't give to go back in time and relive those moments.

Her mother locked gazes with her. She reached out and tenderly ran her hand across her cheek. "Baby. My baby."

Harlow placed her hand over her mother's and sighed. "Always, Mom. Always."

* * *

"Nice catch, Miles," Nick shouted as he watched Miles land the baseball in his mitt. His son was steadily improving his athletic abilities. Although football had been big in the Keegan household growing up, his son preferred soccer and baseball. Zeus was running beside Miles, trying his best to reach the ball first by jumping in the air. Nick got a kick out of their dog's unbridled enthusiasm.

"Thanks, Dad," Miles called back to him before throwing the baseball in Nick's direction. Nick let out a low whistle as he caught the ball. Miles also possessed a killer throwing arm. Ever since he was able to toss a ball, Miles had talked about playing for the Red Sox. Nick had always told him that his dreams could take him anywhere. And he believed his son could do anything, be anything. President. Astronaut. Pitcher for the Red Sox.

Nick beckoned him to come back toward the house. When Miles reached his side, Nick said, "Hey bud. I wanted to talk to you about something. Why don't we go sit down on the front steps?"

"Uh-oh," Miles said, letting out a groan. "Am I in trouble?"

Nick chuckled as he sat down. "Not at all. I just wanted to make sure you're feeling okay about me and Harlow. Like we talked about, you're always going to be my main priority."

Miles nodded. "I totally get it now. You need adult companionship and it doesn't mean I'm being replaced." Miles pointed to his dimples. "Because who could replace all of this?" he asked cheekily.

"No one in the world," Nick said, getting a little choked up by how fast Miles was growing. Every time he looked at him, Miles was sprouting a few inches and sounding older and wiser. *Where had his baby gone?*

"I like Doc Harlow." He shrugged. "It was just scary thinking if you two ended up together there might not be room for me. Do you know what I mean?"

Nick placed his arm around Miles and pulled him close to his side. "Of course I do. For almost four years it's been just the two of us getting used to life without your mom. The dynamic duo. I don't know what's going to happen between me and Harlow, but there's no doubt in my mind about the two of us. You're stuck with me, buddy. At least until your fortieth birthday."

Miles let out a squeal. "I'll be the crypt creeper. Ancient."

Nick laughed so hard his sides hurt. Spending time with his son was life affirming. These moments were etched on his soul like permanent tattoos.

"I just don't want Mom to ever be replaced," Miles said. Worry emanated from his eyes.

"That could never and will never happen. We'll never stop celebrating your mom's life and what she'll always mean to us." He reached out his pinky finger so Miles could loop his own around Nick's.

"Dad, I'm going to be late for the soccer party if we don't get a move on."

"Okay, let's go. Just text me later for the pickup time."

"Is it all right if I go over Jaden's house afterward? He's invited a few of us over."

"That's fine," Nick said, running his hand over Miles's 'fro. "Let me get my keys."

After dropping off Miles, Nick's thoughts turned to Harlow. Not seeing her over the weekend was a kick in the butt. He missed her. Seeing her mother was an important step for Harlow. She had a lot to process and no matter what her needs might be, he wanted to be present for her. Nick hoped that Harlow would seize the moments she had left with her mother and make the most of them, as difficult as it might be. Every moment they spent together would be part of a goodbye. He often wished he'd been able to say goodbye to Kara. Sometimes he wondered if he'd cherished their shared moments in real time. If he could go back in time, he would love her a little harder and let her know how much he valued her.

Nick knew from his own experiences that Harlow would need support on this journey, and he intended to be by her side every step of the way.

Since he had no Saturday plans, Nick got to work digging into the rumors about Harlow by talking to a few friends in town. A few of them had heard the gossip, which was disheartening, but no one could pinpoint exactly what Harlow was being accused of doing. The only names he'd heard as the rumor spreaders were Gillian and Patsy. He wasn't the least bit surprised.

Based on the information he'd gathered, Nick figured he would start with the original source. Nick had known Gillian for most of his life. He was perplexed as to why she would start trouble with Harlow. It hadn't been too long ago that she had been leaving messages on his answering machine about Luke. When his older brother retired as a SEAL and headed home to Mistletoe, the single ladies in town had lined up to date him. Gillian had been quite persistent until Stella and Luke had become a thing.

The florist's shop sat on the corner of Main and Elm. A beautiful pink canopy framed the entrance to the shop, along with a pink-and-cream sign

welcoming customers to Bloom's. A ding heralded
Nick's entrance. Seconds later, Gillian appeared.
"Nick. It's good to see you. Welcome to Bloom's."

"Thanks. You've got a nice place here," Nick
noted. He hadn't been inside in years. Back in the
day, he'd ordered Kara flowers on a weekly basis,
and for a long time, he'd avoided coming here due
to the memories.

"I don't want to waste your time." He glanced
around at the empty shop. "I'd like to talk to you
before customers interrupt us." Bloom's was a very
successful shop. It was only a matter of time before
customers came through.

"Shoot. What's going on? If this is a fundraiser for
youth soccer, I've already made a sizable donation,"
Gillian said with a smile.

"This isn't about a fundraiser. It's about the new
vet in town, Harlow Jones, and the nasty rumors
swirling around town about her." Nick put on his
most intimidating expression. This really sucked.
He'd been in kindergarten with Gillian. But this
was about Harlow's reputation in Mistletoe. He was
invested in her staying here. "You wouldn't happen
to know anything about them would you?"

Gillian shifted from one foot to the other. She
looked down at the floor rather than making eye
contact. "It wasn't me." She bit her lip. "I mean it
was, but it wasn't."

"What does that even mean?" Nick folded his
arms across his chest.

"I did tell a friend about her and how bad she made me feel about Elvis, but I didn't say she hurt my dog." Gillian shook her head.

Nick frowned. "What do you mean she made you feel bad?"

"She was borderline rude to me. To be honest, I didn't like her tone or the fact that she's new to town and being condescending to me." Tears pricked in Gillian's eyes and Nick sensed they were born of anger. "I know when someone's treating me like I'm an idiot." She huffed air out through her nose.

"Is that what you told your friend?" Nick asked. He was still trying to figure out how Harlow's professional skills had been called into question. Not once had Gillian mentioned anything about Harlow endangering Elvis.

"Yes, but somehow she turned everything around and made it sound as if Harlow was unfit as a veterinarian." She made a tsking sound and held up her hands. "She spun that story on her own. I wasn't even trying to go there!"

"And who would that friend be?" Nick asked, although he was pretty sure he knew already.

"Who else?" Gillian asked, twisting her mouth. "Patsy. I should never have discussed it with her, but I was angry and I ran my mouth. I acted childishly that day at the festival when I didn't speak to Doc Harlow."

Nick ran a hand over his face. A groan escaped his lips. He should have known Patsy was at the heart of this. Patsy was the queen of town gossip. She lived on Blackberry Beach right next door to Stella and Luke, and she thrived on the rumor mill. She had been responsible for an abundance of tall tales that had run rampant through their small town. She was also quite ornery and not the type of person to see reason. Unlike Gillian, the older woman wouldn't even acknowledge her role in the matter. To Nick, she seemed to get nastier by the week.

"Thanks for being straight with me," Nick said. "I appreciate your candor." Knowing that she was taking responsibility for her part in the rumors was a relief. Gillian hadn't always behaved well over the years, but she hadn't ever gone this low. Nick believed her version of events.

"Nick. Let me know if there's anything I can do to help." She shrugged. "After all, I got the ball rolling by being negative about someone I interacted with only one time. That's on me. And I do plan to apologize in person to Doc Harlow. It's the least I can do."

"Harlow would love to talk to you any time you feel like reaching out. I may just take you up on that offer if you're serious about helping." An idea was forming in his mind, one that might just help restore Harlow's professional reputation in town. With Gillian's help, this whole mess might just blow over like a Maine nor'easter.

CHAPTER TWENTY-ONE

K eep your head up." Malcolm's parting words served as Harlow's mantra the moment she walked into Paws. She was going to keep it together no matter what went down today. Even if she didn't have a single client on her schedule, she wasn't going to wallow in feelings of not being good enough. She was determined to hold her head high.

Jon greeted her effusively at the front desk. Harlow sensed he was trying to cheer her up. On impulse she leaned down and pressed a kiss on his cheek. He was a good egg.

"I've got something that might make you smile," Jon said, beaming at her.

"Do tell. I'll take all the smiles I can get."

Jon handed her the day's client list. Harlow couldn't believe her eyes. Ten clients. Ten actual people who'd made appointments with her.

"Oh, this is a beautiful sight to behold," she said, tears pricking her eyes. She had honestly feared the worst today—zero clients. But she actually had a full day of appointments. Her eyes nearly bulged out of her head when she saw one name in particular. Gillian Robinson.

"Go check out your office." Jon was definitely smirking at her now.

As she made the walk down the hall, Jon, quickly followed by Whitney, trailed behind her. Not knowing what to expect, Harlow slowly turned the knob of her office door, then pushed it wide open. She let out a gasp as she looked around her. Flowers. Gifts. Cakes. Pies. Her office was overflowing with things.

Flabbergasted, she turned toward Jon and Whitney. "What is all this...stuff? What's going on?" She let out a nervous laugh. "It's not my birthday or anything."

Whitney raised a hand in the air in a celebratory gesture. "If I had to guess, I'd say you have a lot of great friends here in Mistletoe who want to see you soar. Harlow, never forget that you're very much wanted and needed in this town. Having you here has made all the difference at this practice."

She placed her hand above her rapidly beating heart. "I nearly passed out when I saw Gillian's name on my docket. She's bringing Elvis in for a checkup. How did that happen?"

"I think Nick Keegan could explain it better than

we can. He's been working overtime on all of this,"
Jon said, wiggling his eyebrows. "I'm calling dibs
on those Godiva chocolates over there."

Whitney and Jon disappeared, leaving Harlow
alone with her thoughts. She cast another look around
her office, finally noticing the cards and drawings.
She picked up a colorful picture of a poodle and a
brown-skinned little boy. The words *Thanks, Doc
Harlow* had been scrawled at the bottom, along with
Jimmy's name.

"Oh my heart," Harlow said out loud. This was
the first time she knew with a deep certainty that her
vet services had impacted people in Mistletoe. And
it felt amazing. Even though she had told Nick she
wanted to leave Mistletoe, she hadn't really meant
it. She'd spoken out of anger and frustration. Now,
more than ever, she felt conflicted about her future
plans. If nothing else, Harlow now believed this
town was different than Chestnut Ridge.

The day went by at a spectacularly fast speed with
almost all of her clients taking time to let her know
how valued she was as their pet's vet. Tess and her
mother even popped in to bring Harlow lemon bars,
which were her favorite. Elvis's appointment was
a surprise. She and Gillian had ended up having a
heart-to-heart talk.

"Like I told Nick," Gillian said, "I'm really
sorry about my part in the rumors." Gillian's expression was sheepish. "The truth is, I felt foolish
about allowing Elvis to eat the chocolate. Instead

of admitting that during our visit I sort of acted indifferent. You were only trying to educate me, but I ended up feeling judged."

Harlow let out a tutting sound. "Never in a million years would I ever want a client to feel that way. And I'm sorry if I made you feel bad. There's a fine line between preaching and educating. I may have blurred the lines. And for that I'm sorry too."

"Well, thanks for taking such good care of Elvis," Gillian said. "I know you must be a special person because Nick cares about you a lot. And, in case you haven't figured it out yet, he's a keeper."

With a wave, Gillian and Elvis sailed out the door, leaving Harlow astounded by the turn of events. If anyone had told her this reconciliation with Gillian was even a remote possibility, she would have laughed in their face.

At noon a text from Nick reminded her of Mistletoe's town event, the fiftieth annual lobster boil—the same event Agatha had raved about at the farmers' market.

Welcome back! I'm aiming to be at the beach by 7. Make sure to bring a warm coat.

Of course, with everything going on in her world, she'd completely forgotten about the lobster boil at Blackberry Beach. A few weeks ago when Nick had invited her, she'd been excited to attend. According to Nick and Agatha, the event was highly anticipated

by the residents. To Harlow it seemed a bit odd to
hold the event at the beach in November. But who
was she to buck town tradition? And lobster was
always an incentive.

She should be more excited about attending tonight and seeing Nick, but all she felt was this
pressure resting against her chest. Harlow still had
moments when she felt breathless and out of sorts.
Progress had been made today at Paws, but she
knew all too well the power that rumors held. Even
if you could convince 50 percent of people not to
believe them, you still had half who did.

Before leaving Paws that evening, Harlow took a
long look at the myriad of offerings that graced her
office. If she lived to be 105, she would never forget
these beautiful gestures. She'd received them all
with a grateful heart. Sometimes a person thought
they knew just how things were, only to find out
they were wrong. Was that going to be her Mistletoe
story? She had brought all of her biases with her
when she'd come to Maine, but now they were being
struck down, brick by brick.

Everything was falling into place, but she couldn't
completely settle into that knowledge. Her stomach
still twisted with tension. She knew what this feeling was as someone who had experienced childhood
trauma. It was almost as if she was waiting for
catastrophe to strike.

The wind kicked up the moment she landed on
the beach. Thankfully, torches had been set up, so

she wasn't fumbling around in the dark. After a few minutes of searching, Harlow spotted Nick standing by the edge of the water.

"Nick!" she called out as she quickly strode toward him. Although she hadn't felt as if he'd listened to her the night of their ill-fated movie date, clearly he was responsible for the outpouring of love from the community. Not to mention that she knew he'd been behind Gillian's sudden change of heart.

He turned toward her at the sound of her voice, then greeted her with a sizzling kiss on the lips. Harlow eagerly returned the kiss, matching his intensity measure for measure. The chemistry between them had always been fiery. This time was no exception. It was almost as if their time apart had added an extra level of passion. Light and easy, she reminded herself. Stick to your goal of being in an uncomplicated relationship.

"I missed you," he said, looking her over with appreciative eyes.

"Me too," she murmured. "First, I want to thank you for whatever you did to stem the tide of those rumors. Half of Mistletoe sent gifts to me. And I know you must have arranged the visit, but Gillian brought Elvis in for a wellness checkup. It was fairly shocking."

Nick didn't appear surprised at all. He simply nodded his head as she spoke. "I figured that would be a surefire way to win back the town's confidence. If Gillian still takes Elvis to see you, most people will realize that the rumors aren't true. For what it's worth, I don't think Gillian accused you of improper care." He made a face. "Stories tend to get altered as they spread."

Harlow made an annoyed sound with her lips. "It was really above and beyond of you."

Nick played with one of her curls, wrapping it around his finger. "It was done with love. Plain and simple."

Bam. Nick had just dropped the *L* word, and she had no idea what it meant.

Love. As in love with her love?

She took a step away from him, fighting the urge to flee. Harlow couldn't even look Nick in the eyes. She hadn't been expecting this, and she had no defenses against his declaration.

"Harlow, stay with me," he said in a low voice. "I didn't mean to make you uncomfortable. I'm just a big believer in speaking what's on my mind. And you're in my thoughts all the time. At night. In the daytime. When I brush my teeth in the morning. It's all you."

For a few solid minutes, she didn't say a word. She wasn't ready for this. She hadn't seen this coming. Not this soon!

"I'm sorry. There's just been so much going on. I've been grieving the loss of my mother, Nick. I know that might sound strange, but we can't deny the fact that she's fading away from us. There's no hope of her being cured." She ran a shaky hand through her hair. "This wasn't supposed to be anything serious." She buried her face in her hands. "We weren't supposed to be using the *L* word."

"According to who? I don't remember getting that memo." There was a layer of irritation laced in Nick's voice. He sounded upset. "There's no plan for falling in love. Sometimes it just happens."

He was right to dispute her. She hadn't said those exact words to him. And now he'd been blindsided. He had fallen in love with her. It was the very last thing she wanted.

"Everything between us has been wonderful. I've never felt so drawn to someone."

Nick's jawline hardened. "But? I can hear a *but* coming."

"But I'm feeling overwhelmed. With everything. And everyone." A slow hiss-like sigh escaped her lips.

Nick's eyes widened. He reached out and placed his hand on the side of her neck. He gazed deeply into her eyes. "Things happen, Harlow. Feelings grow. It's okay to go where your feelings lead you. You don't need to be afraid. I'm never going to hurt you."

But she was afraid. Terrified. How could she not be? This was everything she'd spent her life avoiding. Intimacy. Closeness. Love. She didn't deserve Nick. How could she trust in what she'd been building with him when it was only a matter of time before he came to that realization too? How could she trust herself to unconditionally love someone like Nick, when she'd never once had a successful relationship?

She fiercely shook her head. "Nick, I'm not staying in Mistletoe. My work agreement is only for a year. After that I'm headed back to Seattle."

"You could stay. I know you've grown to love it. We could make this work. Or at least try."

"I-I can't see myself in a small town. Too many bad things happened in Chestnut Ridge. I just can't shake it. And what certain people tried to do to my reputation brought it all back up again. I've been down that road before when accusations were made about my father."

"Harlow, a town can't hurt you. I won't let it."

"But people can." She let out a brittle laugh. "My dad—"

"What happened to him was horrific. It was a huge wrecking ball to your childhood. But if you let it get in the way of your happiness, that means you're just stuck. You're not growing. Something tells me your dad wouldn't want that for you."

"Maybe I am stuck, Nick. Permanently." Harlow looked away from Nick's intense gaze. Tears were burning her eyes. *Please don't cry. It will be so much worse if you cry. Stuff your feelings down. That way it won't hurt as much.*

She felt Nick's fingers on her chin, gently turning her face back toward him. What she saw reflected back at her was shocking to her core. Harlow nearly let out a gasp. "I'm in love with you. That's not something I could ever say lightly. I never thought I'd want to walk through life with someone after losing Kara." Nick's voice sounded raspy with emotion. "But you're all I see when I think about the future. You're all I want, Harlow. I'll never need anything more than you. You're enough, baby."

Harlow squeezed her eyes shut. Nick's words sounded perfect. She wanted so badly to believe that she was worthy of being with him. But at her core, she was screwed up and damaged. The past still had a grip on her. Nick deserved better than she could ever give him.

"As an adult I've never dreamed of the white picket fence or getting married and raising a family. Those were childhood dreams."

"So what? It's never too late to switch up your dreams."

She took a step away from him. "You're not hear-ing me. I don't want that. We don't want the same things, Nick. You're meant for all that. I'm not."

"Harlow. Please," Nick said, his voice breaking. "Don't do this."

"I'm not going to change my mind."

Fear was leading her now. Buying into happily ever after with Nick was too scary. If it didn't work out between them she would be gutted. Losing Nick down the road would be far more agonizing than if she ended things now. Harlow knew she was protecting herself. She'd done this hundreds of times ever since she was a child. But this was by far the most painful, because it meant she wouldn't have Nick in her life.

She could see the shattered expression etched on his face. His eyes were devoid of their usual light and his shoulders were slightly slumped. His body shuddered. All because of her. He took a few steps away from her, slowly shaking his head as he did so.

"Goodbye, Harlow," Nick said as he walked down the beach and away from her.

Harlow tore her eyes away from Nick. Her words had ravaged him. She hated herself for hurting him. Of all people, Nick didn't deserve it.

Nick. *Sweet, gorgeous, wonderful Nick.* What was she going to do without his corny jokes and his cooking lessons? Who would hold hands with her now or lift her spirits when she was down?

Harlow sniffed back her tears. She'd made the right decision, as difficult as it had been. Or at least that's what she was trying to tell herself. It would hurt less this way to know she'd let him go so he could find someone else to wholeheartedly love him. Right now she needed to find a way to move on from Nick, even as her heart was aching.

CHAPTER TWENTY-TWO

For the next few days, Nick wasn't sure if he was coming or going. He felt like one of the zombies from his favorite television show, *The Walking Dead*. Miles sensed something was up with him, and Nick knew it was only a matter of time before he would have to tell his son he and Harlow were over. Miles liked Harlow. The two had really bonded over taking care of Zeus, stuffed-crust pizza, and football games. Once he'd been reassured by Nick that Harlow could never take his place, Miles had accepted her with open arms. And although neither one would admit it, Nick was convinced that they had hashed things out in private.

Nick had no one to blame but himself. Harlow hadn't made him any promises. His heart had led him to believe that she'd fallen in love with him.

He'd been living in this fantasy world where he had imagined Harlow giving up her life in Seattle to make Mistletoe her home with him and Miles at the center of it all. Maybe it wasn't fair of him to think that way, but it had almost seemed as if the rug had been pulled out from underneath him. But he'd moved on from that way of looking at the situation. Love wasn't a right. He couldn't demand that of Harlow, no matter how much this hurt.

Love wasn't for the faint of heart—a lesson he was now learning.

"Why hasn't Harlow come over? Maybe we can go to her house," Miles suggested, dragging Nick out of his thoughts.

Ugh. He'd known Miles would bring up Harlow sooner or later. He had to tell him the truth about their breakup.

He sat down on the front stoop next to his son. "Hey, Miles. We probably won't be seeing that much of Harlow other than at Zeus's appointments."

Miles looked up at him with wide eyes. "Why?"

"We broke up," he said, feeling a pang in the region of his heart as he said the words out loud. When would it get easier to talk about it? At the moment, it was still uncomfortable to put it out there in the universe. He didn't want it to be his reality, but it was.

"You did? But I thought you really, really liked each other. That's the way it seemed."

"We did. I did." He let out a sigh. "I can't speak

for her, but I haven't liked anyone as much since your mom," he confessed.

"Is it my fault?" Miles asked, lips quivering.

Nick ran his hand over his son's short-cropped Afro. Miles looked distraught. "Of course not, buddy. Why would you think that?"

His son let out a huff of air. "I wasn't so nice to Harlow. Maybe she thought I would be too much to deal with down the road if you two stuck together."

"No, buddy. She didn't think that. Her decision was about her not sticking around Mistletoe, Miles. She's going to be heading back to Seattle after her term is up at Paws. Harlow didn't want to complicate things by being in a relationship."

"Couldn't you convince her to stay?" Miles's eyes were as wide as an owl's.

"I tried," he admitted. "That's not what she wants, and I have to accept that. Even though it hurts knowing she's not going to be a part of our lives moving forward, I do want her to be happy. She deserves it." After enduring so much pain and loss in her childhood, Harlow should have joy in her life.

"Even if it's with someone else?"

Ugh. Sucker punch to the gut. Nick didn't even want to think about Harlow finding love with anyone but him. Their breakup was too fresh and the wounds were still raw and open.

"Yep. Even if it's with someone else," he answered, forcing the words out of his mouth. He wasn't even certain if he was lying or telling the truth. His mouth felt like it was filled with sawdust. Who was he trying to kid? Loving someone did mean you wanted the best for them, but it would be pure torture to see her walking around Mistletoe with some other dude.

Buck up, he reminded himself. All was fair in love and war.

Falling in love with Harlow had been easy.

Falling out of love with her was going to be nearly impossible.

* * *

It was a beautiful Saturday afternoon in November with a wintry chill in the air. Today's weather indicated a shift in the direction of winter. Harlow overheard a few locals saying it smelled as if snow was on the way. Hearing this chatter took Harlow all the way back to being a kid in Vermont and listening to her parents say the same thing.

"Time to pull out the snow boots, Dee. It smells like snow." Her father's deep voice had been robust and joyful.

"I know, Jack," her mother responded. "We'll have to take the kids shopping for new ones along with snowsuits."

"Absolutely. I just made the reservation for our ski weekend at Mount Snow. The kids are going to love it." Her father's grin stretched from ear to ear.

"No one's going to enjoy it more than you," her mother had said, pressing a kiss on her husband's face.

The memory seized her by the heartstrings. They'd been happy together. A love match. Why was it that the good memories had been stuffed down alongside the bad ones? Why was this remembrance popping up right now? A week later, he'd been killed in the car accident. The trip to Mount Snow had never taken place.

At the moment, Harlow was kicking herself for not canceling her brunch date with Stella and Lucy. She was trying to act normal and pretend as if she wasn't completely falling apart, but it was becoming increasingly difficult to plaster a smile on her face and keep up the happy-go-lucky façade. She was absolutely miserable on the inside and it was shocking that her feelings weren't oozing out for all the world to see.

She needed to focus on what her friends were saying instead of letting her mind wander back to Nick. Never in her life had she felt this aching sense of loss after a breakup. The only thing she could compare it to was grief. Harlow felt as if the bottom had fallen out of her world. Dealing with deep emotions was something she always avoided. It had been her pattern since her father's death. But lately, stuffing everything down wasn't working. Things kept bubbling up to the surface.

"I was thinking we could do a movie date night

at Casablanca's," Lucy said as she reached for a berry-flavored scone. "Dante comes back from Los Angeles next Friday."

"Oh, that would be great. I can ask Mom and Dad to watch Jade," Stella said, clapping her hands together. "Tess has been begging to babysit. I still think she's a little too young for that solo responsibility, but she can help them out and get some pointers."

"Are you in, Harlow?" Lucy asked before taking a sip of her mint tea.

Harlow fiddled with her teacup. "That might be kind of awkward. Nick and I broke up."

"What happened?" Stella asked. Her tone radiated shock. "You two seemed blissful."

"Nick is such an idiot!" Lucy said, twisting her mouth. "He doesn't know what he wants or needs."

"It wasn't Nick. I was the one who ended things," Harlow admitted. Just saying the words out loud made her feel foolish.

Both sisters gasped and stared at her as if they couldn't comprehend what she'd told them.

"Why, Harlow?" Lucy finally asked, brows knit together. "You two are great together."

Stella shook her head. "I'm shocked. Did something happen?"

Harlow paused for a moment. "He told me that he was in love with me."

"And that's a bad thing?" Lucy's voice came out as a screech.

"No, of course it isn't," Harlow quickly answered. "Love is a wonderful thing. It's precious and rare. And any women worth a damn would be lucky to be loved by a man like Nick."

Unexpected tears slid down her cheeks. As soon as she brushed them away, more tears fell. "Don't mind me. I have no idea of why I'm crying."

"Don't you?" Stella asked, narrowing her gaze as she looked at her.

Lucy handed her a tissue. Harlow dabbed at her eyes and sniffled, willing herself not to shed any more tears. "No offense, but you don't seem happy with your decision."

Harlow bowed her head. She couldn't even bear to lock eyes with Stella and Lucy. What was going on with her? She was blubbering like a big ol' baby.

"Harlow. What's wrong?" Stella asked. "You don't look so good."

The truth was that she didn't feel very good. She was sick to her stomach. What had she done by breaking up with the best thing that had ever come into her life? She'd been a fool to allow fear to get in the way of her relationship with Nick. Fear and doubt and anxiety.

All of a sudden, it came to her like a flash of lightning in a rainstorm. She knew exactly what was wrong. Nick was what she wanted more than anything else in this world. She had just been so afraid to trust. To believe that her future could be filled with love and stability. Because of her past hurts, Harlow had never allowed herself to hope for normalcy, for the love of a good, strong man. In truth, she had never felt worthy of what Nick was offering her. Love. Acceptance. Strong arms to hold her. Everything she'd always wanted.

She met Stella's gaze. Concern radiated from her eyes. "I made a mistake, Stella. I-I shouldn't have ended things with Nick."

Stella reached for Harlow's hands and squeezed them. "Then reach out to him. Make things right. Sit Nick down and talk everything through."

But what would she say? That she'd been an idiot? That she was totally head over heels in love with him?

Just then Stella's cell phone buzzed and she held up her hand. "One second. I've got to take this," she said with a frown. Lucy came over to Harlow and gave her a hug.

"It's all going to work out, Harlow. You'll just have to do a little groveling," Lucy said, patting her on the back.

"I'm not above groveling," Harlow answered. If Nick forgave her for her complete lapse in judgment, Harlow would tap dance in a bikini on the town green.

Stella let out a gasp and turned toward them. Her cell phone slipped out of her hand and fell to the ground.

"Stella! What's wrong?" Lucy asked, rushing toward her.

Stella's big brown eyes were as wide as saucers. She let out a moan and said, "There's been a rockslide at the site of the search and rescue mission. That was Luke's superior on the phone." Stella made a fist and placed it over her mouth. Blinking back tears, Stella pulled her hand away from her mouth. "Luke is in trouble. He was buried under the rubble. Nick managed to free him but he's been taken to the hospital with serious injuries."

"Okay, what do you need?" Lucy asked, scrambling to mobilize.

"I need to get there as soon as possible," Stella said as Lucy bent down to pick up her phone.

"I'm so sorry, Stella," Harlow said. "What can we do? Do you want me to stay behind and look after Jade?"

Stella shook her head. "No, I'm going to bring her with me. Harlow, I need you to come along for Nick's sake. At a time like this, he's really going to need you."

Nick! She had been so busy thinking about Luke, she hadn't had a moment to consider how Nick must feel right now. From the early days of their relationship, she'd known how deeply he loved his brother. How close the ties were that bound them together. Nick had told her about all the years when Luke had been overseas as a Navy SEAL and how grateful he was to have him back in Mistletoe. And now, without warning, Luke's life could be hanging in the balance. Her place was by Nick's side.

"Of course," Harlow said, grabbing her coat and purse. "I wouldn't want to be anywhere else." Or with anyone else. This was her crew. Stella, Luke, Lucy... and Nick. After Stella gathered up Jade, the three women got in Harlow's car and raced to the hospital, offering prayers the whole way over.

* * *

Nick paced back and forth in the hospital's waiting room as he anticipated word on his brother's condition. He was still shaking from the events on the mountain. They had been rescuing three hikers who had been lost overnight. One moment they had been standing on the mountain, and in the next a rockslide had come out of nowhere, burying Luke along with the hikers. With the help of other team members, Nick had dug Luke out as quickly as possible before the paramedics mobilized. He had ridden in the ambulance with his brother, who hadn't regained consciousness the entire time. One of the hikers had died at the location, which was a heartbreaking outcome.

Luke had to make it. Nick couldn't imagine his life without him. He was his best friend in the entire world. *Who else would he share his deepest thoughts with?* Not too long ago, Luke had found the love of his life, Stella, after serving heroically for so many years as a SEAL. He couldn't die from a random rockslide on a Maine mountain. Not after winning the Medal of Honor for heroism in Afghanistan. Not after bringing Jade into the world. Luke deserved a chance to be a father for his little girl and to live out his incredible love story with his wife.

We can't lose him! Nick didn't even want to think about living in a world without Luke in it. All he could think about was Kara's accident and receiving the terrible news of her death. He didn't want to go through that torture all over again, nor did he want Stella and his folks to endure such trauma.

Pretty soon he was going to have to make the call to his parents to tell them about the accident. He'd been waiting until he heard an update from Luke's doctor. If the news was good, he could lead with that information. Nick's mind wouldn't allow him to go toward a negative outcome.

The moment Stella burst through the waiting room doors she threw herself at Nick's chest, wrapping her arms so tightly around his neck he could barely breathe. He looked past her shoulder, surprised by the sight of Harlow standing with Lucy, who was cradling his niece in her arms. Stella abruptly let go of him before asking, "What are the doctors saying?" she asked, stress lines creasing her features.

He placed his arm around her. "I'm waiting for news from the doctors."

Stella shuddered and wrapped her arms around her middle, tears falling from her cheeks. Lucy strode to her side to comfort her, then led her to a nearby sofa, where they both sat down with the baby.

Harlow stepped toward Nick and he instinctively opened his arms to her. That's where he wanted her to be—pressed up against his heart. As she rested against his chest, the smell of her hair product rose to his nostrils. It was something fruity, like mango or coconut. Whatever the scent was, he breathed the aroma in, allowing himself to bask in the comforting smell that always surrounded her like a halo.

For Nick, all that mattered right now was that she was here with him. She'd smashed his heart into smithereens, but the very sight of her caused pure adrenaline to pulse through his veins. He came to life just looking at her. Nick had no pride where Harlow was concerned. He couldn't even pretend to be unemotional about her being here. He needed her, which was way deeper than wanting her.

When their embrace ended she placed her hands on either side of his face. "Oh, Nick. I'm so sorry you're going through this." Her touch on his skin caused shivers of awareness to flood his body. Despite the drama swirling around him, Harlow's contact felt invigorating.

"Thanks for being here," he murmured. He was trying to still his thumping heart, as hard as it might be. For a man who wore his heart on his sleeve, he wasn't used to playing it cool. The last thing he wanted to do was overstep boundaries with Harlow now that she'd made her feelings toward him clear.

"Of course. I care about what happens to Luke...

and Stella. And you, Nick." Her voice was buttery soft, and it flowed over him like a soothing balm.

She still cared about him. He hadn't been imagining the romantic vibes between them. Nick tried not to get his hopes up too high. Maybe she was just being nice and comforting him about his brother. "I'm just praying he pulls through. Waiting for news is the hardest part." He grimaced. "He has to be all right."

"He will be," she said, fiercely shaking her head. "Try to focus on that. Don't let your mind take you to scary places."

Nick shifted from one foot to the other. He couldn't seem to stand still. "That's what my dad always says."

Harlow knitted her brows together. "Where are your parents? Do they know about the accident?"

"Not yet," he said, knowing he would have to make the important phone call sooner rather than later. "I wanted to wait until we received some solid news." He knew they would both be beside themselves with fear and worry. They had been through a lot of over the years as parents of a Navy SEAL. When Luke had been seriously injured in an explosion in Afghanistan, the entire Keegan family had been in panic mode. Thankfully, he'd pulled through then. They needed another miracle now.

Just then a doctor wearing scrubs and a white jacket entered the waiting room. "Keegan. Luke Keegan."

Please, please. Let there be good news. Stella jumped up from her seat and stepped forward with Nick placing himself beside her. He felt someone tightly gripping his hand. Harlow! Thank God she wasn't going to make him face this moment without her.

"I'm Luke's wife, Stella. And this is his brother, Nick," Stella said in a quivering voice. She seemed so nervous and unsteady on her feet. He placed a steadying hand around his sister-in-law's waist. No matter what happened, Nick would be there for Stella.

"Hello. I'm Doctor Griffith," the woman said with a nod as she stood before them. "Mr. Keegan lost consciousness after being hit by rocks and debris during the rockslide." Stella let out a little moan. "He's conscious and alert now."

Stella let out a cry of relief at the news. "Oh, thank God. My baby's awake."

Nick shut his eyes as relief swept over him. Hot tears pricked his eyes.

"We're treating him for a concussion. He needs a lot of rest and relaxation. I've spoken to him about avoiding all devices, like cell phones, iPads, and television, but we can give you some literature to take home with you. He also sustained some bruised ribs and facial lacerations, but they look way worse than they are." Dr. Griffith smiled at them. "You can go back and see him if you like. We're hydrating him at the moment, but he's raring to go.

He basically said it's hard to keep a good Navy SEAL down."

"Sounds like Luke," Nick said with a chuckle. When he looked over at Harlow, she was wiping away tears.

Nick turned back toward Harlow. He didn't say anything, but he was hoping his eyes did the talking for him.

"I'm not going anywhere," she said, reading his mind. "Tell Luke hello from me and that I'll see him soon."

* * *

The joy Harlow had felt humming and pulsing in the air around her after the doctor's announcement was effusive. She couldn't keep her eyes off Nick as he hugged Stella, then made the phone call to his parents. All was right in Nick's world, and she couldn't be happier for everyone who loved Luke. She couldn't imagine how Nick would have handled another loss in his life. He'd been through enough tragedy to last a lifetime.

Nick and Stella quickly headed off to see Luke while she, Lucy, and the baby stayed behind in the waiting room. Harlow helped Lucy keep Jade occupied by playing peekaboo with her and rocking her on her hip as she sang an upbeat tune.

Time seemed to drag on as they waited for confirmation that Luke was doing okay. Even though the doctor had delivered the good news, it would be nice to hear it from a family member's perspective. When the door finally swung open and Nick came through the doors grinning, she knew everything was going to be okay.

"How is he?" she asked as he strode toward her. Nick looked like a completely different person. Before he'd been on the verge of cracking. Now he was lit up like pure sunshine.

"As ornery as ever," he said, chuckling. "Can you believe he was trying to get up out of his hospital bed so he could go home?"

"You can't keep a Keegan man down," Harlow quipped.

"Ain't that the truth," Lucy said. "I'm going to change Jade's diaper before she gets fussy." Lucy placed the baby on her hip and headed toward the bathroom with the diaper bag looped over her shoulder.

Now that she and Nick were alone, Harlow felt tongue-tied. There was so much she wanted to say, but where did she start? "I acted the fool" or "Forgive me" sounded about right, but what if Nick didn't want to hear it?

"I'm so happy Luke is doing well. I know you must have been scared to death."

Nick shuddered. "I don't think I'll be able to talk about those moments on the mountain for a very long time. I thought I'd lost him." He ran his hand across his jaw. "I never wanted to feel that way again."

She touched his arm. "I know, Nick. It's obvious how much you two love each other." She also knew that this accident must have brought back terrible memories of losing Kara. All she wanted to do at this moment was wrap her arms around him.

"You don't have to stick around, Harlow, now that Luke's out of the ICU. It's getting late," he said, glancing at his watch.

"I didn't just come here for Stella. I mainly came for you, Nick." She tilted her chin up and locked eyes with him, then quickly tore her gaze away. She was too nervous to see his reaction. Every insecurity she had was rising to the surface.

Nick looked down at her with a quizzical expression on his face.

"I've been a fool." The words leapt from her mouth.

"You have?" Nick asked. "How?"

"Ending things with you…breaking up wasn't what I truly wanted." She twisted her fingers around. "I was afraid."

"Of me?" Nick asked in a gentle voice.

"Not exactly. Of what I was feeling. It was too real. Too strong. And when you said that you loved me, it just seemed overwhelming. It felt like I was barely holding on with my mom being terminally ill and the stress of the rumors about me…so I crumbled. And I want to tell you all about my dad and what happened to us back in Vermont. It's always been so painful to discuss, but I'm trying to be better about dealing with my issues." The look in his eyes was so intense she was tempted to look away.

Say something, Nick. Please don't leave me hanging.

"And why would you want to be with someone who makes such rash decisions? I get that, and it's totally understandable if you tell me to kick rocks. I'm not expecting anything, Nick. I just needed to tell you how I feel and why I did what I did. Because I love you, and it's ridiculous to walk away from love."

She took a deep breath. At this point she had veered into rambling territory. Honestly, she should just slink out of the waiting room and disappear. Or maybe falling through the floor was an option?

Nick was just gaping at her. Dear God, she should have just kept her mouth shut. This was humiliating. It would be far better if he rejected her, because his silence was a killer. All of a sudden, her fight or flight response kicked in. She didn't have the strength to fight, so she was going to dash.

"Well, thanks for listening. Good night," she said, turning on her heel and moving toward the exit. She was walking as fast as she could, desperate to get away.

"Where do you think you're going?" Nick's voice called out to her. Harlow stopped in her tracks, then turned back toward Nick. "You can't say all that stuff and then walk away." His face broke wide open with the biggest smile she'd ever seen. Harlow let out a cry and ran toward him, flying into his arms. Nick lifted her up off the ground and held her against his chest. Being in his arms was the safest harbor she'd ever found. All of her tension melted away until she felt almost weightless. Joy raced through her veins. When he finally put her back down on her feet, Nick placed his hands on either side of her face and said, "You had me at 'I've been a fool,' but telling me you love me is the icing on the cake."

She stood on her tippy-toes and pressed a searing kiss on her man's lips. Once they came up for air, Harlow said, "You're mine, Keegan. And I'm yours. For as long as you'll have me."

"I just got you back. You're not going anywhere. I'm looking at forever," he said, pulling her into his arms. "Can you handle that?"

"Before I met you, I would have said absolutely not," Harlow admitted. "But you changed my life, Nick, in every imaginable way. All this time I've been wanting something solid and true…a home. A soft place to fall. I was just afraid to go after it, because I wasn't sure I was worthy of it."

"You pushed past all of those worries, baby, to fight for us. And you're here with me when I needed you the most. After all you've been through, that's brave." He placed a kiss on her forehead, then rained kisses on her cheeks and jawline.

"Oh, Nick. I'll do battle for us any day of the week. That's what forever means."

"Forever," he murmured against her lips. "We're not settling for anything less."

Their intentions were sealed with a searing kiss that celebrated all of the wonderful things to come. The future was theirs. All they had to do was reach out and grab ahold of it and never let go.

EPILOGUE

Summer is a glorious season in Mistletoe, Maine. Flowers were in full bloom and the skies were as radiant as a robin's egg. Boats were docked at the harbor, along with fishing vessels that graced the waters of Mistletoe Bay in search of lobsters, shrimp, and crabs. Carefree afternoons were spent at Blackberry Beach swimming and kayaking. Nick and Harlow loved sitting at the marina, looking out across the water as they enjoyed a shared plate of fried clams and French fries.

On a hot day in June, Harlow and Nick hosted their wedding at her house on Sweetwater Lane. Harlow felt like a little kid again as she selected the perfect white dress and floral centerpieces. She enjoyed planning every detail of their special day.

"Are you sure about this?" Malcolm whispered in her ear right before it was time for him to walk

Harlow down the aisle. "I can definitely be your sidekick if you want to pull a runaway bride." His smile was full of mischief.

Harlow swallowed past her nervousness and turned toward her brother. "Despite my jitters, I know I'm marrying my other half today. No doubts. No questions. Just a deep certainty that he's the one. And I'm his."

"Then let's do this thing," Malcolm said, holding out his arm so she could loop hers through it.

To the strains of "What a Wonderful World" by Louis Armstrong, Harlow walked toward her destiny. Nick, dressed to perfection in a black tux, stood with Miles and Luke at his side. Stella was there also as Harlow's maid of honor.

The ceremony was simple and heartwarming due to the vows they'd written for each other that spoke poignantly of their devotion. "I do," they said in unison as they were pronounced man and wife.

"I'm madly in love with you, Harlow. And that's never going to change," Nick whispered to her as they shared their first dance at the wedding reception. "And if you ever start to doubt you're worthy of a happy ending, I'm here to straighten you out."

"I love you too, Nick. I never thought I'd be a wife, but I think I was born to be yours. And I'm so grateful to be Miles's bonus mom. That's icing on the cake."

Harlow had made a promise to Miles to honor the memory of his mother. And she meant it. She never wanted Miles to believe she was trying to replace Kara. If she and Nick decided to have children, she wouldn't treat them any differently than Miles. He was hers, to be cherished and adored. Always.

Life was good! Marrying Nick was proving to be the best decision of Harlow's life. Every day spent with him showed her that he really was her person. She could tell him all about her fears without feeling judged. Harlow planned to be Nick's wife and best friend for the rest of her days. Nick had taught her that together they could face any curveballs life threw at them. And she'd stopped getting in her head about their relationship. She'd switched up fear and anxiety for trust.

Believe was the word that now grounded her. Every time she started to doubt whether she deserved all the blessings she'd been given, she took time to get her mind right. She was a work in progress, but she had made the decision to love abundantly and to accept Nick's devotion without reservations.

* * *

Harlow and Malcolm had made the decision to move their mother from Bay Shore to a nursing home in Maine. Harlow was able to visit her mother regularly, and due to his flexible schedule, Malcolm drove up frequently. Harlow no longer dwelled on her mother's grim diagnosis or her past. She had decided to live in the moment and try to help her mother live out the rest of her days with dignity and grace. That decision had given her peace. Although her mother rarely remembered Harlow, there were precious moments when she did. And in those moments, Harlow rejoiced.

Whitney had offered Harlow a partnership in Paws, which she'd gratefully accepted. Paws was now officially a haven for rescue dogs as well as being a top-notch veterinary practice. Nick was helping out in his spare time and recommending certain dogs to be trained for search and rescue. Zeus was healthy and cancer-free. And Miles was over the moon about his best friend's recovery.

Due to his many visits to Mistletoe, most of the single women in town had their sights set on Malcolm. Harlow, Stella, and Lucy were determined to play matchmaker for him, although they hadn't disclosed that information to her brother. Harlow figured he would thank them after they'd hooked him up with his other half.

Harlow hadn't done a complete turnaround in her thinking. She still didn't consider herself a white-picket-fence, fairy-tale-wedding kind of girl. But she did believe in love. And her life with Nick and Miles. In the end, she'd decided that her life was better with Nick in it.

Thanks to her husband, she finally believed in happily ever afters.

ABOUT THE AUTHOR

Belle Calhoune grew up in a small town in Massachusetts as one of five children. Although both her parents worked in the medical field, Belle never considered science as the pathway to her future. Growing up across the street from a public library was a huge influence on her life. Married to her college sweetheart, she is raising two lovely daughters in Connecticut. A dog lover, she has one mini poodle named Copper and a black Lab named Beau.

She is a *Publishers Weekly* bestselling author as well as a member of RWA's Honor Roll. In 2019, her book *An Alaskan Christmas* was made into a movie (*Love, Alaska*) by Brain Power Studio and aired on UPtv. She is the author of more than forty novels and is published by Harlequin Love Inspired and Grand Central Forever Publishing.

Looking for more second chances and small towns?
Check out Forever's heartwarming contemporary
romances!

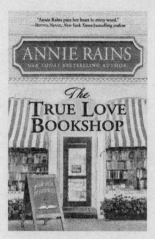

THE TRUE LOVE BOOKSHOP
by Annie Rains

For Tess Lane, owning Lakeside Books is a dream come true, but it's the weekly book club she hosts for the women in town that Tess enjoys the most. The gatherings have been her lifeline over the past three years, since she became a widow. But when secrets surrounding her husband's death are revealed, can Tess find it in her heart to forgive the mistakes of the past... and maybe even open herself up to love again?

THE MAGNOLIA SISTERS
by Alys Murray

Harper Anderson has one priority: caring for her family's farm. So when an arrogant tech mogul insists the farm host his sister's wedding, she turns him *and* his money down flat—an event like that would wreck their crops! But then Luke makes an offer she can't refuse: He'll work *for free* if Harper just considers his deal. Neither is prepared for chemistry to bloom between them as they labor side by side... but can Harper trust this city boy to put down country roots?

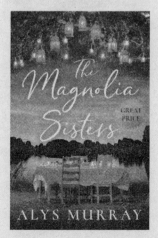

HER AMISH PATCHWORK FAMILY
by Winnie Griggs

Martha Eicher, formerly a schoolteacher in Hope's Haven, has always put her family first. But now everyone's happily married, and Martha isn't sure where she fits in...until she hears that Asher Lantz needs a nanny. As a single father to his niece and nephews, Asher struggles to be enough for his new family. Although a misunderstanding ended their childhood friendship, he's grateful for Martha's help. Slowly both begin to realize Martha is exactly what his family needs. Could together be where they belong?

FALLING IN LOVE ON SWEETWATER LANE
by Belle Calhoune

Nick Keegan knows all about unexpected, life-altering detours. He lost his wife in the blink of an eye, and he's spent the years since being the best single dad he can be. He's also learned to not take anything for granted, so when sparks start to fly with Harlow, the new veterinarian, Nick is all in. He senses Harlow feels it too, but she insists romance isn't on her agenda. He'll have to pull out all the stops to show her that love is worth changing the best-laid plans.

RETURN TO HUMMINGBIRD WAY
by Reese Ryan

Ambitious real estate agent Sinclair Buchanan is thrilled her childhood best friend is marrying her first love. But the former beauty queen and party planner extraordinaire hadn't anticipated being asked to work with her high-school hate crush, Garrett Davenport, to plan the wedding. Five years ago, they spent one *incredible* night together—a mistake she won't make again. But when her plans for partnership in her firm require her to work with Rett to renovate his grandmother's seaside cottage, it becomes much harder to ignore their complicated history.

THE HOUSE ON MULBERRY STREET
by Jeannie Chin

Between helping at her family's inn and teaching painting, Elizabeth Wu has put her dream of being an artist on the back burner. But her plan to launch an arts festival will boost the local Blue Cedar Falls arts scene and give her a showcase for her own work. If only she can get the town council on board. At least she can rely on her dependable best friend, Graham, to support her. Except lately, he hasn't been acting like his old self, and she has no idea why...

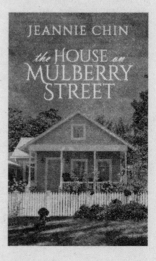

STARTING OVER ON SUNSHINE CORNER
by Phoebe Mills

Single mom Rebecca Hayes isn't getting her hopes up after she has one unforgettable night with Jackson, a very close—and very attractive—friend. She knows Jackson's unattached bachelor lifestyle too well. But in his heart, Jackson Lowe longs to build a family with Rebecca—his secret crush and the real reason he never settled down. So when Rebecca discovers she's pregnant with his baby, he knows he's got a lot of work to do before he can prove he's ready to be the man she needs.

A TABLE FOR TWO
(MM reissue) by Sheryl Lister

Serenity Wheeler's Supper Club is all about great friends, incredible food, and a whole lot of dishing—not hooking up. So when Serenity invites her friend's brother to one of her dinners, it's just good manners. But the ultra-fine, hazel-eyed Gabriel Cunningham has a gift for saying all the wrong things, causing heated exchanges and even hotter chemistry between them. But Serenity can't let herself fall for Gabriel: Cooking with love is one thing, but trusting it is quite another...